MERCILESS MONSTER

LYDIA HALL

Copyright © 2023 by Lydia Hall

All rights reserved.

No part of this book may be reproduced in any form or by any electronic or mechanical means, including information storage and retrieval systems, without written permission from the author, except for the use of brief quotations in a book review.

❦ Created with Vellum

ALSO BY LYDIA HALL

Series: Spicy Office Secrets

New Beginnings || Corporate Connection || Caught in the Middle || Faking It For The Boss || Baby Makes Three || The Boss's Secret || My Best Friend's Dad

Series: The Wounded Hearts

Ruthless Beast

Series: The Big Bad Braddock Brothers

Burning Love || Tell Me You Love Me || Second Chance at Love || Pregnant: Who is the Father? || Pregnant with the Bad Boy

Series: The Forbidden Attraction

My Mommy's Boyfriend || Daddy's Best Friend || Daddy Undercover || The Doctor's Twins || She's Mine || Tangled Trust

Series: Corrupt Bloodlines

Dangerous Games || Dangerous Refuge || Dangerous Obsession || Dangerous Vengeance || Dangerous Secrets

BLURB

I have to bear the consequences of sleeping with a merciless monster.

Dante is the father of my child.

He has no idea I kept that secret after our sizzling night in Italy.

It was my best friend's wedding and he was her cousin that I couldn't resist.

Dante looked like a strong man who would protect me.

But a relationship couldn't be in the cards.

I had to get back to the US.

Little did I know that I was carrying a part of him along.

Not just his child… but also the dangerous world he can't escape.

If I've got an unspeakable secret, Dante has a few of his own.

Ending up in the same city as him five years later would remove all veils.

It would force us to confront the truth.

And it would push him to protect his new family with everything he's got.

But first, could this merciless monster find a way to forgive me for a mistake that would change his world forever?

1

MIA

Another wedding. Swell. I'll be the one again, dressed in an outfit that makes me look like I've stepped off a set of a Disney movie—and I'm not talking about being Cinderella either. No. I'm one of the ugly stepsisters, dressed in a turd. Oh, well.

I exaggerate for effect. The dress isn't that bad. I'm just so sick and tired of being the one who catches the bouquet for no bloody reason every time. Where the hell is my Prince Charming? What did I do to piss off the Fairy Godmother?

Of course, I am happy for Gina. Plus, I'm going to Italy! I've always wanted to walk the narrow, cobbled streets of Venice and Sicily. Who knows? Perhaps I'll meet my Romeo. Crazier things have happened.

"What's with the sad face, mio amico? Tell me you're not still pining after that loser of an ex of yours," Gina comments while we're doing the pharmacy's inventory.

It's midnight, so the place is all but deserted. Occasionally, someone in need of an emergency item pops in briefly, but for the most part, Gina and I are left to fly solo.

"No. I most certainly am not!"

"Good. That guy doesn't deserve you, Mia. He never did."

"When am I going to learn?" I remark more to myself than to my best friend.

"Hey, you're a bad boy magnet. I get it."

"Thanks a lot."

"I'm serious. You're like Sandy in Grease. You just won't be satisfied until you find your Danny," she chuckles.

"I wish. I could do worse than John Travolta."

Gina and her fiancé graciously paid for my ticket to Italy. They've also arranged accommodation for me with Gina's family. I was overwhelmed when she handed me the envelope with the flight ticket inside. Granted, I'd just broken up with Sam, the man I thought I'd spend the rest of my life with. So much for that fantasy.

Sam and I were together for almost two years. It wasn't a perfect relationship by any means, but then again, what relationship is? I feel silly now that I know the truth about him. Rotten cheater.

"I know it's been a tough year for you, M. You deserve better."

"I can't believe we'll be in Italy in less than two weeks. I can't wait to meet your family, Gina."

"They're Italian. You know that, right?"

"Duh!" I laugh.

"Okay, don't say I didn't warn you. They're loud and opinionated, and they will feed you to within an inch of your waistline."

"Perfect."

Gina looks at her watch.

"Ugh. Will this torture ever end? I'm tired. I don't know how I let George talk me into doing the graveyard shift. I should be in bed right now, snuggled up against Jeff's tight buns."

"Rub it in, why don't you? Anyway, I'm used to the late nights."

"Uh-huh. You'd make a great vampire. Pass me that box over there, please."

"Look, I'm good with blood, but I think vampirism is a bit of a stretch," I laugh.

"Hey, don't knock it til you've tried it."

"Has Jeff been to Italy?"

"No. He's looking forward to it. I just hope my family doesn't scare the crap out of him. He's so very English."

"It's a crazy match. Isn't it strange how opposites attract? I would never have put the two of you together."

"Yup. Jeff's the butter in my espresso, that's for sure. But it works."

"You're so lucky, Gina. He's a wonderful guy."

"Jeff isn't perfect. But he sure is perfect for me."

"He's a prince compared to the guys I seem to attract."

"Sam is a master manipulator, M. Even I fell for his bullshit. You can't blame yourself."

"I guess. Anyway, he's history. Thank God. Can you believe he had the nerve to send me flowers for my birthday?"

"What! He's such an asshole. As if flowers could make up for what he did. Honestly, I don't know how you've managed to keep it cool. I would have gone full Italian vengeance on his ass."

"Does Jeff know about the extent of your Sicilian verve?" I giggle.

LYDIA HALL

"Oh, yeah. Why do you think he's so good to me? One dinner with the famiglia was all it took. My brothers gave him the hairy eyeball, and that was that."

I laugh as Gina runs her thumb across her throat and sticks out her tongue. She's such a nut. I love her so much.

"It's a pity Georgio is too young for you, M. How nice would it be if we were related?"

"You've just warned me about them, and now you want me to join the crazy. Yeah, I don't think so. But thanks for the offer."

"Yeah, you're right. You're way too Californian for the Fontanas. Too vanilla, dare I say."

"Way too much."

I just turned twenty five. My plan was to be married by now. Maybe even pregnant. But I don't know if that's ever going to happen. I'll probably end up an old maid with twenty cats, the way my luck has been going. Damn you, Sam!

It's 4 a.m. when the next team arrives. I'm too wired to sleep, so I go to the bakery around the corner from my apartment for a fresh donut and a mug of hot chocolate. The orange glow of sunrise will brighten the horizon soon, welcoming the morning runners as they make their way along the promenade.

I love the ocean. It's my happy place. There's something about the salty scent in the air and the sound of the waves crashing onto the shore that resonates with my soul. My mom says I used to sit in the shallows for hours when I was a toddler, staring out to sea and grabbing handfuls of beach sand. I can't remember a time when I wasn't either swimming in the ocean or surfing the break.

It's been a little difficult lately to get to the beach. Working the graveyard shift at the pharmacy takes it out of me. But it pays the bills.

Another spectacular California sunrise.

See. It could have been worse. You could have had your heart broken inland, away from all this beauty.

* * *

"Oh, wow! Your village is gorgeous, Gina!"

The flight took forever, and we've just stepped out of a cab after a long drive, but I am instantly smitten with Sicily. It feels like I'm in a remake of an old gangster movie. The cobbled street and the sandstone colored buildings seem as if they've been here since the dawn of time.

"Welcome to Erice, my friend. She's a beauty, alright."

"Why would you ever leave such a place?"

"It's too small for me. I like the hustle and bustle of city life. Besides, California is just far enough away from my nutty family," she winks.

"Oh, my goodness! Look at that beautiful cathedral. I'm in love."

"Erice isn't known as the City of a Hundred Churches for nothing. This medieval town was once a sacred place dedicated to the goddess of fertility, Venus."

"No wonder you have such a large family," I chuckle.

"Yeah. I'd be careful if I were you. Erice does things to a woman's fertility. One kiss, and you're in danger of giving birth to an entire litter."

"Thanks for the heads up. I'll be sure to keep my legs crossed while I'm here."

"Yeah. You do that."

Jeff looks like he's about to fall asleep on his feet. Not ideal, seeing as he's the man of the hour. I imagine Gina's extended family is super excited about meeting the man who stole their Gina's heart.

LYDIA HALL

"Are you ready for this?" I whisper to the man, who looks like a deer caught in the headlights of a pantechnicon.

"I guess we'll find out together," he whispers.

"You have the advantage here," I whisper back. "You speak Italian. Unless you say otherwise, I plan on smiling and nodding."

"Stick with me, kid."

A rush of noise bursts forth from the medieval building as Gina's family approaches us as soon as we exit the cab. Everyone is talking all at once. Gina wasn't kidding. It looks like the whole village is here to greet us. I'm overwhelmed, so I stand back and wait for the chaos to subside.

Gina pulls me into the family and introduces me to her aunts, uncles, cousins, and family friends who have all gathered for this momentous occasion.

"Come! Let's eat," one of the older women announces and grabs me by the arm.

I'm not complaining. I'm starving, and whatever they've prepared smells wonderful.

"Are all these people family?" I ask Gina once the storm of chatter has subsided a bit.

"Most of them. My wedding is an event, so everyone who's ever known me and my family is here to celebrate. I'm the only daughter, so it's a big deal."

"This is quite something," I grin. "I had no idea you were a minor celebrity."

"What can I say? I'm the golden girl."

"Poor Jeff is surrounded by a horde of old women. He looks rather nervous."

"Yeah. They're probably grilling him about impregnating me as soon as possible," she laughs.

"Poor guy."

"Come on. I'll show you to your room. It overlooks the Mediterranean Sea. You're going to love it."

"How old is this house?"

"Older than time."

"It's so beautiful, Gina."

"I'm so happy you are here to share it with us, M."

"Thank you."

"For what?"

"For giving me something to look forward to this year."

"Oh, come now. It's going to be a great vacation. You're going to have a great time. No more sad face. Okay?"

"You got it."

I'm all settled in in no time, so I go downstairs. I pass Gina's mother on the staircase.

"Hi, Mia. How are you, my love?"

"A little tired from the trip, but excited," I say, kissing Gina's mom on the cheek.

"When did you get here?"

"Two days ago. It's good to be back home."

"Do you miss it?"

"I do. But I get itchy feet. I'm already looking forward to my next trip abroad."

Gina's mom is a doctor. She travels all over the place, working with doctors without borders. She gave up her practice after Gina's father passed. She's a lovely person. I could talk to her for hours.

"You must be so excited to see Gina walking down the aisle."

"I am. I just wish her father could be here to see his baby getting married."

"I'm so sorry."

"It's alright. Thank you for being such a good friend to my Gina."

"Are you kidding? She is like the sister I never had."

"We love you, sweet girl. Come on. I could eat a horse on toast. Let's go rummage through the pots."

* * *

"Good morning, you beautiful human. Are you ready to get hitched?"

"Oh, absolutely. How did you sleep, M?"

"Like a baby. You?"

"Good, considering it was my last night as a free woman."

"Oh, stop it. You can't wait to be Mrs. Barlow."

"Mrs. Gina Barlow. Can you bloody believe it?"

"Come on. Let's get your warpaint on so we can hand you over to your groom."

"You owe me, you know."

"Yes, and I will be eternally grateful that you're not making me wear an awful bridesmaid dress. I'll try and return the favor one day when I get married."

"You'd better. I was really into those poofy purple dresses with the serious shoulder pads until you squealed."

"Sure you were. How's Jeff?"

"He'd still be drunk off his ass if my brothers had their way. I dragged him off to bed at midnight. He clearly doesn't have the legs for our locally brewed tipple. I must say, though, that his Italian gets better the more he drinks."

I laugh hysterically at the mental image of Bridezilla Gina dragging Jeff off to bed. I'm sorry I missed it.

"What time are we leaving?" I ask as we head down to breakfast.

"Noon."

"Are you nervous?"

"Not as much as I thought I'd be."

"You're going to look like a princess in your wedding dress."

"I'd better, considering how much I paid for it."

"Pittance, considering."

Gina comes from a wealthy family. Not that she lords it over anyone. She's humble and generous. I couldn't be her friend if she were any different. I hate pretense. Wealth is great as long as you're not a dick about it.

I decide to go for a walk after breakfast while Gina talks to her mom and aunt. I stop at a shop and buy some pistachio gelato. It tastes divine. I keep an eye on the time. It wouldn't be right for the maid of honor to be late on the big day.

Okay, it's time to marry Gina off, Mia. Who knows? Your very own Prince Charming may be waiting for you somewhere in the crowd of celebratory guests. If not, a good shag would do just as nicely.

2

DANTE

The knuckle on my middle finger is gushing blood where my fist connected with the man's snaggletooth. Man, it feels good! I've been itching to deck this asshole for a long time now, and today his proverbial chickens have come home to roost.

"Get this piece of shit out of my sight before I kill him," I growl, standing over the lump of flesh cowering at my feet.

"Yes, Boss."

"And tell Bruno I want to see him," I bark.

Damn it! There's blood on my new Egyptian cotton shirt. I rip it off, watching in frustration as the delicate buttons fly off in all directions. I hate starting my day off this way. It sours my mood unnecessarily.

"Leila! Get me a new shirt!" I yell to my assistant in the other room.

A tall, gangly girl with big tits rushes in a few moments later carrying a new shirt, still in its packaging. She unwraps it, takes out the pins, unfolds the delicate white cotton, and hands it to me.

"Thank you."

"You have a spot of blood on your chest," she remarks and hands me a Kleenex.

"Oh, yeah. Thanks."

"Shall I have this one cleaned?" she asks me, picking the soiled shirt up.

"No. Throw it out."

She nods and leaves my office, taking with her the proof that Dante De Luca doesn't suffer fools lightly. And why should I? I'm not an unreasonable man. I hold others to the same standards as I do myself. Work hard, show loyalty, and, above all, do what's expected. Why is it so hard for my underlings to adhere to these simple principles? It's not fucking rocket science!

"You wanted to see me, Boss."

"Yeah. Come in, Bruno."

Bruno is my consigliere. He's been with me from the word go. I trust him implicitly, as he's never given me a reason to doubt his loyalty. I'd never tell him this, but I consider Bruno an equal. He's the closest thing to a best friend a boss in the mafia could hope for.

"What happened?" he asks, pointing to my hand. "I passed a rather defeated looking lump of meat in the hallway."

"I finally lost my sense of humor with the moron. Nephew of a made man or no, he's gotta go, Bruno. That fool is going to get someone killed."

"I agree. What do you want me to do with him?"

"Use your imagination."

"Okay."

"By the way, I have to go to Erice next week."

"Business?"

"No. A family affair. A wedding."

"I see. Is your mother putting the screws on you again?" Bruno grins.

"Of course. I swear, that woman is the only person on this earth who can bully me into doing whatever she wants."

"She's a feisty old gal," Bruno chuckles. "Who's getting married?"

"My distant cousin, Gina. I haven't seen her since she was a sprig of a girl, but her mother is mine's favorite cousin, so I guess I'm going."

"What a good son you are."

"Careful. I'm warmed up now. I'll whip your ass."

"Yes, Boss," Bruno grins. "Will your brother be joining you?"

"Yes, Elio wouldn't dare say no to his mother. I'll leave you to run things while I'm away."

"Of course."

"Don't fuck up."

"Have I ever?" he smiles, getting up to leave.

"Smartass."

"Are you taking Francesca with you?"

"Are you nuts? I'm keeping that crazy bitch as far away from my family as possible. She's good for a shag, but I'd never hear the end of it if I introduced her to my mother."

"So, no wedding bells in your immediate future, then?"

"Fuck off."

Bruno cackles loudly and leaves my office.

* * *

I haven't been to Erice in a while. It's quiet here. Quiet and beautiful. Not at all like the hustle and bustle of Rome I've grown accustomed to. One can breathe out here.

"So, I suppose the whole family will be here for the wedding," Elio says on our way to the grand villa I booked for our mother and us for the weekend.

"I hear they've crawled out from every hole in the kingdom for this," I sigh.

"I'm surprised we even made it onto the guest list," he snorts. "We're not exactly popular with the extended family."

"I suppose the fact that you and I are at the pinnacle of the mafia organization does present a love-hate scenario with the other side of the family. We wouldn't be here if it weren't for our mother."

"So you tried to get out of it too, did you?" Elio grins.

"Yup."

"What good sons we are."

"More like a pair of pussies."

"Hey, I'd take on a legion of tough guys if I had to. But mother scares the shit out of me."

"Ain't that the truth?"

"You're flying solo for this occasion. What's the matter? Couldn't scare up a date?"

"Funny. No. I thought I'd scope out the local talent for a change. Why isn't Lisa with you?"

"She had a previous engagement."

"Speaking of engagement, isn't it about time you put a ring on that girl's finger?"

"You should talk. You are the oldest. You're the one who's expected to carry on the proud De Luca lineage. I'm the baby brother. All I'm required to do is show up and smile."

"You're dodging the question, little brother."

"Lisa and I love each other. A ring isn't going to make any difference."

"Have you told her that?"

"Lisa is a modern woman. She gets it."

"Uh-huh. She's a modern woman whose biological clock is no doubt ticking loudly in her ears."

"Slow down, bro. No one is talking about kids."

"All women want kids. They can't help it. It's nature. Like earthquakes and tsunamis."

"Is that your educated opinion, Dr. De Luca?"

"You joke, but I bet Lisa will be up the duff before the end of the year. Watch my words."

"You're full of shit. I'm amazed there aren't scores of little Dantes running around Rome."

"Not this De Luca. A broad would have to be pretty cunning to catch me out that way."

"Famous last words."

* * *

"Dante! My goodness. It's so good to see you."

"Congratulations, Gina. You make a beautiful bride."

"Thank you. May I introduce you to my husband, Jeff? Jeff, this is Dante, my mother's cousin's son. He lives in Rome."

"It's a pleasure, Dante."

"Welcome to the family, Jeff. You must be a tough man, seeing as you've survived the family thus far."

"It's been an interesting few days; I'll give you that," Jeff chuckles.

He seems like a nice guy. Not at all what I'd expected when I heard that Gina was marrying a foreigner. I didn't expect him to be so very English, but, hey, different strokes. Gina sure has filled out since the last time I saw her. I wouldn't have recognized her if we passed each other on the street. She's very attractive.

"Mother tells me you are doing well in Rome," Gina says.

"Yeah. We're keeping the wolves from the door."

"Dante here is being very modest, babe," Gina says to Jeff.

I guess the family grapevine has done its best, as always. I suppose it's to be expected. I am De Lucas' first billionaire.

"What do you do, Jeff?"

"I'm in finance."

"Now who's being modest?" Gina coos. "Jeff is an investment banker."

"Interesting work."

"Yeah, I enjoy it."

"Where are you from, Jeff?"

"London, originally. My family moved to the States when I was in high school."

"He's my very own import," Gina swoons.

"Well, congratulations to you both."

I'm not too keen on small talk. Besides, I spotted someone I'd much rather be talking to than my cousin. The dark haired maid of honor has me all hot and bothered. I watched her during the ceremony. In fact, I couldn't take my eyes off her. She's exquisite.

She's standing next to the buffet table, so I make my way over. I look at her left hand to make sure I'm not too late. Good. No ring.

The beautiful woman turns suddenly and bumps into me. The glass of champagne she's holding spills its contents onto my shoe.

"Oh, shit! I'm so sorry," she stammers. "It's my first glass too. Imagine what I'd do after another."

I'm transfixed as the woman's piercing blue eyes rest on mine.

Come on, Dante. What's your problem? Say something.

"Hi. I'm Dante. Don't worry about it. I'm sure my shoe will survive the assault."

"You're too kind. It's nice to meet you, Dante. I'm Mia."

"Ah, è un piacere incontrarti, Mia."

"Oh, sorry. I don't speak Italian."

"Really? With a name like Mia, I just assumed."

"Yeah, you'd think. My mother was a hopeless romantic movie buff. She named me after Mia Farrow."

"So, you're a friend of Gina's."

"Yes. I just adore her. How do you know her?"

"We're distant cousins."

"I see. More family," she chuckles.

"I take it you've met the army."

"Indeed. Not that I'm complaining. It must be wonderful to be a part of such a large family."

"It has its challenges. But, for the most part, it comes with the territory when you're Italian."

"Well, I think it's wonderful. Do you live here in Erice?"

"No. I live in Rome."

"Oh, wow. Rome. A beautiful city, I hear."

"I take it you haven't been?"

"No. I hope to come back to Italy one day and visit all the ancient cities."

"Perhaps I could show you around."

"That would be wonderful."

"Can I refill your glass, American Mia?"

"Yes, please. I promise not to baptize your shoes with the next one."

"In that case," I smile.

The music stops, and someone announces that it's time for the bride and groom's first dance. Gina and Jeff make their way to the dance floor while the rest of the guests look on.

"Would you like to dance?" I ask Mia once the other guests join in.

"Okay, but if you thought the champagne assault was offensive, wait until I step on your foot with these stiletto heels."

"You're not a fan of dangerously pointy footwear, are you?"

"No. I'm more of a sneakers girl."

"I promise not to complain."

"Okay."

Mia smiles, and my gut clenches instantly. Something about this woman has me completely disarmed. I haven't had a strong reaction like this to the opposite sex before. Is it because she's a foreigner?

Surely not. Italian women are as gorgeous as they come. I'm used to dating the hottest beauties around. What is it about this one that has me all thumbs?

"You're not doing too badly," I say into Mia's ear as she's pressing up against me.

"You're a good dancer, cousin Dante."

"I do try. Are you staying with Gina's family?"

"Yes. It's so beautiful. I have a stunning view of the ocean from my room. Is all of Italy this picture postcard perfect?"

"The countryside is special."

"Where are you staying this weekend?"

"A villa not far from here. I'd love to show you. Could I interest you in a nightcap later?"

"Sure."

My heart is thundering in my chest as Mia and I glide across the dance floor. Her hair smells like wildflowers, and her hand is silky soft in mine. I have to suppress the urge to bury my nose in her lustrous black mane and kiss her neck.

I want to take my time with this exotic flower, teasing her petals open one by one until she offers up the sweet nectar that satisfies. I like the hunt. I always have. The primal urge to corner and conquer is strong in the De Luca men.

I run my hand down her back, savoring the curvy contour. I rest my hand in the small of her back as we move as one to the music. It's over too soon.

"Shall we go?" I say, staring into her blue pools.

"Ready when you are."

Oh good. This is going to be fun.

"Where are you off to looking like the cat who got to the saucer of cream?" Elio asks as I pass him.

"Wouldn't you like to know? I'll send the car back to you later. I found something much more entertaining than a wedding reception to keep me occupied."

My brother peers over my shoulder at Mia, who's waiting for me at the exit.

"I see," he smirks. "Stunning creature. That didn't take you long."

"I always take what I want, little brother," I smile back.

"Yeah, I'll be fine. Have fun."

"I intend to."

"Be a gentleman," he chuckles.

"Oh, shut up, you fool."

3

MIA

What the hell am I doing? I hardly know this man. Sure, his rugged good looks and raw sex appeal alone are enough to bring any woman to her knees, but I'm not that kind of woman. Or am I?

It's been a terrible year. I've suffered enough emotionally for two lifetimes. I deserve a little fun; letting down my hair is just what the doctor ordered. Still, I'd hate for Dante to think that I'm some sort of a loose tart, ready to give myself to anyone with an irresistible smile and the voice of an angel.

But here I am, in the back of a luxury SUV with a man I barely know, wishing more than anything that he would touch me. No, ravish me, is more correct.

"That's me over there," he says, pointing to a villa on a hillside.

Wow. Nice place. I bet that set him back a good few thousand euros.

"You must have quite the view over the town from up here," I say, trying to sound calm when inside my heart is racing wildly.

"I do. We'll see the whole of Erice tonight under the light of the full moon."

The only thing I want to see by the light of the moon is your naked body, beautiful stranger.

"I look forward to it. Did you grow up here?" I ask, trying desperately to replace the image of him in my head.

"No. I grew up in Palermo, sixty-nine kilometers away from Erice."

"Oh, it's a big city, isn't it?"

"It is. My family has lived there for four generations. My grandfather worked as a civil servant."

"How wonderful. To have such a rich history, I mean. Are your folks still there?"

"No. My mother lives with my brother and me in Rome. My father died a few years ago."

"I'm sorry."

The car stops, and Dante gets out. I wait for him to open the door for me. I'm not about to compromise on good manners. They say it's the little things about a man's actions that speak volumes about his character. So far, Dante is 't doing too badly. My mother taught me to make a man work for it. She'd be appalled if she knew what I wanted to do to Dante.

My sexy host leads me to the front door of the villa. Dante must be a somebody somewhere, because he is never alone. I've noticed two men close to his side all night. Sure, they watch him discreetly from a distance at times, but nevertheless. Once we're inside the house, the men peel off, leaving Dante and me all alone. Hhmm. What to do now?

"Would you like me to show you around?"

Among other things, sure.

"I'd love that. What a beautiful home."

The house is built into a rockface. It's simply the most beautiful and romantic setting anyone could hope for. White leather furniture, hardwood floors, Italian marble' everything in here screams luxury. But it pales in comparison to the man I'm with.

Dante must be in his early forties, but he could effortlessly rival any man much younger. His flawless olive skin beckons me as I watch him moving around the rooms, pointing at interesting features and ultimately the view.

I feel like a schoolgirl with a debilitating crush. I hope I don't look as witless as I feel around him.

"It's spectacular," I offer up as Dante looks my way.

"How about that nightcap?" he smiles. "Brandy?"

"I'd love one."

My heartrate edges up just a little at the look in his bedroom eyes. This man is dangerously gorgeous. I'm going to have to watch myself. I'm no gusher, but damn!

We're in the living room now I sit down on one of the leather chaise lounges while my host pours brandy from a crystal decanter into two snifters. I watch his catlike movements as he walks over to me and hands me the drink.

"Thank you."

Our hands touch as I take the glass. A shiver runs through me. The sexual tension between us is deliciously palpable.

"So, how do you know little cousin Gina?" he asks as soon as he's seated across from me.

The distance between us is intentional. This man is playing with me. This is clearly not his first delicious seduction. He's an old hand at this. I can always tell.

"We work together. We just clicked from the first day we met. Have you ever met someone and instantly felt as if you've known them your whole life?"

Dante smiles and takes a sip of his brandy.

"Perhaps."

Is he talking about me or am I reading the situation wrong? I decide to steer the conversation into a safer direction. I haven't quite decided yet if I'm going to ravage this spectacular creature tonight or take the high road.

Oh, please, Mia. Who are you trying to kid?

"What do you do? When you're not saving damsels in stiletto distress from Italian wedding receptions, that is?"

Dante laughs and my sex quivers unexpectedly at the sound. With one small gesture he's reached down into my groin and teased me ever so gently without even touching me.

"I'm a businessman. A little bit of this and a bit of that, really. I like to keep busy."

"Not vague at all."

"Is that really what you want to talk about?" he asks, and places his glass down gently on the table next to his chair.

I recognize the look. It's one of the most exciting things about meeting someone new. The look that signals intent. Dante is letting me know, on the most primal level two people can share, that he wants me.

"What *would* you like to talk about?" I counter, playfully.

"I don't know about you, but I don't really want to talk about anything right now," he says in a low voice and gets up.

I watch him closely as he moves across the floor toward me like a panther. Before long the irresistible man who has my insides bouncing around is seated next to me on the chaise lounge.

"I must compliment Gina on her choice of a bridesmaid's dress," he whispers into my ear as he removes the clasp from my hair.

"I take it you're a fan of poofy sleeves," I say, exhaling slowly.

"No, but I am thankful for the way the silky material outlines every one of your perfect curves," he teases, running his hand through my cascading hair.

"Oh, that," I giggle.

"You are very sexy, American Mia," Dante says, running his finger down my back, causing a storm of goosebumps wherever his skin touches mine.

It's too late to turn back now. I couldn't stop this volcano brewing inside me even if I wanted to. Every fiber of my being is screaming out for this man to take me. The sound is positively deafening.

"Your hair smells like wildflowers," he whispers before he kisses my neck.

My head is swimming. I'm dizzy with delight and anticipation. My body is warm all over. The dull ache of desire grows steadily with every breath. I must have him. I deserve this. No one will know. No one will judge me. I'm in a strange land with a stranger. I've been a good girl all my life and look where it's gotten me. I'm twenty-five years old and I'm alone.

"It's bergamot, jasmine, and lilies," I groan, struggling to speak over the noise in my head.

"It's fantastic."

I close my eyes and focus on the trail Dante's blazing across my body with his fingers. His touch is so unexpectedly delicate. I'm trembling.

"Are you cold?" he whispers.

"A little," I lie.

"We'd better warm you up then," he says, takes my hand, and leads me up the staircase.

We're in a bedroom now. There's a fireplace against one of the walls. Dante leaves me standing in the middle of the room for a moment, walks over to it, and flips a switch. A fire roars to life, bathing the room in its soft, amber hues.

"Better?"

"Yes."

"Good. Come here. Stand next to the heat," he commands gently.

I do as he asks. The large room becomes smaller the closer I am to Dante. He's larger than life now, surrounding me with his presence. The object of my desire reaches for me and wraps me in a passionate embrace. I melt into him, effortlessly.

Dante's kiss is sweet. His lips cover mine while his tongue darts around playfully inside my hungry mouth.

"I want you," he coos.

Is he asking for my permission? Dante doesn't seem like the type of man who needs approval from anyone. He simply goes after what he wants. That's my impression of him, anyway. His eyes, though, are searching mine.

I cannot bring myself to say the words so instead I start to unbutton his shirt. I'm afraid that if I speak, I'll break the spell and all this will disappear into vapor. I close my eyes again as he kisses me with such urgency that my legs have difficulty holding me upright.

Dante must sense this because he picks me up and carries me to the bed the moment I free him from his shirt. Now it's my turn to feast.

He steps away, unzips his pants, and allows the garment to fall to the floor. My eyes turn immediately to my prize. He's magnificent!

I want so desperately to leap off the bed and run my fingers over his perfect form, but I don't. I wait patiently and watch. Dante is in excellent shape. His torso is ripped, his broad shoulders dreamy. I have to touch him. I have to.

"Come here," I whisper.

Dante grins and takes off his underwear, freeing his erection for me to see. I breathe in deeply. I've never been so turned on as I am at this moment. My lover watches my eyes. He's pleased with my reaction to him. I can tell.

He moves slowly toward me, reaches under my dress, and pulls my wet panties off. I'm swollen and tight with excitement. Dante slides his finger inside my core. The sensation is earth shatteringly pleasurable. This man knows his way around the female anatomy.

I whimper as he teases me with his touch. I'm trembling all over. I close my eyes and relax against the pillow while I allow Dante free reign. Now he's pleasuring me with his tongue. I moan out loud as he moves against me.

I don't want this to end. It's too delicious. My lover pulls away from me while I pull my dress off over my head. I'm completely naked now. Naked and desperate for him.

Dante gets onto his knees onto the bed. He takes in my nakedness from his vantage point.

"You are exquisite," he says, breathing hard.

I open my legs for him, making room for his magnificent erection. I want him inside me. I want Dante to take me and do whatever he pleases. I've never wanted anyone this much. My body is begging for him to subjugate me.

His shaft is warm and hard as he slides into me. I let out a sharp breath at the forceful, pleasurable shunt and immediately grab onto his firm posterior, riding him like a bucking Bronco.

Nothing else matters at this moment. Nothing! I am alone in a universe with Dante and the two of us are in perfect sync. He's kissing me now, marking me with his scent, like a wild animal does when it rubs itself against a tree trunk in the wild.

'You're mine,' his body says to me in no uncertain terms. I'm his and I yield to him. No greater force exists at this moment in time than the one that is coursing through our bodies. We move as one. We think as one. We want one thing—sweet release.

Faster, harder, and more urgent still, until I can feel my orgasm rising up inside me. It spills out of me with such force that I'm sure I'm going to snap my spine. Out it gushes, like a volcano shooting hot lava into the night sky. I call out his name as I climax. His sweet name rests on my lips as I feel him tense up before he too yields to the force.

Then, all is silent. Only the sound of hard breathing from two lovers who have given their all to the cause. I'm floating in a sea of dopamine, endorphins, and oxytocin. They have me helplessly under their spell.

I open my eyes only to look at my lover. He is propped up on his side, resting on his arm. He smiles while he gazes into my dreamy, post-coital eyes. What should I say? Do I even imagine that I have the appropriate words hidden somewhere in my vocabulary that could match this experience? I doubt it.

"You are a rare and beautiful creature, Mia," Dante says, gently kissing my breast.

How do I top that sentiment? I feel that I must gush. He deserves any and all accolades I can muster, but I remain speechless. All I can do is stare into his beautiful, espresso-like eyes and watch as the tongues of the flames from the fireplace dance around the room.

LYDIA HALL

I close my eyes while he snuggles against my back. Pure Heaven.

4

MIA

It's so quiet, except for the sound of the ocean in the distance. I open my eyes. For a moment, I forget where I am. Then it hits me. Dante. The memories of last night come flooding back all at once, and I have an overwhelming urge to stretch out and purr like a cat.

Dante isn't in bed. The side where he slept is empty and cold. I wonder where he is. I look at my watch. 11 a.m! Yikes! I must have been out for the count. I sit up and look around the room.

The sun is peering through the slit in the drapes. The view must be even more spectacular in the light of day, so I get up so I can open the curtains and look outside. Ugh…I would kill for a cup of coffee. The combination of champagne and brandy has left me feeling a little worse for wear. I desperately need a shower, too.

I notice a piece of paper on the nightstand. It's addressed to me. I open it and read.

Good morning, you gorgeous creature.

I hope you slept well. Thank you for a wonderful time last night. I don't usually do this, but I have a work emergency, so I have to leave early. Please make yourself at home and feel free to stay as long as you like. The villa staff will take good care of you. The driver is at your disposal.

I hope to see you again, Mia.

Warmest regards,

Dante

Damn. I have to admit that I'm disappointed. I was hoping to spend some more time with the irresistible Dante, but I guess that's a bust. Oh, well. We did have one passionate night. I'm sure it's one I won't forget anytime soon.

I pop the note into my bag and head for the shower. There is no sense in moping around on such a beautiful, sunny Mediterranean day. I have a gorgeous villa all to myself and a driver to boot. My day could be a whole lot worse.

* * *

Italy was a rare and exciting treat, but it feels good to be home. I'm excited to see Gina tonight. She and Jeff are back from their honeymoon, and I'm dying to tell her about my dalliance with Dante. I can't get him out of my mind. He made quite an impression on me. I catch myself daydreaming about our night of passionate love making more often than I should.

It was a night I sorely needed. I'm back to my old self again. No more moping about, regretting the colossal waste of time spent with Sam. In fact, I don't have one ounce of regret. Dante liberated me from the mire of self loathing and I'll be eternally grateful to him for that.

"Hi! Come in. Oof, I've missed you, Gina says, hugging so tightly I can hardly breathe.

"Well, hello there. Don't you look amazing? You wear marriage well. So, tell me all about it. How was the honeymoon?"

"Uh, amazing. I highly recommend it, M. But, before we get to the boring bits where I gush and show you all the pictures, I must ask. Where did you disappear to? One minute you were dancing, and the next you were gone. Who is he? Did you have your well deserved holiday romance?"

"More like a wedding inspired hump fest," I grin.

"No! With who?"

"Dante."

I notice a quick reaction in Gina's eyes. It's so subtle, I nearly missed it. I wonder what that's all about.

"Dante? Really? Do tell."

"Let's just say that he liberated me from any feelings I may have for Sam. I'm thoroughly flushed."

"You bad girl!" she laughs. "How was he?"

"A lady never tells."

"Oh, please. Come on. Spill it."

"Incredible."

"I must say, when I encouraged you to have a fling, I didn't expect it to be with someone like Dante."

"What do you mean? Why not Dante?"

"I don't know. He's thirty-seven. I thought you'd go for someone younger, I suppose."

"Are you kidding? Dante has the body of a twenty-something-year-old. He's gorgeous! And what a lover! Oh, my word. I've never felt that way with anyone."

"Yeah, the Italian men know their way around the lady parts. What did you guys talk about?"

"Talking wasn't the aim of the game. You were right. I needed a good shag, and that's what I got."

"Tra-la-la-la-la…"

"Cute. Now, where are the honeymoon pictures?"

I don't want to talk too much about my night with Dante. It was special, even though it was brief. It's something I'll treasure and think back on when I'm feeling particularly disappointed by men in general.

The afternoon spent with Gina gives me hope for the future. I'm sure that someday I'll find the kind of happiness she shares with Jeff. If not, I'll always have Erice.

* * *

"Are you feeling okay? I've seen healthier looking corpses."

"Geez, thanks, Gina. That's so sweet of you to say."

"I'm serious. You're not looking like your usual healthy self. Are you okay?"

"No. I feel awful. You'd think that working in a pharmacy would offer me a little extra defense against the common stomach flu."

"You'd better go home before you infect all of us. George will have a shitfit if there's a breakout of the runs. Here, take some of this and go home. I'll cover for you."

"You're a lifesaver, Gina. Thanks. I'd hug you, but…"

"No thanks. Just take it and go, you carrier," she grins.

"I'll call you later."

"Feel better."

I head straight for bed when I get home. I feel awful. I don't even bother getting out of my work clothes, but I simply flop onto the bed and close my eyes.

A fresh wave of nausea wakes me from my slumber, and I rush over to the bathroom. Bloody hell! What a crappy feeling! Eventually, once my stomach is completely empty, I move into the dry heaving phase. Ugh! Kill me now!

The sound of my cell phone ringing somewhere in the distance pulls me from my pity party for one. I rummage through my bag until I find it, then answer.

"Hello."

"Oh, my goodness. What's wrong, hon? You sound awful."

"Hey, Mom. Yup, I think I may have lost my internal organs through my mouth."

"Oh, darling. Tummy bug?"

"From hell."

"I'll come right over and make some of my famous chicken soup. That will fix you right up."

"Oh, no, please don't talk about food," I groan. My stomach is nice and empty."

"I'm coming anyway. See you soon."

Good old mom. There's no malady she cannot cure with soup. Not that I'm complaining. She's a fabulous cook. It remains to be seen, though, if I can keep down whatever she's planning on serving up.

I fall asleep again while I'm waiting for her. The doorbell wakes me up.

LYDIA HALL

"Hey, Mom," I say when I open the door.

"Wow! That bug's got ya good, huh?"

"Sure has. Come in."

"You go and take a nap, sweetheart, while I get the cauldron brewing."

"No, that's alright. I think I've slept enough. I'll drape myself over the sofa while you cook."

Mom puts down the paper bag she brought with her onto the open plan kitchen counter while I plop down on the sofa.

"Are you taking in enough fluids, my love?"

"Not faster than I can expel it, I'm afraid."

"Do you have a fever?"

"No. I don't think so."

"Good. Here," she says and hands me a glass with an opaque liquid inside it, "home made ginger beer."

"I don't know if this is a good idea, but I'll try. Thanks, Mom."

"Ginger is good for nausea. You'll feel better soon, I promise."

"How long have you felt this way?"

"It's been almost a week now. I must say, I'm over it."

"A week? Sounds serious. Have you been to the doctor? Tummy bugs shouldn't last that long."

"Did you forget where I work? Who knows what kind of superbugs people drag in there off the streets? I'm sure it will pass soon enough. The good news is that I'm one vomit away from my goal weight," I chuckle.

"Oh, rubbish. You'll fall through your own backside if you lose any weight. You're perfect."

"Just a little girly humor."

"Where's your vegetable peeler?"

"In the drawer next to the sink."

"It's a good thing I'm here. Your cupboards are empty. What were you planning on eating?"

"I wasn't."

"We haven't seen each other since your trip to Italy. How was it?"

"Oh, it was wonderful; thanks, Mom. What a beautiful place. And Gina was such a beautiful bride."

"Yes, I saw her photos on Facebook. What a gorgeous dress. She looked like a princess."

I can hardly believe it, but the ginger beer is actually helping. I'm feeling a little better.

"How was her family?" Mom asks, peeling away.

"Large. And, noisy. But very sweet."

I wonder what my mother would say if I told her about Dante.

"Meet any eligible cuties?"

"If I didn't know any better, I'd say you were trying to marry me off, Christine."

"Ha ha. Would that be such a bad thing? You're twenty-five years old, sweetheart. You don't want to wait too long before you have children. The older you are, the tougher pregnancy gets."

"Geez, woman. I'm still young. There is plenty of time for babies. I have to find a decent man first. Who knew it would be so hard?"

"Yeah. They don't make 'em like they used to."

"So you keep saying."

"I take it Sam is out of the picture for good."

"That chapter is closed."

"I'm sorry he hurt you, my love."

"Thanks, Ma. That's sweet of you to say."

"The soup won't be ready for another hour. Why don't you run yourself a nice warm bath?"

"That sounds like a great idea, actually. Thanks, Mom," I say, kissing her on the cheek.

"My pleasure."

"Love ya."

"I love you too, sweetheart."

* * *

"That's it. You're going to see the doctor, and that's final," Mom says a week later, when she pops in for a coffee.

I'm still green around the gills. It's better, but not by much. Mom is on the phone while I get dressed. Forty minutes later, we're in the doctor's waiting room, paging through old magazines while we wait to speak to Dr. Flowers.

"You shouldn't have let it go on for this long, Mia."

"I feel a little better, Mom."

"Well, you don't look it."

"The doctor will see you now, Miss Martin," the assistant says after she takes my vitals and gives me a cup to urinate into.

Mom waits outside while I go in.

"Hi, Mia. It's good to see you again. Please take a seat. What's troubling you, Mia?"

"Hi, Doc. Mom's being a little overly dramatic. I feel okay. I'm just having the darndest time shaking this tummy bug."

"I see."

The doctor looks down at the chart on his desk and flips over a page. He takes a few moments to read and then looks up at me.

"Well, I can see what the problem is," he says.

"What is it?" I ask.

"Nothing a few months won't sort out."

"I'm sorry, I don't understand. A few months? What kind of crazy bug is this?"

"You're pregnant, Mia."

* * *

"You're what?"

Gina is staring at me as if I just told her I was abducted by aliens. I know how she feels. I thought I was going to pass out when Dr. Flowers broke the news to me. I've been in a daze ever since.

"Oh, Lord. It's Dante's, isn't it?" she says again, looking quite pale.

"Uh-huh."

"Oh, Mia. How did this happen?"

"I would have thought you of all people would understand, Gina. You were the one who told me to let down my hair, live a little, blah blah blah."

"I did. But I didn't mean for you to come home with a permanent reminder of your joyous holiday. And, Dante. Oh, my…"

"Okay, I have to ask. Why do you keep saying his name like that? What's wrong with him?"

"There's nothing wrong with him. It's just. Well."

"Well, what?"

"I hate to tell you this, M, but he's the 'bad boy' of the family."

"What are you talking about?"

"Let's just say his business practices are a tad on the fringes of the law."

"I hate it when you talk in code."

"I'm sorry. Just forget about it. Are you going to tell him?"

"I don't know. I have to get used to the idea of being a mother first."

"I'm here for you, M. You don't have to tell him if you're not ready."

"Thanks, Gina. Oh, hell. Why did this have to happen?"

"I warned you about our Italian stallions. Erice didn't get its name for nothing."

"Yeah, you told me. Pity, I couldn't hear it over the sound of Dante's magnificent penis serenading me."

5

DANTE

I'm about to celebrate my forty-second birthday, and life couldn't be better. I haven't found the woman of my dreams yet, but then again, I do alright in the dating department. It's been five years since Gina's wedding, and I must say, I think of Mia often. There was something so sweet and innocent about her. Not to mention that it was possibly the strongest sexual attraction I've ever had toward a woman.

"Hey, old man. Are you ready for your party tonight?" Elio interrupts my thoughts as he enters my office.

"Old man? I could run rings around you, squirt."

"They say that denial is the first step in the grieving process," he grins before he sits down across the desk from me.

"Funny man, hey? So, what? Now, I'm grieving the loss of my youth, am I?"

"If the patent leather shoe fits, Cinderella."

"Smartass. What can I do for you, my pain in the ass brother?"

"Kyle called. They want to see us in LA. I think this deal is going to be good for the family."

"I don't know. I'm a little weary of Kyle. There's something about him. I can't put my finger on it, but..."

"Bullshit. You just don't like him. His offer is solid, though."

"I'm not jumping into bed with anyone until I've had some time to think about it."

"Suit yourself. But don't take too long. If we don't move on this, someone else will."

"Cool your jets, little brother. That's why I'm the boss. Remember?"

"Uh-huh. Okay, I'll get out of your hair. Don't be late tonight, Boss. I'll keep the strippers on ice in the meantime."

"I bet you will."

"Gotcha back, Jack."

"You've seen too many gangster movies, Elio. Anyway, if Kyle so much as breathes at me in a way that makes me uncomfortable, I'll cut off his dick and feed it to him."

"I don't doubt that for a moment. I'll see you later, Dante."

"See you. And, thanks."

"For?"

"The party."

"Of course. You're the man of the hour."

My brother leaves. I send off a few emails before it's time to call it a day. There's a knock on the door. It's my right hand man.

"Happy birthday, Boss."

"Thanks, Bruno. Come in. Sit. How did it go in San Luca?"

"Good."

"Did you have to crack open some heads?"

"No. All good. Stefano's been on his best behavior since you punched out his front teeth."

"Glad to hear it. I'm glad you're here. I wanted to talk to you about Kyle."

"Sure. What's up?"

"Elio said he wants to meet with us in LA."

"Yes, he told me."

"What do you think about this deal?"

"Well, it certainly sounds promising."

"Do you trust him?"

"So, you feel it too?"

"Yeah. I'm not so sure that he isn't trying to pass off his shit as shinola."

"What do you think, Boss? Informant for the cops?"

"I don't know. But I'll tell you one thing, I don't trust the man. Something about him is off."

"You've always had good instincts, Dante. You want me to do a little digging?"

"Yeah. Do me a favor, though. Keep it on the down low."

"Of course."

"Thanks, Bruno. Well, I'd better get out of here. Got a party to get to."

"I hear Elio has gone to a lot of trouble for this one," Bruno smirks.

"Yeah, I believe so. Something tells me I'll be up to my eyeballs in strippers before the night is out."

"I'll make sure to double the muscle tonight. We wouldn't want you to worry about safety on your birthday, Boss."

"Thanks, buddy."

Bruno leaves the office to do what he does best, making sure I have as much intel on both friend and foe.

"Happy birthday, Mr. De Luca."

"Thank you, Donna."

My assistant hands me a small box.

"Enjoy your party, Boss," she smiles.

"Thanks. I'll see you tomorrow."

"Yes, Mr. De Luca."

Donna is cute, and if I'm honest, I think she hero worships me just a little bit. But I don't shit where I eat, so I graciously accept the gift and leave.

* * *

"Okay, so I've checked Kyle out."

"And?"

"The man's no altar boy, but on the plus side, his business is on the up. Perhaps an alliance with him isn't such a bad idea. We have been looking to expand our international business. Kyle's operation is a good place to start."

"Okay. Set it up."

"Will do."

"Except, I'm not taking Elio with me. It's better if he stays behind to run the day to day operations while I'm away."

"Your brother won't be happy to send you off by yourself, Boss."

"He'll be fine. Besides, Elio does what I tell him to do. Everyone knows it's a bad idea for the two of us to travel together. The rules of ascendancy don't permit it."

"I'll set it up."

"Thanks, Bruno."

"You had quite a night, by the looks of it," he smirks.

"Yeah. Elio knows how to throw a party; I'll give him that."

"How are you feeling this morning?"

"Strong like a lion, buddy."

"You De Luca men are chiseled from tough stuff," Bruno chuckles.

"You better believe it."

* * *

I settle in as I gear myself for the fifteen hour flight to LA. One of the perks of being wealthy is owning my own jet. It gives me time to go through some paperwork. I like to be prepared when it comes to business dealings. My degree in finance gives me a good business head, so no one has ever been able to pull the wool over my eyes when it comes to numbers.

I must say, I'm impressed with what Kyke has sent through. He seems to be a savvy entrepreneur. It's not his business acumen that gives me pause. Again, I don't know what it is about the man that makes me uncomfortable. I usually have great instincts when it comes to people. I hope I'm wrong about him.

"Would you like a drink, Mr. De Luca?"

"I'll have a whiskey, thanks, Jenna."

"Dinner will be served in about half an hour," she smiles.

"Thanks."

I'll have a bit to eat and then take a nap. I've been running on fumes lately. I want to be clear headed when we land in LA.

"Gino."

"Yes, Boss."

"I want you boys to be on your game tomorrow."

"Yes, Boss."

"The Americans are on their own turf. I don't want any fuckups. You get me?"

"Yes, Sir."

I keep a gun on me at all times. I've learned the hard way that it pays to be prepared. Never bring a knife to a gunfight, they say. Well, whoever they are, they're right. I'll hide my Sig Sauer P365 in my boot. She's small, but she gets the job done.

In fact, she makes quite a mess if used correctly, as Billy back in Rome will testify. I left that wanker with a permanent hole in his face. He'll never fuck with me again. I should have killed him, but, honestly, Billy is worth more to me alive. He serves as a living reminder to those who would think to fuck with me.

"We'll be landing soon, Mr. De Luca," the pilot announces over the intercom, once I wake up from my nap.

I check my watch. It's midday in LA, so the boys and I will book into our hotel for the afternoon and meet with Kyle and his men at 10 p.m. tonight.

* * *

It's 21:15, and I'm raring to go. Gino and the boys are armed to the teeth. Fat load of good it will do them, as I'm sure Kyle will insist that we leave our firearms at the door once we get to his place. But it's worth a shot.

Our driver punches the warehouse coordinates into the GPS, and we're off. My muscles are well rested, and I'm switched on. It's time to make a deal and expand my operation into LA.

There are four men, armed with automatic weapons, outside the location as we drive up.

"I don't like this, Boss," Gino says, unconsciously resting his hand on his firearm under his jacket.

"It's okay, Gino. Kyle isn't stupid enough to try anything. He'll have the full force of Italy raining down on him if he tries. He knows that."

"Even so, Boss. Are you wearing your vest, Sir?"

"Yeah. It's bloody uncomfortable, but it beats the alternative hands down."

"Stay by my side, please, Boss. Just to be safe."

I nod. The car comes to a stop.

"Okay, boys. We're up," Gino says to the three men with him.

He gets out of the car, goes around to the passenger side, and opens the door for me. I look around the minute I get out of the car. No sudden movements on either side. No one can afford to get antsy' not with the ample firepower around.

I walk behind Gino. One of my bodyguards walks next to me, and two more follow closely behind. We get about halfway across the parking area when, out of nowhere, the sound of a gunshot shatters the calm.

"What the fuck!" Gino screams before he turns around and throws his body onto mine.

The next few minutes are chaotic, with men scrambling in all directions, gunfire blasting away, and the sound of tires screeching on tar as my driver mows men down in his path.

"Mr. De Luca!" he shouts as he stops next to me and flings open the passenger door.

Gino's dead weight keeps me from leaping up. I can feel a hot, sticky liquid running down my neck. It must be Gino's. I use all my strength to push his two-hundred-and-sixty pound frame off me. He doesn't show any signs of life. His eyes are open and vacant.

"Fuck! Gino!" I yell through the noise of gunfire before I slip into the passenger side of the car.

"Leave him, Boss. He's dead," the driver shouts at me.

The other three men aren't any better off. One of them is on his haunches, firing at will. A bullet to the head puts paid to his efforts. He slumps over and stops moving. Gino saved my life with his quick thinking. I'm the only one still alive.

"Drive!" I scream.

I jump over the seat into the back of the car and scootch down so that I'm out of the line of fire. My driver is throwing the car so violently around corners that I nearly knock myself out of the door. Thank God I decided to bring him along on the trip. He's the best driver I've ever seen. If anyone can get me out of this mess, it's the man currently at the wheel.

We get about half a mile away when the car suddenly comes to a stop with the horn blaring.

"Fuck!"

The driver is slumped over the wheel. Blood is pouring from a wound in his neck. I have to get out of here or I'm next, so I jump over the seat, push him out the door, and step on the gas.

I have no idea where I'm going, but I don't care. Anywhere is better than where I am now, so I keep zigzagging the streets until I find myself in a steady stream of traffic. What the fuck just happened? Am I dreaming? Is this a nightmare? Surely, I'll wake up any second now and find myself safely in my hotel room.

But it's not to be. I'm racing through the streets of LA, my men are all dead, and I'm bleeding profusely from a gunshot wound to my arm. I've only just noticed it, actually. The adrenaline is still pumping hard. I know from experience that it's going to hurt like a son of a bitch as soon as the shock wears off.

I have to get the wound treated. It would be a sorry tale if I die of an infection after surviving the attack. I drive until I see the lights of an all night pharmacy up ahead. I park the car.

I don't want to go to a hospital, as they have to report all gunshots to the cops. I can't afford that sort of heat. Not now. I'm losing a lot of blood. I can feel myself getting weaker by the minute.

Come on, Dante. Don't be a pussy. This isn't your first gunshot wound.

I pull myself together, take a deep breath, and walk into the pharmacy. Thankfully, it's empty except for a pharmacist behind the counter and an assistant on the floor.

She looks familiar. I know her. Those eyes. I get as far as the first aisle before my legs buckle, and I go down like a sack of potatoes.

The woman rushes up to me and grabs me by the arm. She's saying something to me. I hear her faintly before I pass out.

"Dante. Oh, Lord."

Mia! But how?

6

MIA

Dante! How is this even possible? I'm trembling all over as I hold his head in my lap.

"Holy, crap," George says as he rushes over and sees me cradling the man bleeding all over his shiny pharmacy floors.

"Is he alive? I'll call the cops," he says.

"Wait!" I urge him to stay put. "I know him."

"What? Who is he?"

"He's Gina's family."

"Shit! Are you serious?"

"Please don't call the cops. Help me."

"Are you nuts? This man's been shot, Mia. I have to call the police."

"Please, George. I'll explain later. I'll owe you big. Just help me."

George doesn't look happy as he stares down at Dante.

"Please," I beg.

"Fine. But you better pray that he doesn't die."

"He won't. Help me."

George hooks his arm under one of Dante's, and I take the other. Together, we drag the unconscious man to the back of the pharmacy and hoist him onto the bed.

"We're going to have to take out the bullet," George barks.

"Okay. I'll get the gauze and the needle."

"Bring the antiseptic so I can clean the wound."

"Your friend is a lucky man. The bullet went straight through and missed the brachial artery by a ball hair," George says once I return with the emergency supplies.

"Oh, thank God."

"He's going to need stitches, though. It's a bloody mess," he moans.

"Thanks, George. I mean it."

"Yeah, yeah. Consider yourself in my debt for at least a year," he says drolly.

"Happily."

"So, you say it's Gina's family?"

"Yes, I met him at her wedding."

"Any idea as to why he'd stumble in here with a gunshot wound?"

"Not the foggiest."

My heart is racing. It's Dante! What are the odds? He is just as handsome as I remember. It's been five years, but it feels as if no time has passed and I'm staring at him again for the first time.

"Okay," George says after having sewn up Dante's arm. "It's the best I can do under the circumstances. He's going to have to take a course of antibiotics, or he'll end up with an infection. I'll prescribe him a course."

"You're my hero, George."

"Hey, if this guy dies, I'll deny ever seeing him. Got that?"

"Got it."

"You'd better get him out of here."

"Will you be okay?"

"Yeah, it's a slow night. Go."

I kiss George on the cheek. His gray beard scratches my face.

"Thank you, George."

"Yeah, yeah. Get out of here. I'll help you get him to your car. You'd better call Gina."

"I will."

I'll call her for sure. But not until I have an opportunity to talk to the father of my child, first. Alone.

*   *   *

"Where am I?"

"Don't get up. You're hurt. You've lost a lot of blood."

Dante sits up and touches his arm where George and I treated his wound. I still can't believe he's in my living room. Dante De Luca! Of all the pharmacies in LA... I have so many questions.

"What happened, Dante?"

"It's you. I can't believe it. How are you, Mia?"

"A damn site better than you, by the looks of it. What happened, Dante? Who shot you?"

"It's a long story."

"Hey, we have all night."

"Is this your home?"

"Yes."

"Do you live here alone? No boyfriend…husband?"

"No, I'm single."

I daren't tell him about our son, Angelo. Thank God he's with the babysitter tonight. I have no doubt that his face will give away his patronage. My son is a carbon copy of his father.

"What happened? Why are you in LA?" I ask again, hoping that this time the man I've been dreaming about for five years will tell me what the hell is going on.

"I'm here on business."

"Does Gina know?"

"No."

"Who shot you?"

"A very stupid man, that's who."

"What happened?"

"I suspect my competitors are out to do away with some healthy competition. I don't want to talk about it, Mia. I'd much rather talk about you. How have you been? I can't believe it's been five years since Gina's wedding."

"So, that's it," I say, suddenly very upset. "You stumble back into my life, wounded and bleeding, on death's door, and you don't want to talk about it!"

"It's for your own safety, Mia. I'm sorry. Thank you for helping me. Truly. I'm more than grateful."

I'm pacing the room. That's what I do when I'm upset and frustrated. This is not how I wanted my day to go.

"I'll go if you tell me to," he says and makes a motion to get up.

"No. You're not well enough. Just stay in bed. We'll talk about it in the morning. I'm exhausted."

"I'm sorry, Mia. This isn't how I hoped we would meet again."

His words sterile a cord. Does he mean to say that he's been thinking about me? Or is he just being polite?

"I've thought about you often, you know," he says, his eyes sincere. "I'm so sorry I had to leave before I had an opportunity to say goodbye, Mia. I had a wonderful night. We shared something amazing."

I stop pacing.

"I thought so too."

"How are you? You haven't changed a bit. You're still as beautiful as the first time I laid eyes on you."

"If you're trying to win brownie points, you're doing a good job," I grin.

"Does that mean I'm forgiven?"

"I'm thinking about it."

"It's true, Mia. You are a vision."

My anger is abating. This man has a curious power of me. It was evident the first time we met and I can tell that my feelings toward him haven't changed a bit.

"Are you in pain? I have painkillers for you."

"No. I'm alright. Thank you."

"This is crazy. I can't believe it's you."

"I know what you mean. I almost had a heart attack when I saw you."

"I don't know about you, but I could do with a drink. Do you have anything?"

"I do, but I'm not going to give you alcohol. You're on some pretty strong meds and alcohol isn't a good idea."

"I wasn't planning on finishing the bottle. One drink? I promise not to drive," he smiles.

"Okay. Just one. I'll be back in a bit."

My hands are trembling while I pour Dante a shot of whiskey. I down a shot to steady my nerves before returning to the room with his drink.

"Here. It's whiskey."

"Uh, you're an angel. Thanks."

I watch as Dante throws back his drink. I can't help staring at him, watching his every move. He is so handsome. His face has aged a little since the last time we were together, but not by much. In fact, Dante is one of those men who is guaranteed to age like a fine wine.

"How is Gina?"

I'm grateful for his question. I'd hate to do something stupid, like throw myself at an injured man.

"She's fine."

"Still happily married?"

"Yeah. Don't you guys talk?"

"Not really, no. Our families aren't that close. Despite appearances, the De Lucas and the Carusos don't see much of each other."

"Why is that?"

"It's complicated."

"Strange."

"What is?"

"That's what Gina said when I asked her the same question."

"So, you asked about me?" he grins.

"Don't get any ideas," I smile back.

"Come on, Mia. You can't deny that we had something pretty racy. An undeniable attraction, even."

"You were a holiday romance, Dante De Luca."

"Ouch. You're a mean nurse."

"Hey, if it weren't for me, George would have called the cops."

"I'm sorry I put you in such an unpleasant predicament. Thank you for taking care of me."

The air is as filled with as much sexual tension as it was the first time he and I were alone in a room. I don't know where to look. I know if I give myself half an inch, I'll end up in his arms again. Would that be so bad?

"You're welcome. Are you hungry?"

"Yes, but not for food."

Oh, crap. He's doing it again. Dante is seducing me and I'm lapping it up. Damn his sexy eyes!

"Come a little closer," he says dreamily. "I'd like to thank you properly."

My legs are on their our mission as I acquiesce to Dante's request. It's as if my mind, and common sense, have no say here. My body is yearning to reunite with Dante's and there's not a damn thing I can do about it.

"You've changed your shampoo," he whispers into my ear.

"I can't believe you remembered."

"I remember everything about you," he breathes hard. "I missed you."

Is this a dream? A rotten trick the universe is playing on a woman who longs to be loved? If it is, I hope I never wake up again.

Dante kisses me softly on the mouth, and teases my lips apart with his tongue. This is really happening. It's as if no time has lapsed. I close my eyes as I take in his scent. My lover's skin smells wonderful. I cannot get enough of him.

The T-shirt I found in my cupboard is tight on him. His shirt was drenched in blood, so I changed him when he was still asleep. I run my hands over the soft material. Over his pecs, along his taut abdomen, all the down to his groin where I ultimately rest my hand.

The feel of Dante's erection sends tingles through my body. I have imagined this often in the past five years. The reality of what's about to happen doesn't disappoint. In fact the fantasy trails a distant second in comparison to the real thing.

The familiar fire ignites within me at this beautiful man's deft touch.

"I missed you, Mia," he whispers.

"I missed you, too."

"I want to make love to you."

His words are an aromatic pleasure. I move away from him so that I can take off my shirt and jeans. I'm burning to be skin to skin with the most exciting man I've ever met. Dante does the same. He shimmies out of his pants and pulls off the T-shirt. He grimaces when he lifts his arm, but doesn't stop undressing.

I want to take away his pain. It's an instinctive reaction. I want to pleasure him. I want to be pleasured by him.

"I'll kiss it better," I whisper.

I start with butterfly kisses on the skin surrounding the bandage before I move steadily and with absolute purpose toward his chest and then down to his beautiful abs. It's a taste sensation as I trail my tongue along his smooth, bare skin.

Dante is making soft moaning noises as I go. He lets out a sudden breath as I get to his proud erection. I tease the head of his shaft with my tongue before I close my mouth around it and move rhythmically up and down.

"Uh, yes," he whispers.

Dante feels for my breasts and tweaks my nipples. I get in a few more delicious mouthfuls before he hooks his hands under my armpits and pulls my body on top of his. Dante positions me onto his shaft and pulls me down hard. The sensation of his hardness sliding into me sends tremors of pleasure through me.

"You're perfect," he moans as I ride him harder, faster.

My lover grabs a hold of my rear as he takes what he wants, what he needs, what we both desire. The headboard is hitting the wall, making a racket, but I don't care. I have what I want, and I don't care who knows it. Let the bed roar! Let the walls come down around us! I have Dante inside me and I'm chasing the pleasure that only an orgasm can deliver.

It's coming! It's so close, I can feel it. I let out a roar of satisfaction while I climax. It's been five years of longing and finally, release is at hand. I bite down on my lower lip as I cum. I shudder and jerk for the longest time. Dante follows closely.

The pain in his arm is long forgotten as we ride the beast with two backs. The experience is intense. Everything about this man is intense.

Finally, we're spent as we lie together, breathing hard. My lover is still inside me and I refuse to move away, afraid that in doing so I'll break the spell. I want to stay this way forever. This is the only place where I have true fulfillment—here in Dante's arms.

I don't care what the morning may bring. All I have is now. And now is more than enough.

7

DANTE

It's morning. The sun is up—I can tell by the light in the room—and my arm hurts like a bitch. The memories of the past twenty-four hours come flooding back. Kyle! He's a dead man. I hope he knows that I will stop at nothing to kill him. And not just him, but those he cares about too. But there are a few things I have to do first.

Mia. Beautiful, sexy, irresistible Mia. She saved my life. I'd hate to think where I'd be had it not been for her quick thinking.

"Good morning."

She is standing at the door, wearing a T-shirt, her legs bare. Such shapely calves.

"Hi."

"How are you feeling?"

"Sore."

"You were sleeping so peacefully, I didn't want to wake you. Coffee?"

"Great, thanks."

"How do you take it?"

"Black with two sugars."

I motion to get up.

"No. Stay in bed. I'll bring it to you."

"That's sweet of you, but I need to stretch my legs."

The blood rushes to the wound as soon as I stand up, sending a sharp pain down my arm.

"Ahia," I seethe, wishing for Kyle's demise.

"I'll throw in a few painkillers too," Mia says before she leaves the room. "You must be hungry," she calls from the other room while I put on my pants.

"Starving."

"I don't have much. Eggs okay?"

"I love eggs."

I look around the room while I dress. It's modest, but tastefully decorated. A lot of throw pillows. Definitely a woman's room. I notice a few photographs on the dresser. There are a few of Mia holding a young child. I wonder who the kid belongs to. Mia said last night that she was single.

I'll ask her about it later. For now, I need to get rid of the throbbing pain in my arm and get some food into my system. I leave the room wearing only my pants. I don't feel like wrestling with a T-shirt now. My arm is too sore.

Mia is in the kitchen, pouring coffee into a mug. She pops two teaspoonfuls of sugar in and stirs before she hands it to me.

"Thanks."

"It's good," she smiles. "I'm a bit of a coffee snob."

"Lucky for me."

"I'll whip up some scrambled eggs. Why don't you take a seat? I'm sure you must be a little fuzzy still."

I sit down at the kitchen counter while I drink the coffee and watch the stunning Mia as she whisks eggs. Amazing how she makes such a mundane task appear erotic. She's wearing her dark hair up in a bun, and I marvel at her high cheekbones and unblemished, olive skin. Mia is a rare beauty. I wonder why she's single. Surely, men must fawn over her wherever she goes. Not that I'm complaining.

"Did you sleep well?" I ask.

"Like the dead. You?"

"Surprisingly well, considering."

"Here. Take these."

Mia places two painkillers and a glass of water on the counter in front of me.

"They'll take the edge off."

"Thanks."

I watch her while she cooks the eggs. I drool as she reaches for a plate on the top shelf, exposing her gorgeous derriere. I'm desperate to leap off my chair and take a bite out of her delicious butt cheek, but the pain is keeping me from it. Fuck you, Kyle! You're going to pay for this. You're going to wish you'd never heard the name De Luca.

I wonder if he's alone in his betrayal. Did he have help? None of it makes sense. Why would Kyle lure me here and then try to kill me? Surely he must know that his actions are tantamount to suicide. Either way, he's a dead man.

"Here you go. Eggs ala Empty Pantry."

"Smells good. Do you have hot sauce?"

"You're in luck," she says and opens the fridge. "A friend brought this back from Mexico. It's delicious, but beware. It will erode your undies from the inside," she giggles.

She is so sweet.

"I promise to make this up to you, Mia."

"Last night was a good start."

"A meager offering," I smirk.

"So, what's the plan? Where to from here?"

"Well, I have to call my brother in Rome and talk to him about a few things before I decide."

"I don't want any trouble here, Dante. Promise to keep me out of whatever this is."

Mia is acting like someone who has something to say, but can't decide on the exact delivery. I can't blame her. What woman would invite this sort of chaos into her home?

"I promise. No trouble."

There's a knock at the door. Mia is flushed. I wonder what's going on.

"Are you expecting anybody?" I ask, hoping that my trust in her is well founded.

"Yes, actually. I'll be back in a sec."

I don't have my gun. I hate being without it.

I hear the chatter of a child as soon as Mia answers the door. I wonder who it is. My answer comes soon enough when a young boy, around four or five, I reckon, walks into the living room. I recognize him from the photos in Mia's room. He's a beautiful boy.

"Hi," he beams up at me with his innocent face. "Who are you?"

"Hi. I'm Dante. Who are you?"

Mia is still at the door. She's talking to a woman.

"I'm Angelo," the boy announces. "I live here."

"Oh…"

A child. Mia never said anything about having a child. Why would she not say?

Why would she tell you, Dante? It's none of your business.

"Hi, Angelo. It's nice to meet you."

"What happened to your arm?"

"I had a little accident."

"Mommy kisses my boo boos and ouchies better. Did she kiss your ouchie?"

Uh-huh. And then some.

"Your mommy fixed my arm, yes."

Mia is standing at the door, watching the kid and me.

"Go get your school bag, darling," she says.

"You have a son," I say as soon as Angelo has left the room.

"I do."

"Why didn't you tell me?"

"I was going to but…you know. You distracted me."

"What about his father?"

"He's no longer in the picture."

"I see. He's a cute kid."

No rival suitor. Excellent news.

"I think so too. I need to get him ready for school. Would you excuse me, please?"

"Of course. Thank you for the eggs."

"Sure."

Mia leaves the room. I can hear the kid laughing and chattering away in the adjacent room. The apartment isn't very big so sound travels. It's a good thing the kid wasn't here last night because his mother and I made quite a racket.

It's not long before little Angelo is back in the living room.

"I'm going to school now."

"Okay. Have fun."

"Come, darling."

Mia is dressed. She's a knockout in blue jeans and a T-shirt.

"I'm going to drop Angelo at school now. I won't be long. Why don't you relax a bit. Take a bath. I have sweatpants in my closet. They're a little big for me, so it will fit you in a pinch."

"You're sweet. Thanks. Would you mind if I use your phone?"

"Sure. The landline in my bedroom next to the bed."

"Thanks, Mia. For everything."

She smiles, catapulting my stomach into a hot mess.

* * *

"Dante! What the fuck is going on? Are you alright? I keep calling and calling your cell phone. The receptionist at your hotel said she hasn't seen any of you since yesterday."

"It's okay, Elio. I'm okay."

"What happened? Why are none of the guys answering their phones either?"

"Kyle happened. The fucker ambushed us. Everyone is dead, Elio."

"Figlio di puttana! I'll kill him! Where are you? Are you hurt?"

"I caught a bullet in the arm, but I'm alright."

"This is unbelievable! Where are you now?"

"You wouldn't believe me if I told you."

"What? Why?"

"I stumbled into a pharmacy and straight into that woman I spent the night with at Gina's wedding. Mia."

"You're kidding!"

"No. She stitched me back up and brought me to her apartment."

"Unbelievable."

"Yeah. Anyway, I'm here now. I don't want to go back to the hotel until I'm sure that Kyle's men aren't waiting for me."

"Fanculo! I don't believe this."

"You'd better batten down the hatches back home, Elio. I don't know if Kyle acted alone. He may have his sights set on you."

"If he's an idiot! Which seems more likely than not after what he's just attempted. I'll rip his lying tongue out before I kill him."

"You won't get that lucky, brother. I'm going to make sure there's nothing left of that fucker long before you ever get yours hands on him."

"You need to come home, Bro. You're not safe there."

"No. I'm staying right here until I figure out what Kyle's up to."

"That's not smart, Dante. You're all alone."

"I want you to send some muscle my way. I'm going to buy a place here in LA and set up a temporary operation."

"Okay, but I'm coming too."

"No, Elio. Stay there. I can't protect you here. That fucker almost killed me. I won't put you in harm's way."

"I'm not a child, Dante. I can take care of myself."

"I know. But I need you there. You can do some investigating on your side while I cover this area. We don't know who's in this with Kyle. Please Elio. Do this for me."

"Fine. I'll send a team."

"Okay. The plane is still here. I'll send it back to you. Fill her up with able bodied men."

"Stay safe, brother. I won't lose you to a prick like Kyle."

"Will do, Elio."

"I'm sorry, Dante."

"For what?"

"I was the one pushing you to meet with him. I should have trusted your instincts."

"It's not your fault, little brother. Keep Mamma safe. Tell Bruno I need him too."

"They'll be on the flight as soon as the plane gets here."

"Thanks, Bro."

* * *

I'm in the bath when Mia gets back. She has a shopping bag in her hands.

LYDIA HALL

"I got you a few things. I thought about you in my sweatpants and couldn't stop giggling."

"Hey, I wouldn't mind getting into your pants, but not literally."

"Yeah, I figured. I bought you a pair of jeans and a few shirts. Oh, and sneakers. I figure your dress shoes would look a little odd with the outfit."

"Are you always this thoughtful?"

"Well, my motives aren't totally altruistic. I refuse to be seen out with a man dressed in a woman's pants and Italian dress shoes. Call me a snob if you must."

"You're cute."

"Did you get hold of your brother?"

"Yeah. Thanks."

"What are your plans?"

"I was thinking of sticking around for a while."

Mia smiles. I can tell that my news pleases her. I have to be honest with myself. Kyle isn't my only motivation for lingering in LA. I'm not ready to say goodbye to her again. Not just yet.

"In fact, I could use your help. If that's okay."

"Of course. What can I do?"

"I'm going to need a place to stay. I thought you could come with me and help me decide."

Is she disappointed? Did she assume that I would stay with her? I couldn't impose like that. She has a kid. Motherhood is hard enough without a houseguest who attracts trouble.

"Sure."

"I'd love to stay here, but you have a son and I don't want to impose."

"Of course. I understand. I'll call an estate agent friend of mine."

"Do you have to work tonight?"

"No. I called George and asked if I could take a few days off. I figured you'd need me."

"Mia, I've said it once and I'll say it again. You are perfect."

"You'll sing a different tune when I'm drawing my PMS sorrows in chocolate and red wine," she chuckles.

"Impossible. Now, come over here. I can't reach my back with one bum arm and there's a dirty spot that needs cleaning. You'd better take off your clothes too. I don't want you getting all wet."

"You, Dante De Luca, are a bad man," she grins, taking off her T-shirt and sliding off her jeans.

"And just like that there's an extra bit for you to wash," I purr as she gets into the tub with me.

"I have a feeling I'm going to be dirtier than I was by the time this bath is done," she giggles.

"Beautiful and smart. Who's the lucky patient?"

8

MIA

My life has been a whirlwind since Dante stumbled into it. It's odd how one person can cause such a drastic shift in one's existence simply by being there. Dante has changed my life in a profound way. And not just mine but Angelo's too. Our son seems to be drawn instinctively to his father without knowing why.

Dante is so gentle with him. I'm starting to wonder if I did the right thing by not telling him about his son. I'm wracked with guilt at the moment. Seeing them together is torture. How am I going to explain my selfish decision to Dante when the time comes? Damn it!

"What do you think?"

Dante interrupts my mental flatulations. We're looking at a house in the hills. The property isn't officially on the market just yet, but Candice decided to show it to Dante when I called her and explained to her what he was looking for.

"It's incredible. A dream home. Do you like it?"

"Yeah. I do."

Candice is outside in the garden. She's an excellent sales person. I hate it when agents walk you through a house, pointing out the obvious features. I mean, I know what a kitchen looks like for Heaven's sake. Not every buyer enjoys it when a stranger hangs around when they're trying to make up their mind about a new home. It's irritating.

"Are you going to make an offer?" I ask, trying my best to focus.

"Well, the place is rather big. I'm not sure I want to live here all by myself. I'd feel a bit like a fart in a windstorm."

"It is expansive."

"I *do* have an idea," he says, like a cat that got into the cream.

"Oh, do you now?"

"Uh-huh. It would be a waste, me living here all alone. What would you say about moving in with me? You and little Angelo."

Moving in together! The thought makes my insides shake. It's a big step.

"I know it's a big step…"

Mind reader.

"But it would be great to spend more time together. You have your hands full between your job and ferrying Angelo to school and back. Moving in with me would make your life easier. You can bring his nanny here to live with us. There's plenty of room."

"Goodness. I don't know what to say."

"Look, I don't want to put you on the spot, Mia. Please promise me you'll at least think about it. I must tell you, though, that I don't want to waste time. We've already lost five years. Just saying."

"Okay. I'll think about it."

"Great."

"Wow! Mommy! Dante! Come see the pool," Angelo yells, running into the living room.

It would be wonderful to afford my son, our son, a chance at a better life. Our apartment is small and there's no lawn, so poor Angelo is missing out on the things little boys should be doing, like playing outside. Maybe I can get him a dog. He's always wanted one.

"Looks like I have at least one of you on my side," Dante laughs as Angelo jumps into his arms.

"It's so cool! Is this our new house, Mommy?" my angel asks with excited eyes.

Shit. What should I say? This is so hard.

"Uhm, well. We'll see, sweetheart."

"Ah, a firm fan," Candice smiles.

"At least two," Dante winks.

Great. Nothing like being ganged up on. I can see that saying no to the father and son duo is going to something I'm going to have to get wise to.

* * *

"I still can't believe what you're telling me, M. Dante! Here in LA! It would have been nice if he'd called and told me."

"I don't think he was planning on staying that long, Gina. It's a miracle he found me."

"From what you're saying, I think you turned out to be *his* miracle. Is he okay?"

"Yeah, he's fine."

"What happened?"

"Dante was vague when I asked him. I don't want to push. I'm sure he'll tell me when he's ready."

"And? How are things between you two? Have you told him about Angelo?"

"Are you crazy? I'm not ready to do that. Even if I were, how the hell will I break the news to him that I've been hiding his child from him for five years?"

"Good point."

"What should I do, Gina? Dante wants Angelo and me to move in with him."

"So soon. That's a big step, M."

"No shit! Come on. He's your family. You must have some useful advice for me."

Gina looks like a cornered animal. Why does she always get that look when I ask her about Dante? Is she hiding something from me?

"What aren't you telling me, Gina?"

"It's not my place to talk to you about Dante. I don't really know him that well, anyway. We're distant relatives. I grew up here in the States and he in Italy. We used to see each other every now and again when we were kids. I don't know the grown up Dante well enough to comment on his character."

"Are you sure that's all?"

"Look, M. I know Dante and his brother, Elio, are tough businessmen. As I've said, it's up to him to talk to you about it. I won't speculate."

"Ugh! You're no help."

"Sorry, babe. You're going to have to navigate this pothole all on your own," she winks.

"That's it. I'm downgrading your best friend status. I want my airfryer back."

"Indian giver," Gina giggles, hugging me tightly. "You'll figure it out. You've made it this far on your own. You're a tough chick."

"Yeah, sure. Hand me that bottle of aspirin, will you? The price tag has come off."

I want to know more about Dante before I decide to move in with him. It's only natural. But I find myself all thumbs when I want to ask him personal questions. Is it my guilt over Angelo that's muddying the waters?

The truth is I'd love nothing more than to be a family, living in a home together—Dante, Angelo, and me. Like we're supposed to be. Ah, hell! This is driving me nuts.

* * *

"Nanna!"

Angelo throws himself around my mother's leg. He adores her and the feeling is more than mutual. It's a beautiful thing, watching the relationship between a child and its grandparents. I catch myself being almost jealous at times when I see them together.

My parents worked throughout my childhood, so I didn't get to enjoy them the way that Angelo does. I guess that's just the way life goes. I'm thankful for our closeness now that they're retired and I'm an adult. My parents are so dear to me.

They were so supportive when I told them that I was going to be a single mother. It took me some time to tell my mother who Angelo's father is. I don't know what she's going to say when I share my latest news with her.

"My little munchkin. Oh, my goodness! You've grown so heavy," my mother groans, picking up her grandson and popping him onto her hip.

"I eat all my veggies, Nanna," he grins proudly.

"That's a very good boy. Why don't you go find grandpa? He's in the garage."

"Okay," he smiles and runs off as soon as his little feet hit the ground.

"What's the matter, Mia?" my mother asks after she hugs me.

"Why do you ask?"

"Come on. I know that look. I am your mother, you know. You used to get that same look when you did badly on a test and tried to hide it from me. Fess up."

"You've become much tougher since you became a grandmother," I chuckle.

"Come, let's have some tea. I baked your favorite. Apple pie."

"You always know just how to get me to spill the beans, don't you?"

"So, you are hiding something. I knew it. How big of a slice of apple pie are we talking, here?"

"Just bring the pie dish, the tub of cream, and a spoon."

"Hmmm. I'm almost afraid to ask."

My mom and I walk, arms linked, to the kitchen. She smells like Jasmine and Vanilla. I could find her in a crowd if I blindfolded.

"How's Dad?"

"He's fine. He and Bill are working on another model train out there in the garage. The place is a minefield of miniature locomotive parts. But it keeps him busy so I daren't complain."

"You must be looking forward to your trip to see Aunt Maddy next month."

"I am. She's taking your Dad and me on a trip through the winelands."

"That sounds amazing."

"I know, right. Flip the switch on the kettle, please, sweetheart."

"Sure."

Mom slices the pie, while I pop two teabags into a teapot. I'm not sure how I'm going to start this delicate conversation off, so I'm a little rattled.

"So," she says once we're seated at the nook. "What's on your mind, Mia?"

I take a bite of apple pie before I start talking. Heaven knows I need the feel of comfort food on my tongue right about now.

"It's about Angelo's father."

"I get the feeling we should be drinking something a little weightier than tea."

"I know I haven't spoken much about him, but I feel I need to now."

"Why? What happened?"

My mother looks worried.

"He's here. In LA."

"Oh. I see."

Mom waits patiently for me to speak. I take a sip of tea before I feel brave enough to speak on.

"He's met Angelo. But I haven't told him that he's the father."

"Mia! That's terrible. You have to tell him, sweetheart."

"I know! But, how? I feel awful. What am I going to say?"

"That depends on what kind of man he is, Mia. Which brings me to a question that I've never asked you because I respect the fact that this is a difficult situation for you. But what kind of a man is he?"

"Truthfully, Mom...I don't know. I don't know him well enough. It was a mistake, Mom. It isn't something I'm proud of. I'm not a one night stand kind of girl. You know that. But, I was vulnerable and he was so good for me at the time. Ugh! It's all a mess!"

"Shhh, my love. It's alright. I'm not judging you. Heaven knows, none of us are perfect. Don't beat yourself up. You're a terrific mom."

"I called him once."

"Really? When?"

"When I was about eight months pregnant. I found out where he lives and I called his house."

"And?"

"I hung up as soon as I heard his voice. I didn't know what to say."

"Oh, Mia. My darling."

"Now he's here in LA and he's met his son and you should see how well they get along, Mom," I start rambling. "Angelo adores him and he doesn't even know that the man is his father."

"Kids are instinctive, Mia. They know things. What are you going to do?"

"I wish I knew."

"I'm going to put off our trip to Aunt Maddy. You need me."

"No, Mom. Don't you dare. You and Dad deserve this break. You've been planning it for months. I'll be just fine. I promise."

"Will you bring him around so I can lay eyes on him?"

"And say what? Hey, do you want to meet your child's grandparents?"

"Okay, smartypants. You know that's not what I meant."

"Sorry. I'm a little antsy. Okay. Let me see what I can do."

"Is he here to stay?"

"Well, he's buying a house, so I guess he's planning on sticking around for a while at least."

"In that case, you'll have to tell him sooner rather than later."

"I know."

"How are things between the two of you?"

"Wonderful. I'm crazy about him, Mom. I know it's insane, but I've never felt this way about a man before. And, he's equally smitten. He's asked me to move in with him."

"Goodness. That's heavy."

I chuckle at my mother's choice of words. She sounds like a hippy.

"What can I do, my darling? How can I help you?"

"That's sweet, Mom. But, I made this bed and now I have to lie in it. If you pardon the pun."

"Bring him around for lunch on Sunday. We'll figure something out."

"Okay. Thanks, Mom."

"I love you, Mia. I'll do whatever I can to make this as painless as possible for you."

"Don't tell Dad yet, please. I don't want to have to explain myself to him."

"I won't. You can tell him when you're ready."

"Thanks, Mom. I think I need another slice of pie."

"Coming right up. Extra whipped cream?"

"You read my mind."

9

DANTE

"I was wondering when you'd get around to seeing me," Gina smiles and kisses me on the cheek.

She and I are at a coffee shop near the new house I just bought. I was hoping that Mia and Angelo would be living there with me by now, but I don't want to push. I'll give Mia as much time as she needs. I don't want to scare her off by being overbearing.

"Hi, Gina. I'm sorry. How are you? Married life seems to agree with you. You look happy."

"I am, thanks."

A waitress comes over to our table. Gina and I place our order and then carry on talking.

"You need to level with me, Dante. What happened? Ordinarily, I wouldn't ask. I know it's none of my business. But Mia is my best friend. I love her. I don't want to see her hurt."

"I see you inherited the family's cutting-through-the-bullshit gene."

"Would you be more comfortable if we engaged in meaningless small talk?"

"Hell, no."

"Okay then. What are your plans, Dante?"

"I had no idea I'd bump into Mia again. To tell you the truth, I've never forgotten her."

"That brings me to my next question? What happened? Why are you in LA and why were you shot?"

"Do you mind if I have a sip of my coffee before we carry on with this interrogation?"

Gina smiles. Her face lightens up just enough for me to be able to relax. She's a tough cookie just like all the women in my family. You don't mess with a De Luca. Gina may be a distant cousin, but she's clearly made of the same spit and vinegar.

"Okay, cuz."

Gina isn't afraid of me. Or she doesn't seem to be. Most people are. It's refreshing.

"Okay. I came to LA to meet with a potential business partner."

"From what Mia told me, I take it that things didn't go according to plan."

"It could have gone better, yes. As far as my intentions toward Mia are concerned, I think that's between her and I."

"Be careful with her, Dante. She's a sweet person. And she has a child. You and I both know that your world doesn't leave much room for peace and tranquility."

"I care very much for her and Angelo. I'll never let anything bad happen to them."

"That may be so, Dante. But you know that's not up to you."

"What have you told Mia about me?"

"I haven't told her the truth, if that's what you're asking. And I feel awful about lying to her. You have to come clean, Dante."

"You're right. This is none of your business. You may be family, Gina, but you don't know me at all."

"I know you're in the mob. That's no life for Mia and Angelo."

"Don't you think that's something she should decide for herself? She's not a child."

"If you're so sure then why haven't you told her yet? What will you do if this business partner of yours comes after Mia?"

"I told you, that won't happen?"

"Are you sure, Dante?"

* * *

"I told my mom about us. She's like to meet you," Mia says one afternoon.

"Meeting the parents, hey? I didn't realize we were there yet," I chuckle, kissing her in her soft neck.

"Don't distract me, you horny devil. What do you say? Are you ready to meet my parents?"

"Sure."

"Great. They've invited us for lunch on Sunday."

"I'll be on my best behavior. I promise," I wink. "I have a little surprise for you."

"Ooh, I love surprises. What is it?"

"Can you take a few days off next week? I thought I'd take you away."

"I'm sure I can ask Gina to fill in for me. Where are we going? Can I bring Angelo along?"

"Do you think your mother would mind looking after him for a few days? I was hoping we could be alone."

"Oh, really?" she purrs and nuzzles my neck.

"Yeah. I'd love to have you all to myself."

"Okay, I'll ask her."

"Great."

* * *

"What's happening? Have you found him yet?"

"No, if Kyle is still in LA, he's in deep hiding. The men and I have been looking, but no luck so far."

"Yeah, he'd better hide. The bastard. How are you doing?"

"I'm frustrated. I want to get back to Italy."

"Don't worry about us on this side. Everything is fine. You've established a good team here."

"I'm sending Bruno back to you. He's of little use to me here."

"Alright. Did you buy that house you were talking about?"

"Yes. It's got great security. No one will get in there."

"I worry about you, brother. When will you come home?"

"Soon."

"How's Mia?"

"Incredible. You've never heard me say this about anyone before, Elio, but I think she may be the one."

"The woman must be something else."

"Oh, she is."

"Does she feel the same?"

"I think so."

"What about the kid?"

"Angelo is a good kid. He looks a lot like Mia."

"Has she said anything about his father?"

"No. It doesn't matter to me, as long as he doesn't interfere. Mia says he's out of the picture."

"Do you believe her?"

"She hasn't given me any reason not to."

"Oh, by the way, you'd better be back here by the end of the year."

"Of course. Why?"

"Because your baby brother is getting hitched."

"What? I don't believe it."

"Lisa is finally making an honest man out of me."

"Congrats. I'm happy for you, Elio. Please give Lisa my love."

"I will. Talk to you soon."

"Okay."

My brother is getting married. That's great. Not so much for me. My mother will no doubt be all over my ass soon about doing the same. It's our duty to have scores of children while we forge ahead and build a legacy.

I wonder what Mia would think of the whole Italian mob lifestyle. Gina was right. I'll have to tell Mia sooner rather than later but I'm in

LYDIA HALL

no rush. She's American. All she knows about the mafia is what she's seen in movies.

It's a merciless life and I don't know if she'll understand our ways. But, nonetheless, I want her by my side. All I have to do is figure out how to get her there.

* * *

"It's very nice to meet you, Dante."

Mia's mother is a beauty. She has such soft eyes. Her father is ogling me. I wonder what he must think of the Italian man moving in on his princess. I imagine I wouldn't be any different if I had a daughter. He's polite enough though.

"Good to meet you, Dante, he says, extending his hand to me.

"So nice to meet you both," I smile.

"Can I get you a drink, Dante?" he offers.

"Thank you."

"Beer? Wine? Whiskey?"

"A beer sounds good. Thanks."

"Mia tells us you live in Rome?" her mother says.

"Yes. My family lives there. Have you been?"

"Harold and I went there when we were first married. It's a beautiful city. I'm sure much has changed since then."

"Yes, as with all cities, change is inevitable, I suppose."

"Christine is a hopeless romantic," Harold grins. "I wanted to go to Sicily and see where they filmed that great Italian movie, In the Name of the Law. But my dear wife here wanted to see the great cathedrals of Rome. No prizes for guessing who won that argument."

"Don't forget the Colosseum and the Pantheon, you brute," Catherine chuckles. "Not all of us are obsessed with gangster movies, Harold."

The irony of this conversation isn't lost on me. I wonder what Harold would say if he knew who I was. I imagine he'd be less of a fan of the arts then.

"What do you do in Rome, Dante?" Harold asks.

"I own a few businesses."

"He's being modest, Dad. Dante does very well," Mia says with a smile.

"Mia tells me you and Catherine are retired. Are you enjoying it?"

"It took a bit of getting used to at first. I almost drove my poor wife nuts. But I have my hobbies now so I keep out of her hair."

I laugh as Mia's mother throws her husband a cheeky look. They're a nice couple who seem to be in love even after many years together. Such relationships are a rarity.

My father was killed when I was in my twenties, so I had to take over from him. There wasn't time for anything but work. He and my mother were close too. I know she misses him terribly. But that's life.

"I hope you're hungry, Dante," Christine says.

"Yeah. She made enough food to feed an army," Harold chirps. "You'd better eat or I'll be having lasagne for dinner for the next week."

"They're adorable," I whisper to Mia while her parents are talking to each other.

"They are indeed."

***

The clerk at the front desk is staring at Mia. I'm going to knock his block off if he keeps doing that.

We've just arrived at the wine farm and I'm irritated. My efforts to find Kyle have all come to nought. All I need now is for this horny asshole to push me. No one fuck with my woman. No one.

"Good afternoon," he grins. "Welcome to The Grape Escape. Do you have a reservation?"

He's talking to me but he keeps looking at Mia.

"Yeah. De Luca," I half growl.

"Ah, yes. You are in the private suite, Sir. My name is Raúl. Please let me know if there's anything I can do for you while you're here with us."

Oh, hell, no! Did he just look at Mia's tits? This dirty Spanish fucker needs to be taught some manners. I won't make a scene here in front of Mia, but I'm not going to let this go.

"The porter will show you to your suite, Mr. De Luca," he smiles and hands me a key.

"Thank you," Mia says kindly, clearly having missed the creep's innuendo.

I say nothing. It's safer if I keep my mouth shut at this point. Anything I say will make Mia uncomfortable, and I don't want to do that to her.

The porter shows us to our suite, overlooking the vineyards. It's the best money can buy. I wanted to spoil Mia. I know she's never been away from Angelo. She told me as much. I want to distract her. This weekend is special.

"Oh, wow. This is gorgeous, Dante."

"No. You're gorgeous."

"You've earned yourself plenty of points, Mr. De Luca," she grins.

"Job done," I grin, pulling her closer. "Let's see if we can press some things in here while the workers are pressing grapes out there," I purr.

"What an excellent idea," Mia giggles.

My lover and I spend the next hour taking full advantage of the peace, quiet, and isolation this suite affords us. I explore every nook and cranny on her magnificent body and I don't quit until she screams my name while she's in the throes of her orgasm.

We lie together afterward, soaking up the magnificent afterglow.

"I'm starving," Mia says eventually, breaking the silence.

"Shall we order in or would you like to go to the restaurant?"

"My hair is a mess and I don't feel much like dressing up. How about we order in and go out tomorrow?"

"This weekend is all about you, my gorgeous. We'll do whatever you like."

"There you go again. Points. Lots and lots of points," she grins, kissing my chest.

"Careful. Don't start something you can't finish."

"Oh, you are so bad."

Mia, you have no idea!

* * *

Mia's asleep. It's close to midnight. I get up quietly. I have something to take care of before I can sleep soundly.

I make my way to the reception area. It's quiet. The Spaniard is alone at the reception desk. Good.

He doesn't see me coming until it's too late. I grab him by the hair and bash his head down onto the marble countertop.

"You look at my woman like that again and I'll break more than your fucking nose. Nod if you get my meaning," I growl into the Spanniard's ear.

He nods while covering his bleeding nose with his hand. I let go of his hair and I disappear as quickly as I appeared.

There. I feel much better. Now I can sleep soundly.

10

MIA

So, this is living the highlife. I can get used to it. How wonderful to wake up and have your every whim pandered to. I'm afraid what will happen when this bubble shatters. Will I ever be able to go back to tolerating the nine-to-five existence I've eked out since becoming a single mom?

Raising a child on your own is exhausting. Two parents share the load, but when there's just one of you, it gets tricky. I don't know how I would have survived without my parents' help. Not that I take advantage of their love for Angelo. They're retired and I want them to enjoy their freedom. Saddling them with a baby, then a toddler, and now a busy five-year-old, doesn't seem fair to me no matter how much they insist on it.

Dante has truly spoiled me rotten. I think about how unexpected and surreal this all is while I'm lying next to the swimming pool, sunbathing under the California sun. I slept like the dead. Why wouldn't I? Earth shattering orgasms, delicious food, expensive wine —it's a pill.

"Hey, gorgeous woman," he purrs and hands me a glass of freshly squeezed orange juice.

"Hey yourself," I smile.

I'm lying on my stomach. I'm sunbathing topless, taking full advantage of the privacy the suite provides.

"Can I rub some sunscreen on your back?" Dante coos.

"Uh-huh. I know what that means," I giggle. "You just want to touch me again, don't you?"

"You should have been a detective," he chuckles.

"No rocket science here, my friend."

"Okay, but don't blame me if you get a nasty sunburn."

"That's unlikely."

"Oh, and why's that?"

"Because your body will shield me from the rays. In fact, why don't you put some sunscreen on that cute bottom of yours. I have a feeling you're going to need it."

"Aren't you the clever one," Dante groans as he takes off his bathing suit, and slips me out of mine.

This is exactly how I got myself into a pickle in the first place. If I had resisted the temptation to throw myself at this man five years ago, I wouldn't have returned to LA carrying a little memento of our time together. Not that I have any regrets. Angelo is the love of my life. I wouldn't change that part of my life for anything. Sure, it's been hard at times, but still.

We make love next to the pool. It's amazing. Sex with Dante is indescribable. I lose myself completely every time he touches me. I'm falling head over heels in love with this man.

Dante and I are on our way to the dining area for dinner. We pass the reception desk on the way there. The guy who booked us in when we arrived is standing behind the counter. He looks downward as soon as he sees us coming. I wonder what happened to him. His nose is bandaged and his eyes are bruised. Probably a nose job. It isn't uncommon to see in La La Land. Everyone is on the hunt for the perfect facial features.

"Ouch," I whisper to Dante once we've passed the poor young man. "Looks like that hurts."

"Yeah," he says before taking one last look at the guy who is suddenly very busy with his paperwork.

Oh well, just another example of vanity over sanity.

The waiter seats us at a table out on a private deck. The lights are on in the vineyard, casting the groves in a fairytale haze. I must say, I enjoy all this exclusivity. It's nice not to have to fight for a table in a bustling restaurant or squeeze into small spaces, elbows touching.

"Thank you," I say once he pulls out the chair for me.

"Oh, Dante. This is perfect. How beautiful."

"You look beautiful, Mia. I could just stare at you all night and forget the vineyard altogether."

"How's your rear?" I giggle.

"A little warm."

"You should have lathered it with sunscreen like I told you."

"I'm sure I have finger marks burned into my butt," he laughs.

"Do we have to go home?" I sigh. "Couldn't we stay here? Imagine how much fun Angelo would have running through the groves."

"I'll buy this place for you, lock, stock, and barrel, if that's what you want my sweet."

"Ah, that's so nice."

"Do you miss Angelo?"

"Always. But I know he's fine with my parents. He loves going there for sleepovers. They spoil him rotten. Dad takes him fishing down at the lake near their house. He loves that."

"What's it like?"

"What?"

"Having a child."

Tread carefully, Mia.

"It hasn't been easy. Single parenting isn't for everyone. But, I would change it. I love Angelo so much. He's quite the character, as I'm sure you've noticed."

"Yeah. He is a bright little boy. You've done an amazing job with him, Mia."

"Thank you. Have you thought of having children?" I ask, tentatively dipping my toe into the murky waters."

If he says no, I'm screwed.

"I have, yes. But the time hasn't been right. Also, it does help to find a partner worthy of bearing one's seed," he grins.

"Good point. I take it you haven't found such a creature back in Italy."

"If you're curious about my love life, all you need to do is ask," he chuckles.

"Okay. Tell me about your love life."

"Only if you tell me about yours."

"There isn't much to tell, really. I seem to have a rotten picker."

"How so?"

"Well, my last relationship ended badly. It took me a while to realize that he was a consummate liar and a rogue."

"Lucky for me, the man's an idiot. I must remember to send him a thank you card."

"What about you? Have you ever come close to taking it to the next level?"

"I take it that by the next level you mean marriage?"

"Yes."

"No. To be fair, I haven't had much time for that sort of thing. My life is very busy."

"Everyone's life is busy. I think if you're in love you'll move mountains to be with someone."

"I'm starting to understand what you mean."

Dante smiles and covers my hand with his.

"Have you given the move much thought?"

"I have."

"Come on. Don't keep me in suspense."

"As I've said before, it's a big step. Angelo is my top priority, Dante."

"I wouldn't expect it to be any other way. You're a brilliant mother. I do think that it would be good for the two of you to move in with me. There's so much space and a young boy like Angelo needs the space."

"All good points, and I assure you, I have taken every conceivable point into consideration."

"You're killing me here, Mia."

"Sorry," I laugh. "I don't mean to."

"Will you move in with me? Please?"

I take a deep breath. There's no going back after this.

"Yes."

Dante smiles brightly, his brilliant pearly whites on full display. He gets up from his chair, comes around to me, offers me his hand, and then pulls me gently to my feet.

"You have made me so happy, Mia," he says, cupping my face in his strong, warm hands. "I'm going to make you happier than you've ever been."

"That's a tall order. I'm pretty happy right now."

"This is only the beginning. I promise," my beautiful man says before he kisses me passionately.

I lose myself once more in the arms of the man who stumbled back into my life.

* * *

I'm still on cloud nine. I'm convinced that my feet haven't hit the ground yet, as I float around the pharmacy in blissful memories of the weekend away with Dante.

"Good grief. Hello! Earth to Mia!" Gina laughs.

"Huh? What? Sorry, I was deep in thought. What did you say?"

"You seem to be more absent these days than present. I take it that things are hotting up with Dante."

"Like a brushfire, my friend."

"I see."

"I agreed to move in with him."

Gina looks at me for a moment before she responds. What is it with her and Dante?

"Okay."

"You don't look nearly as excited as I thought you would."

"No. I am. Really. When is the big day?"

"He's arranged a moving van for the weekend."

"Is Angelo happy?"

"Is he happy? He adores Dante. He's telling everyone he knows that we're moving into a palace with a pool," I laugh.

"He's so cute. How are things between him and Dante?"

"Peas in a pod."

"I'm happy for you, M. I really am."

"Thanks, Gina. I don't know where this is going just yet, but I'm trying not to look too far ahead into the future. I seem to do that everytime I date a man and look where it's gotten me so far. So, this time I'm taking it one day at a time."

"Smart."

***

"I'm moving in with Dante, Mom."

My mother is quiet on the other end of the phone call.

"Are you sure, my love?" she asks me after the protracted silence during which I imagine she's biting down on the lip so as not to react in haste.

"I'm sure, Mom. We're in love and Angelo is crazy about Dante. It will be good for the two of them to spend time together. They need to get to know each other."

"When are you going to tell Dante that he's Angelo's father?"

Ouch! Trust a mother to deliver a slap that jerks you right back into the real world.

"Soon, Mom. I'm trying to find the right moment to tell him."

"I don't see why this is so difficult, my darling. You tell me that Dante is crazy about Angelo. Surely he'll be glad when you tell him."

"Come on, Mom. There's a vast difference between liking your girlfriend's kid and finding out that you're his father."

"I'm just saying that perhaps you're driving yourself nuts for nothing. Dante may surprise you. He seems like a nice person."

"I know. Ugh! I know you're right, Mom. Honestly, I don't know why this is so hard for me."

"Dante isn't Sam, Mia. Now that one was trouble from the start."

"Really? Sam had us all fooled."

"Not me."

"Oh, nice one, Catherine. If you were so sure about Sam then why didn't you say anything to me?"

"You were so determined to make that relationship work, my darling. I didn't want to meddle."

"I wish you had."

"And be the bad guy? Oh, no. No thank you."

"Anyway, this discussion is moot. Dante is not Sam, and we're moving in with him."

"Okay, darling. I'm happy for you. I mean that sincerely."

"Thank you, Mom. I love you."

"I love you too."

"Gotta run."

"Okay. Chat soon."

I'll tell him soon. I will. Just not right now. Hey, this may not work out and then I won't have to tell him.

Oh, wow! That's a mature way of looking at the situation, Mia.

Oh, hell. Whatever. I can't stand around here fighting with the little voice of reason in my head. I have to pack.

"Mommy!"

"Yes, my love. I'm in the kitchen."

"Can I bring my dinosaur?"

"Of course, sweetheart. You can bring all your toys."

"Oh, good. Because I think he'll be scared if we leave him here. He likes to sleep with me at night."

I never stopped to think about how this move would impact my young son. He seemed more than ready and terribly excited when Dante and I told him we were moving, but kids don't always tell you what they're really thinking.

"Are you okay with us moving, Angelo?"

"Yes. Will you swim in the pool with me when we get there, Mommy?"

And just like that, my son puts my fears to rest.

"Of course."

"Yay!"

"Here. Take this box. You can pack your cars in here."

Lord let this be a good thing. I'm tired of being alone. I need this relationship with Dante to work. Not just for me but for Angelo too.

I look up to find Dante watching me.

"Geez! You nearly gave me a heart attack."

"Sorry," he chuckles. "The door was wide open."

"Angelo is allergic to closing doors," I smile.

"It looks like you've got this packing thing down to a fine art."

"Indeed. When you pack and repack a busy five-year-old's closets and toy box as often as I do, you get the hang of it pretty quickly."

"Super Mom."

"I don't know about that. I still can't get him to close a door."

"You're so cute. Come here."

"Careful," I whisper. "Angelo is in the other room."

"We'll be quiet," he purrs.

Well, this is the best moving gift I'm ever going to get, I guess. Italian style.

11

MIA

"Cannonball!" Angelo yells as he dive bombs into the pool.

He's so skinny that he hardly makes a splash, but both Dante and I applaud enthusiastically.

This is my son's new playroom. He insisted on sleeping under the gazebo the first night we moved in. Dante graciously offered to join him while I flopped onto the king size bed in the master bedroom and died for a solid eight hours of blissful sleep.

We've been here for a week now and thankfully the novelty of it all hasn't worn off yet. Angelo spends hours outside, riding his little bicycle around the estate and swimming until dark. That's when he isn't exploring the grounds and climbing trees.

"Do all kids have this much energy?" Dante asks me as he watches Angelo through the kitchen window.

"Apparently so. That's why he sleeps so soundly. There's nothing left in the tank at the end of each day."

"I'm going to have to up my game if I hope to keep up with him."

My heart warms instantly as I watch him smile. Dante is so perfect.

"I was thinking of getting him a dog," I say, testing the waters. "What do you think?"

"Yeah, sure. I love dogs. What breed were you thinking?"

"I had a golden retriever when I was a girl. They're great with kids."

"Perfect. Is it a surprise?"

"Yes."

"Excellent. Let's go choose a puppy this afternoon."

"That will be nice."

I love that we're doing things together. I was a little irritated when I first moved in and found that we weren't alone. But Dante explained to me that he wasn't going to take any chances when it came to our safety and I suppose it makes sense. Especially considering the way in which we found each other again.

Whoever the business partner is who crossed him, I'd hate it if anything had to happen to my son. So, I've gotten used to the bodyguards and so has Angelo.

Dante insisted we hire a live-in helper to watch over Angelo. I must say it's great to have help after all the years of trying to manage by myself.

"We'll tell Faith to keep an eye on Angelo. Maybe you and I can pop out for a snack before we buy a puppy," he suggests.

"That sounds heavenly."

Lately, I find myself on the brink of telling Dante the truth about his son often. They get along great, we all live together, and we're about to invest in a family pet. What more do I need when it comes to confirmation that Dante is in this for the long haul?

"I need to make a few phone calls first. I'll be done in an hour. Okay?"

"Perfect."

"Oh, and I wanted to talk to you about something. We'll do it over lunch."

"Is something wrong?"

"No, nothing's wrong."

"Okay."

Better not be. I'm invested in this now. Boots and all.

* * *

The restaurant is packed. It's summertime in LA and everyone is out. We come here often and one of the waitresses has taken a shine to Dante—what woman wouldn't—so she seats us at a table in the back, away from the madding crowd.

"Your usual?" she gushes.

"I'll have a white wine spritzer, thanks," I answer.

Not that she cares, I'm sure.

"Yes, thanks, Lillian," Dante smiles, hardly noticing the girl. He only has eyes for me. Thank God.

"So," I say tentatively once we have our drinks. "What did you want to talk to me about?"

"Don't look so nervous," he chuckles.

"You'd be nervous too if you were a woman used to dating assholes," I smirk.

"Well, you can relax. I'm not an asshole. Or at least I don't think so."

"No. You're not."

"I want you to consider something for me, please."

"I'm listening."

"I would love it if you would consider giving up your job. I have more than enough money to take care of you, and you would get to spend so much more time with me and Angelo if you didn't have to work."

I did not see this coming. I like having my independence. Making my own money is important to me.

"Uhm…"

"Just think about it. I don't want to put you under any pressure. Whatever you decide is fine with me. Just think about it, Okay?"

"What would I do with myself all day long?"

"Whatever your heart desires. Isn't there anything you've always wanted to do but had no time to commit to?"

"Well…I do love pottery. I've always wanted to have my own studio but who has the time or money?"

"If you give up your job at the pharmacy, you'll have the time. And, as I said already, I have plenty of money."

"I don't know, Dante."

"Again. No pressure. Just know that the offer stands. You decide if it's something you want."

"You're being very generous, Dante."

"Think of it as an investment in your future. I want to see you happy, Mia."

"Oh, Dante. I just love you."

Oh crap! The words flowed from my heart, snuck up on my tongue, and spilled out before I could think about it.

Dante smiles at me, leans over, and kisses me.

"I love you too, Mia."

My heart is beating wildly in my chest. He loves me! Dante De Luca, the man of my dreams, loves me. I could die happy right here on the restaurant floor.

"You'll have to be patient with me," I say after we kiss.

"Why?"

"I've always earned my own way. I don't know what I'm going to be like if I have to ask you for money. I may be a little weird about it."

"Don't be ridiculous. I'll open an account for you and you can do whatever you like with the money. It's yours."

"I feel a bit like a kept woman now."

Dante laughs and kisses the tip of my nose.

"You can invoice me for services rendered if you like," he grins.

"You dirty old man," I counter.

"Yup. That's me. The horny Italian."

"Okay. I'll do it."

"Excellent."

"Thank you, Dante. This is an amazing gift."

"It's my pleasure, gorgeous. Whatever you want is yours."

"I'll start with a nicoise salad," I wink.

* * *

"This is the one," I purr as the puppy nozzles my neck. "He's perfect."

"I agree. Angelo is going to love him. What shall we name him?"

"We'd better let his master decide."

"Excellent choice," the breeder smiles. "This one is lively. Perfect for a busy boy," she says.

"That's good because my son is going to run him ragged," I laugh as the puppy barks and wags his tail.

"He likes you," Dante says. "The dog has exquisite taste."

Twenty minutes later, we're in the car with the dog, dog food, and dog toys galore.

"Angelo is going to bust a gut," I giggle. "He's been begging me for a dog for years."

"I can't imagine trying to keep a busy child and his dog happy in an apartment," Dante says, negotiating traffic.

"Yeah. My ex-landlord would have a cow."

Angelo is in the pool when we get home. Of course.

"Let's take the puppy out to him," Dante says and picks up the dog.

"Okay, but we prepared to get wet. He's bound to go a little mental."

"I've got this," he laughs.

"Hey, champ," Dante calls to get Angelo's attention. "We have a surprise for you."

Dante puts the puppy down and before we can stop it, it takes off, charges the pool and dives straight in.

"Okay, I guess the dog likes water," Dante laughs.

"Talk about a great fit," I chuckle.

"What! What!" is all Angelo can manage.

"He's yours, sweetheart," I call out.

This is the first time I've ever seen Angelo speechless. He looks at the puppy splashing about and then at Dante and me.

"Do you like him?" Dante asks.

"My dog! I have a dog!" he babbles on excitedly.

"Isn't he cute?" I ask.

"He's great, Mommy. What's his name?"

"You decide, Angelo," Dante says.

"Splash. His name is Splash."

"Okay, then. Splash it is."

The dog barks excitedly as Angelo splashes water.

"Right, then. Looks like we're about to enjoy some undisturbed adult time," Dante smirks.

"Totally deserved after such a clever move," I giggle. "These two will be busy for hours."

"It's time for my treat," Dante says, taking my hand.

"And what a treat it's going to be."

"Did the puppy come with a collar? I can think of at least one use for it."

"You're a bad man, Dante De Luca. A bad man!"

"You have no idea, woman," he grins and slaps me on the bottom.

* * *

I can't do this anymore. My heart breaks everytime I see Dante and Angelo together. I feel rotten. I must tell the man I've fallen so deeply in love with the truth. I just have to figure out how.

"I'm going to tell Dante the truth," I blurt out to Gina.

She's with me at the house while Dante and Angelo are out together. The two are shopping for a new baseball mitt after Splash chewed up the last one.

"Wow. Okay. Are you sure you're ready?"

"No, but I can't keep putting this off. My nerves are shot. I planned a nice dinner first. Soften him up, you know," I say wryly.

"It better be some kinda dinner," Gina snorts.

"Thanks for that. You're not helping."

"Sorry, you're right. I'm proud of you, M. This is a big step."

"Do me a favor. Please keep your spare room open just in case he takes the news badly and tosses me to the curb."

"Now you're being over dramatic. Dante is nuts about you. It's obvious to all. I'm sure he'll be thrilled to know that he shares a child with the woman he loves."

"I hope so. Damn! Why did I wait so long?"

"Doesn't he have any idea?"

"Nope."

"Honestly. Men are clueless. I mean the kid looks just like him, for fuck's sake. How can he be so blind?"

"I guess we see what we want to see."

"Will Angelo be here when you tell Dante?"

"Yes. I'll wait until he's asleep."

"What are you going to tell your son?"

"One hurdle at a time, please. I'll figure something out."

"I'm here if you need me, Mia," she says, then squeezes my hand tenderly.

"I know. Thank you."

12

DANTE

"Are you enjoying yourself, big brother? You're the last guy I imagined to happily play house."

"Says the man about to get married."

"Good point. It's good to hear from you, Dante. We miss you around here. Any news on Kyle?

"No. I'm starting to think he's done a runner. Lots of space to hide here in America."

"He must be a little nervous."

"The man would be shitting himself if he had even half a brain cell. He can't hide forever. How's Mamma?"

"Getting old. Not that age is slowing her down much. She's a firecracker, our mother."

"I'm not planning on staying here in the States for too long, Elio. If I haven't learned anything new after six months, I'm coming home."

"What about Mia?"

"I'll cross that bridge when I get to it."

"How are things between the two of you?"

"You mean the three of us."

"Yeah."

"Better than I ever could have imagined. I did break some Spanish asshole's nose at a wine farm the other day."

"Sounds about right. I'm sure you must miss the action. What did the fool do?"

"He was shamelessly ogling Mia when we checked in. Couldn't take his eyes off her tits."

"I wish I was there to see it," Elio laughs.

"I wanted to kill the little sleaze, but I can't afford that kind of heat here. If we were back in Rome, he'd be six feet under."

"Yeah. There's something to be said for hometown advantage. Bruno's here. He wants to talk to you."

"Sure. Put him on."

"Hey, Boss. You own a pair of Stetsons yet?"

"Funny. I'm in California, you numbskull. Not Texas."

"Like that's ever stopped the yanks. Anyway, I spoke to a colleague of mine. He heard a birdie whisper that Kyle had help."

"I suspected as much. That moron couldn't pull off something like this by himself. Who is it?"

"I don't know yet. But I'm on it."

"Thanks, Bruno."

"Sure thing. Are you homesick yet?"

"I've had enough fucking fake Italian food, that's for sure. I'd kill for a decent Tonnarelli Cacio e Pepe."

"I hear you, brother," he laughs. "Anyway, I'll keep you updated on the whole Kyle situation."

"Grazie."

The call leaves me antsy. I had my suspicions about Kyle. He's a wannabe player without the proper balls to take on a family like the De Lucas. It's evident in the spectacular way he botched my assassination. I never miss. If I want you dead, you're fucking dead. And you stay dead.

"Hey, babe. Are you okay?"

Mia is standing in the doorway to my office. She looks like a supermodel when all she's wearing is a pair of jeans and a white T-shirt.

"Yeah, I'm fine."

"Was that your brother?"

"Yup. He's getting married."

"That's wonderful. What's his fiancé like?"

"Lisa's a honey. They've been together for a long time. Elio is the faithful sort."

"Are you?" she purrs as she slides onto my lap.

"When I'm properly motivated, " I grin.

"Well, let's see if I can give you a little encouragement, shall we?"

The goddess on my lap slowly slips her hand into the front of my pants.

"Oh, yes," she purrs. "I think I can work with this."

"Lock the door. I'm about to suck up all the motivation without breaking the law."

LYDIA HALL

Mia giggles, get's up, locks the door, and takes off her shirt.

"Vieni da papà, you sexpot."

"You say the nicest things," she laughs and slips out of her jeans.

* * *

"Boss! We got him!"

It's late afternoon when Paolo comes running into the house. Mia and Angelo are in town and I'm in my office going through the latest financial reports Elio emailed through to me.

"What? Where?"

I assume Paolo is talking about Kyle. Who else would have him this excited. The boys have been making inroads into the local scene, getting to know the local gangs, asking questions without raising suspicion, and so on.

"This is good news, Paolo. Where is he?"

"He's hiding in a house in the valley. My new bestie tells me he's been there since the botched attack, Boss."

"Excellent. Who's with him?"

"He has about ten of his men with him. Oh, and his girlfriend too."

"Perfect. Let's go."

"Are you sure you want to risk it, Boss?"

My blood boils as soon as his words are out.

"Paolo, I'm going to let that one go. Bit if you ever ask me a stupid fucking question like that again, I'll cutt off your balls and feed them to you. Do you understand me?"

"Yes, Boss. I'm sorry."

"Get the men together."

"Yes, Sir."

Today is the day that Kyle gets to know the real Dante De Luca and not the watered down version he must have mistaken me for. No one fuck with me and gets away with it. No one.

We're in the car within the next half hour. My body is on high alert. I haven't been out in the trenches for a while. Usually I have men who do the killing for me, but today is special. Today, I will remind the men who follow me, and all the other dickheads out there who think that they can challenge my authority, just why I'm the Don.

"Is that it?" I ask as we stop down the road from a large house.

"Yes, Boss."

"Okay. You all know what to do?"

"Yes, Sir."

"No one, and I mean, no one, touches him but me."

Everyone nods.

"Okay. Let's dance."

It's amazing what you can accomplish when the enemy isn't expecting you. We're inside the house so quickly, Kyle barely has time to wipe the shit out of his eyes. A young blonde, his girlfriend presumably, is screaming her head off while she stares down the barrel of my gun. I slap her across the face to shut her up.

"What the fuck!" Kyle barks at me.

"Shut up!" I growl back.

The girl whimpers while she crouches in the corner of the room.

"Shall I get her out of here, Boss?" Paolo asks me.

"No. I want the little cupcake to see what happens to fools who fuck with a De Luca."

Paolo goes over to where the girl is covering, grabs her by the hair, and yanks her to her feet.

"Watch bitch," he snarls.

"Come on, man," Kyle snaps. "She has nothing to do with this. Let her go."

"Who are you working with?" I demand from him, ignoring his request. "You're too much of a fool to have tried to kill me without backup."

"Fuck you," he snaps.

I didn't expect him to give up the goods without a little resistance. On the contrary, I was hoping he'd give me a reason to rough him up. I punch him in the mouth with such force that I knock out his front tooth. He spits it out, blood dripping onto the shaggy white carpet.

"I'll ask you one more time."

"Fuck you!" he yells, defiantly.

I'm surprised. The little worm has more verve than I expected.

"Paolo, bring the blonde a little closer."

"No!" Kyle shouts.

Paolo does as he's told and brings the trembling girl closer.

"I'll ask you one more time. Who are you working with?"

Kyle's lips are pressed together in open defiance but his eyes are pleading with me not to hurt the girl. I shove the business end of the silencer against her temple.

"You'd better start talking, Kyle, or she's going to be the prettiest stiff in the morgue tonight."

"I can't."

"Yes, you can."

It's clear that whoever Kyle took orders from scares the shit out of him. I think he needs a bit more convincing before he'll start seeing things my way.

"They'll kill my family," he pleads.

"And I won't?"

A look of fresh panic darkens his brow, as if he never considered the fact that I am as capable of destroying his world as any other.

"There is no one else," he whimpers. "I did it by myself."

"Bullshit! You're a nobody, a skidmark on the underpants of society! You couldn't think of this on your own even on your best day!" I shout at him.

I'm getting bored with this. If Kyle isn't going to talk, I may as well get rid of him. That will send a clear message to the others.

I nod at Paolo, who snaps the girl's neck like a twig. Her lifeless body collapses to the ground. Kyle cries out in frustration.

"I told you," I say before I put a bullet between his eyes.

"Let's get out of here," I sigh.

"Shall I clean up?" Paolo asks.

"No. I want the others to know I'm coming for them."

"Yes, Boss."

* * *

Mia

LYDIA HALL

Dante is out. It gives me time to cook while Angelo and Splash chase each other around outside. I'm a ball of nerves. Tonight is the night I'm finally going to tell the man I'm so in love with that my son is also his.

I pour myself a glass of Chardonnay before I start chopping away at the vegetables. I decided on Steak and roast veggies. It's my signature dish, so I'm comfortable with it. This is no time to try something new. The way I feel I'm guaranteed to make a hash of anything unfamiliar.

Angelo rushes into the kitchen with Splash hot on his heels, nearly knocking me off my feet.

"Boys! Not now, I'm cooking."

"Sorry, Mommy. I need a snack and Splash is thirsty."

"Yeah, okay. Here."

Angelo stares at the object I just handed him. He looks at it for a while then back to me.

"A carrot?" he says, incredulously.

"Yes, Angelo. It's a carrot."

"But I'm hungry."

"Yes, and that's food. Now run along and eat it."

"But..."

"No butts, my boy. You need veggies."

"Ahhh, Mommy!" he moans.

"Just eat the damn carrot," I say and gently nudge him out of the kitchen.

"You said a bad word," he says with all the childlike verve of a five-year old.

"Sorry, sweetheart. I'll put a dollar in the swear jar."

The way I feel now, I may as well put a hundred dollar note. I don't know why I'm so nervous. Dante loves me and he is crazy about Angelo. How hard can this be?

It's my own fault for having dragged this out for so long. If I had just fessed up the morning Dante first met Angelo I wouldn't be in this mess. It feels like my insides are fighting to get out. Ugh!

I hear the tires of the car on the gravel outside an hour later. Dinner is done. All that's left is to pop the meat into the steak pan for a few minutes. Angelo is bathed and in bed and Splash has finally come to rest on his bed next to his master's. It's a go!

"Hi, babe," I say as I hear Dante's footsteps behind me.

I'm in the living room, nursing my third glass of chardonnay.

"Hi. It smells good in here. What have you been up to?" he says and comes over to the couch to kiss me.

"I thought I'd make my hard working man dinner," I purr as his fingers run along my neck.

"She cooks, she contorts her body like a pretzel…tell me, Mia. Is there anything you cannot do?" he coos.

Yeah, tell the truth right off the bat.

"Would you like a whiskey?" I offer.

"I'd love one."

"Great. I'll organize that for you. Are you hungry?"

"Famished."

"Wash up. I'll get your drink for you. What's that?"

I point to a spot on his sleeve.

"Is that blood?"

"Oh, yeah," he says. "I had a nose bleed earlier. Must be the heat."

"Oh, okay."

"I'll just change my shirt. Be back in a flash."

"Okay."

"Alright, Mia. Take a breath You'll be fine," I whisper to myself once Dante is out of the room. "You can do this. Remember. He loves you."

I pop a few blocks of ice into a tumbler and pour some twenty-year-old whiskey over it. Dante likes his whiskey. He buys the best of everything. I appreciate a man with good taste.

Dante is dressed in a fresh shirt when he comes back. I hand him the glass.

"I popped my head into Angelo's room. He's fast asleep. Splash was happy to see me. Did the two have a good afternoon?"

"Yup. They ran each other ragged. Angelo passed out the minute his head hit the pillow."

"And what did you do with your day? Apart from cooking up a storm, that is."

"I had coffee with Gina this morning."

"Oh, okay. How is my feisty cousin?"

"She's fine. I think she and Jeff are going on a trip soon to see his family."

"Okay."

"Does she miss you at work?"

"Oh, I forgot to tell you. She's not working there anymore either. She's helping Jeff with a few projects."

"Poor George must be beside himself. Losing his dream team and all."

"Yeah, he's positively suicidal," I giggle. "Let's eat."

"Are you alright, Mia?"

"Yeah, fine. Why?"

"You look a little nervous. Are you sure you're okay?"

"Yeah. Just a little tired."

Liar!

"I'll put on the steaks."

"I'll come to the kitchen with you. Looks like you need a refill on your wine."

"Thanks, babe. The bottle is in the wine fridge."

I get the steak pan up to temperature while Dante pours me another glass. I'm going to have to be careful. Too much chardonnay and I'll spill the beans before we've had a chance to eat the ones I prepared earlier.

"Here you go, gorgeous," he says and hands me my wine.

"This wine is delicious."

"Is it the chardonnay we brought back with us from the wine farm?"

"Yes."

"I'd better order a few more bottles for you, then."

"That will be great. Thanks."

Am I engaging in small talk? Really? Now? I want to close my eyes, tell Dante that Angelo is our son, and then wait for whatever reaction may follow. But that's a silly idea, so I sip my wine and hold my tongue while I finish cooking the steaks.

Afterall, I have all night.

13

DANTE

There's definitely something going on with Mia. She's all over the place. I wonder if she has some crazy female intuition about what I did earlier. My mother is like that. One misstep as a child and she'd be all over my ass, as if she knew exactly what I'd been up to.

Her hands are trembling as she cuts through her steak. I can't take it anymore.

"What's wrong, Mia? And don't tell me you're tired because I'm not buying it."

She takes a large sip of wine and sets the glass down next to her plate on the table. Then, she takes a big breath.

"I have to tell you something, Dante."

My stomach is clenched. I hope this isn't bad news. I've had my fill of bad news for a while.

"What is it?" I encourage her gently.

"It's about Angelo."

"Angelo? Is he okay?"

"Oh, yeah, sorry. He's fine."

"Go ahead."

"Give me a minute," she says.

"Take your time."

It must be big news because she takes a while before she starts speaking again.

"It's about his father."

"What happened? Did he contact you? What does he want?"

If Angelo's loser father is sniffing around, he'd better think twice before moving in on the good thing I've got here. Mia and Angelo are my family now. He had his chance.

"Oh, no. Nothing like that. I…"

"For shit's sake, Mia. You're freaking me out. What is it? Just tell me."

"You're Angelo's father, Dante. He's your son. Our son."

Did she just say what I thought she just said? Did Mia just say that I'm Angelo's father?

"What?" I say softly.

"You are his father, Dante."

"But…"

"I'm so sorry I didn't tell you sooner. It's just that. Well, I wanted to, but the time never seemed quite right. I tried to call you when I found out I was pregnant, but I lost my nerve. I didn't want you to think that I was some sort of social climber who traps a wealthy man with a child. Then, after Angelo was born, I had my hands full and, well, frankly I didn't think you'd…"

Mia is rambling on like a freight train gone rogue. Her eyes are darting back and forth and she's writing her hands. She's clearly upset about this.

"Mia. Stop."

I get up and make my way over to her. She's shaking when I take her hands and pull her gently to her feet.

"Shhh. It's okay. Stop talking for a second."

"But…" she protests softly.

"It's alright. I'm not angry."

I pull her close and hold her tightly against my chest.

"I love you, Mia. This is unexpected, sure. But, I'm happy. I love Angelo. I'm so happy that he's mine."

"Oh, Dante," she says and buries her head in my chest. "I'm so sorry I took so long to tell you. I love you so much."

She's sobbing now.

"Those better be happy tears," I whisper.

"Are you kidding?" she says and smiles up at me.

"Does he know?"

"No. I haven't told him yet," Mia sniffles.

"It's alright. I'm sure we'll come up with something."

"You mean together?"

"Yes. We'll tell him together. If you want to."

"Of course I want to. That's amazing. Thank you, Dante."

"Wow. I'm a father."

The weight of it hits me like a sledgehammer. I'm responsible for another. This is no small thing. We Italians live for our family and their honor.

"You're a good one to boot."

This changes everything. I'm scared shitless all of a sudden. I have to protect my son at all costs. This calls for a change of plan.

* * *

"Gina. It's Dante. Can we meet for a drink? There's something I want to discuss with you."

"Hi, Dante. Uhm, yeah, sure."

"Can you make it this morning? I'm sorry it's a bit short notice, but it's important."

"Okay. How about Giovanis at ten?"

"Great. Thanks."

I have to talk to my cousin. She's known Mia for a long time. She's the best person to bounce my ideas off.

"Good morning, Champ. Did you sleep well?"

"Hey, Dad. Yup. Splash woke me up. He licked my face until I opened my eyes."

"That sounds awful," I laugh.

"Nah, we share kisses. I don't mind."

"We'd better remind Mommy to give you some dewormer."

It's been a month since Mia and I told our son that I am his father. He took it better than we could have expected. In fact, we've slipped seamlessly into our own brand of family closeness. Who knew?

"Who needs dewormer?" Mia asks as she walks into the kitchen and hoists Angelo up into the air.

He squeals with delight as she holds him upside down and shakes him playfully.

"Our boy wonder has been sharing kisses with Splash," I answer.

"Oh, ugh!" Mia says and pulls a face at Angelo. "That's disgusting."

"No it's not," the boy giggles hysterically while his mother tickles him.

"Okay, we'll stop off at the pharmacy before I drop you off at school," Mia says once she's put Angelo down.

"Can we say hi to George?" he asks. "I miss him."

"Uh-huh. You miss the lollipops he gives you," Mia chuckles.

Angelo gives Mia a wry grin. He's so damned cute. And just as good with the ladies as his old man.

"Go get your bag, sweetheart," Mia tells him.

"Okay."

"Hey, sexy. You snuck out early," Mia purrs and kisses my neck.

"Yeah, sorry. I had a few calls to make. Did you sleep well, my love?"

"Like the dead. You?"

"How could I not after an orgasm like that?" I grin.

"Sshh, Angelo will hear you," Mia blushes.

"Good. The boy should know how much his parents dig each other."

"And he will. I just don't want him repeating it at school. You know what kids are like. They say the most inappropriate things in class."

"Let him shout it from the rooftops. I don't care who knows how pretty your little ass is or how badly I want to bite it," I smirk and tap her on her tush.

"Okay, that's it. I'm getting you a muzzle," she laughs.

"I'm ready to go," Angelo announces.

"Ciao, Angelo."

"Ciao, Dad."

"Mommy, what's a norgasiam?" I hear him ask Mia as they leave the house.

Mia looks back at me and gives me the stink eye.

"I told you!" she mouths silently to me.

"My bad!" I mouth back and throw my hands into the air.

"Uhm, nothing my boy. Come, we have to hurry if we're going to stop off and say hi to George before school."

I wait until the pair is out of earshot before I burst out laughing. Kids say the damndest things!

It's 10 a.m. and I'm at Giovanis, waiting for Gina. This is going to be a serious conversation, and I hope Gina will give me what I need. After all, what is family for if not to help each other out, right?

"Hi, Dante," Gina greets me when she arrives fifteen minutes late. "I'm so sorry. I got stuck behind a broken down truck. I tell you, traffic in this town can be murder."

"Hi, Gina. It's okay. Thanks for meeting with me."

"Sure."

"How's your husband?"

"Jeff's well. He's out of town at the moment so I'm holding down the fort."

"He seems like a good man. Is he testing you well?"

"The implication being that if he isn't you'll put an end to him?" she grins.

"There is that, yes," I smile.

"Jeff is a sweetheart. I couldn't have chosen better. At the risk of being brutally honest, what are we doing here, Dante?"

"Straight to the point. I see the Sicilian blood courses strongly through your veins."

"Uh-huh. Let's face it, you and I haven't really seen much of each other since we were kids. So, I wonder what I can do for you now."

"It's about Mia."

"I thought as much. What's up?"

"I love her."

"Yeah, I heard."

"Am I sensing just a smidgen of animosity, Gina?"

"If this is going to be a frank and honest conversation, then yes. I am a little pissed at you, cousin."

"I see. And why might that be?"

"Well, for a start, I think that you dropping in on Mia's life in the way that you did, puts her in the center of a world that she simply isn't cut out for."

"Okay, I get that."

"I take it you know that Angelo is yours."

"Yes, and I'm thrilled about that."

"That's great. But have you told Mia exactly who you are? Or shall I say, what you are? If I know Mia, she's probably poured her heart out to you by now. Have you done her the same courtesy?"

"You're being awfully familiar here, cousin. I'd tread a little lighter if I were you."

"Oh, are you threatening me now? This isn't Italy, Dante. You're in my country now."

"No. I'm not threatening you, Gina. I'm merely pointing out that you are being rather presumptuous in your estimation of me."

"In that case, I apologize. What are your intentions toward Mia and Angelo?"

"I love them. I want to build a life with them. Does that answer your question?"

"Yes."

"You don't look happy."

"I'm not. May I speak candidly, cousin?"

"You mean up until now you've been holding back?" I smirk.

Gina gives me a wry smile.

"Please, Gina. Feel free to speak your mind."

"I know that you're the Don. That position comes with a crap load of danger. All I'm saying is that I don't think that Mia is suited to your world. I don't want to see her hurt, Dante. I must insist that you come clean with her. Tell her the whole truth. That's my point."

I stare over Gina's shoulder at the people passing on the street outside. Every one of them has a story to tell. I wonder what they would think if I knew my story. Would they run? Will Mia?

"What was it you were hoping to get from me, Dante?"

"I was hoping to get some more insight into Mia's life and situation. You know her better than anyone."

"I know she loves you. What you do with that is up to you. I do wish that you weren't in the mafia. I don't want to see my best friend hurt."

"I'm not going to hurt her, Gina."

"I'm sure you have no intention of doing so. It's a pity the same can't be said for the people who hate you?"

* * *

"I'm going to tell her."

"Are you sure that's wise, Dante?"

"I have to, Elio. I can't keep hiding the truth from the woman I love. I know you know what I'm talking about. You wouldn't lie to Lisa, would you?"

"It's not the same. Lisa knew who I was from the start. Mia is American. She may not understand."

"It's a chance I have to take. Angelo is my son. I'm not going to abandon him or his mother."

"All I'm saying, brother, is think carefully about this before you act."

"I will. Have you found out anything about who was helping Kyle?"

"No. Whoever it was, has fallen off the planet. I have a feeling it was someone with serious connections."

"Yeah, well that someone better stay down. I got to Kyle, and I'll get to them, too."

"When are you coming home, Dante?"

"Any day now. I have to talk to Mia."

"Okay. Don't take too long."

"I won't."

It's a beautiful evening, so I move outside to the pool area for a bit of fresh air. Angelo and Splash are occupying themselves in the swimming pool. Mia is in her pottery studio. She's made a few bowls and plates and I must say, she does have a knack for this pottery thing.

I'm sorry to leave this lifestyle behind. It's been very cathartic. But real life is waiting for me back in Rome. That's where I belong. I'm good at what I do. My family needs me. I'll have to convince Mia that she belongs with me.

Come on, Dante. You command an army of men. Surely you can convince the woman you love to follow you.

14

MIA

"Those are stunning, Mia. You have such a flair for pottery."

"Thanks, George."

"What a lovely gift. Thank you, so much."

"I wanted to thank you for not calling the cops the night Dante stumbled into the pharmacy. You took a big chance. Thank you, George. You changed my life for the better."

"I'm glad you're happy," he says, rolling his eyes. "I, on the other hand, am a little miffed that he stole my best worker and good friend away from me."

"Oh, come now, you big baby. It can't be that bad."

"You have no idea. It was almost impossible replacing you and Gina. If I have to listen to one more WOKE tale, I think I may vomit right there behind the counter."

"Ah, George," I chuckle. "You're funny. I miss that wit."

"So, how are things going with your dream boy?"

"It's so wonderful, George. I can't believe how lucky I am. Dante is amazing."

"How is he with Angelo?"

"Fantastic."

I haven't told Geroge the truth about Dante and Angelo yet. It's not that I'm hiding it, but I'm not ready to shout it from the rooftops just yet.

I enjoy my cup of coffee with George. We talk about how things are going at the pharmacy. He catches me up on all the doctor, patient gossip, and I tell him about my new life as a potter.

"It's been so nice catching up, Mia. You should come see me again soon."

"I will. I miss you too, George."

"Here. Take this with you. It's for Angelo."

"Ah, thanks, George. Grape. His favorite lollipop flavor."

"That kid of yours is a gem, Mia. He's grown into a beautiful boy."

"He has, hasn't he?" I beam.

"I have to dash, but thanks for the lovely serving bowl, Mia. You're a doll."

"Enjoy it."

I check my watch once I'm outside. It's time to fetch Angelo from school. He's been so happy and bubbly lately. It must be all the fresh air, puppy love, and of course having his very own dad around that brings out the best in him. I know how he feels. I haven't been this happy since…well, ever, if I'm honest.

My cell phone rings.

"Hey, I was just thinking about you," I say as I answer the call.

"Good things, I hope."

"Of course."

"Where are you?"

"I'm on my way to fetch Angelo. Why?"

"Do you mind if his nanny fetches him today? I thought we could meet for a drink."

"Uhm. Okay, I guess that will be alright."

"Great. Meet me at the pier in twenty minutes."

"Sure. Is everything alright?"

"Yeah. Why?"

"I don't know. You sound a little off."

"All good. Just wanted to chat with you about something."

"No problem. I'll see you in a bit."

Something's up with Dante. He's been acting sas little oddly the last few days. I wonder if it has anything to do with the chat he had with Gina. I didn't want to pry when he came home afterward, but I could see he was far away. I hope the cousins didn't fall out. Navigating the intricacies of family relationships can be tricky. I want them to get along. They are two very important people in my life.

I decide to give Mom a quick call while I'm driving to the pier. I connect my phone to bluetooth and dial her number. It rings for a while. She must be in the garden. I'm just about to hang up when she answers.

"Hello," she says out of breath.

"Hey, Mom. Sorry, I hope I'm not disturbing you."

"Hi, darling. No, I was outside, tilling the soil in the rose garden."

"I thought you might be. Can you chat or shall I call you later?"

"That's okay. I'm inside now. I need a cold drink anyway. What's on your mind?"

"I was just with George. I made him a serving bowl. He seemed to like it."

"I would think so. Your work is beautiful, darling. How is George? Is he missing you?"

"He says so. He's fine."

"What are your plans for the rest of the day?"

"I'm meeting Dante at the pier. I'm on my way there now."

"That's very romantic."

"Yeah. He says he wants to talk to me about something."

"Any idea what it could be?"

"Not really. He's been a little quiet since he spoke to Gina."

"I see. Do you think they had an argument?"

"I don't think so. Besides, knowing Gina, she would have told me the minute they parted if there had been an issue between them."

"You have me on tenterhooks now. You better call me later and tell me what happened."

"I will, nosy Rosie. How are you and Dad?"

"Same old same old."

Mom and I chat until I arrive at the pier. She lets me go as soon as she's satisfied that I'll deliver the skinny later.

The end of summer is upon us. The color of the sky is changing ever so slightly. As a local, I notice it immediately. I get out of my car and walk over to a bench. I'll wait here for Dante and enjoy the view of the ocean.

"Is this seat taken?" he says, startling me.

"Goodness. I was far away. Hi, babe."

"Hi, yourself. You look so beautiful in this light."

"You say the sweetest things, Mr. De Luca."

"Let's walk."

"Okay."

I take off my sandals and carry them in my hand. Dante takes off his shoes, rolls up his jeans, and takes my hand as we walk along the shore.

"It's spectacular down here," he muses.

"I know. This is my favorite beach. The surfers will be out soon."

"Surfing was never my game but I appreciate the skill."

"So, what did you want to talk about?"

"Our future."

"Ooh, the future. Sounds serious."

I'm being whimsical but the topic has me nervous. The future is a scary subject. I knew it would come up eventually. I was hoping for later rather than sooner. I don't know if I'm ready to move to Italy. I assume that is something that Dante would want, seeing as his business and family are there.

"Let's sit down for a bit," Dante says and stops.

"Okay."

His face is different. It's as if he's suddenly carrying the weight of the world on his shoulders. The poor thing must worry that I won't follow him to his homeland, when the truth is I'd follow this man just about anywhere in the world. Dante needn't worry.

"I need to tell you something," he says once we're seated on the sand.

I don't say anything. I figure it will be easier if I let him speak.

"I've told you very little about what I do for a living. You have opened up to me and trusted me wholeheartedly about Angelo. So, I feel it's only fair that I adopt the same policy of honesty with you."

I take his hand and squeeze his fingers as a way of encouraging him to speak his mind.

"I'm an important man in Italy, Mia. As such, I have many friends and associates, but I also have my fair share of enemies."

"Yeah, I gathered as much when you stumbled back into my life with a bullet wound."

"That wasn't supposed to happen, but, yes, that illustrates my point perfectly."

"It's alright, Dante. The world is a scary place sometimes. I get that. But my world is tough. I need you to know that but I also want to share the beauty and privilege with you. If you stay with me and join me when I go back to Italy, you'll be a queen, Mia. You and Angelo will have anything and everything your hearts desire."

"That's quite a promise, Dante."

"It's true. I will give you anything you ask for."

"That's sweet, Dante, and very generous. But I don't need vast amounts of wealth and privilege. Sure, it's great, but that's not why I'm with you. I love you and that's enough for me."

"You're making this so hard, Mia," he sighs.

"Why? Because I love you?"

"No, because of what I need to tell you next."

I have an awful feeling in the pit of my stomach. What is he trying to tell me?

"What is it, Dante?"

"I'm a Don."

"A what?"

"The De Lucas are the most powerful mafia family in Italy."

It feels like he's just slapped me. He may as well have. I'm sure it would have been less painful than the dagger he just plunged into my soul.

Angelo is the son of a mafia kingpin! Oh, Lord! No! Anything but this.

"Mia. Are you alright? You're very pale."

I hear his question, but I cannot bring myself to speak for fear of what I may say. This is a nightmare. Am I dreaming? Please let this be a dream, God. Surely, my life cannot go from soaring heights to the depths of the abyss in an instant.

"Mia."

"What did you say? You're in the mob?"

"Yes."

"What the fuck, Dante? How could you keep this from me? You let me fall in love with you. You made my son fall in love with you. And NOW you tell me this! How could you do that?"

I grab my sandals and get up.

"Mia, wait. Please. We have to talk about this."

"Not now, Dante. I need to be alone."

"But," he says and gets up to follow me.

"Alone, Dante!"

***

I'm heartbroken all over again. How could Dante lie to my face? Finance! In finance, he said. This isn;t fucking finance. It's crime!

I'm as mad as a snake right now. I could just punch his fucking lights out as I stomp across the sand to get back to my car. I don't know where I'm going to go when I get there. I'm too upset to go home. Angelo will read me like a book. He always knows when his mommy is upset.

Gina! Does she know about this?

Come on, Mia. Grow up! Of course she knows. She's his cousin, you idiot!

I have to talk to her so I drive over to her and Jeff's house. I know he's away at the moment so she's likely to be alone.

My phone rings. It's Dante. I switch off the phone. I cannot talk to him right now. The drive to Gina's only makes my rage worse. I ring the gate buzzer once I get to her housing estate.

"Hello," she answers into the intercom.

"Gina, it's me. Open up."

"Mia?"

"Yeah."

The gate opens slowly. It seems to take forever. She's standing at the door when I get there.

"Hey, you. This is a nice surprise. What are you…"

"We need to talk, Gina!" I bark.

"What's wrong? Come inside."

"How could you lie to me, Gina? How?!"

"What are you talking about?"

"Dante! Why didn't you tell me the truth about him?"

"Oh. I see. He told you."

"Yes, he bloody told me. What I want to know is, why didn't you?"

"I'm sorry, Mia. It wasn't my place to tell you."

"Are you fucking serious, Gina? You're my best friend. I specifically asked you about him. You lied to me!"

"Okay, this isn't getting us anywhere. Come on, sit down. I'm getting us a drink."

Gina disappears into the kitchen and comes back with a bottle of wine. She opens it and pours out two glasses.

"Here, drink this."

"I don't think that wine is the answer to this particular problem. It's not going to help."

"No, but it will help me."

"Why didn't you say anything, Gina?" I ask once I've calmed down a little.

"When you first spent the night with him, I thought it was sweet. You were so excited about it. Who was I to rain on your parade? Later, when you told me you were pregnant with his child, I didn't know what to say. You were so determined to raise Angelo on your own, I didn;t see a reason to tell you."

"And when he appeared on the scene six months ago?"

"At first, I thought it was another fling. I was sure Dante would go back to Italy and that would be it. How was I to know that the two of you would fall in love?"

"Damn it! I can't believe this. And it was going so well."

"He loves you, Mia. And he's Angelo's father. Give him a chance. Dante will move heaven and earth for you. He'll keep you safe."

"Sure. Like he kept himself safe."

"Things are different now that he knows he has a son and a woman who loves him. He'll take less chances."

"I hope so, Gina. I hope so."

15

DANTE

"Please, Mia. Come with me."

"Not yet, Dante. I need time to think about all of this. What you're asking of me is no small thing. This is another life changing decision. I don't want to do the wrong thing for my son. Please don't rush me."

"*Our* son, Mia. Don't forget that. I love him too and I will never allow any harm to come to him. Or to you, my love. I can protect you both in Italy. My family is there. I want you to be a part of that."

Mia's eyes are downcast. She's been distant since I shared my secret with her at the pier. My heart aches, but I know I have to give her time to process no matter how hard this is for me. I'm a man who gets what he wants. People acquiesce to my every command. I'm not accustomed to taking no or maybe for an answer. But love does crazy things to a man's resolve.

"I'll leave a man behind to keep an eye on you and our son."

"That's not necessary, babe. No one cares about me. You're the one who seems to attract trouble."

That statement hurts. I suspect it's because Mia's right. I *am* the object of conflict. It would seem as if I was born with a target on my back.

"Just in case. Please, my love."

"Okay," she sighs. "Do you have everything?"

"Yeah, I'm all packed."

I'm leaving today. The hollow feeling in the pit of my stomach won't go away no matter how much I tell myself that I'm doing the right thing. I've been in America, away from my business and family, for six months now. I can't stay any longer. If it weren't for Mia and Angelo I would have left the moment I killed Kyle. But I just couldn't bring myself to do so. Now, it's time.

Angelo is at school. Mia and I sat him down last night and told him that Daddy had to go away on a trip. He's too little to understand the implications of what's happening and neither Mia nor I wish to upset him. So, until Mia decides she's ready to join me in Rome, she and I will maintain a united front for the sake of our son.

"I don't want to leave you behind, Mia. I love you," I say, hugging her tightly, storing up lungfuls of her fragrant hair.

"I don't want you to go, either, Dante. I just need some time to adjust to my new reality."

"Don't take too long, my love. I'll call you when I get to Rome."

"Thank you. Be safe. Take care of yourself, Dante. Stay out of trouble. No more bullets, okay?"

"Sure," I smile. "Thank you for saving my life, my gorgeous woman. I'll miss you terribly."

"I'll miss you too."

"Take good care of our boy."

"Always."

I wipe a tear from her cheeks and give her one last kiss before I get into the car that will take me away from the love of my life. I watch Mia standing in the driveway, waving, as the car pulls off. I keep looking until the vehicle enters the bend and I cannot see her anymore. She's gone. It feels like someone has just reached into my chest and ripped out my heart. I've never felt pain like this before, and I've been stabbed, shot, and severely beaten in my lifetime. This pain is different. It's far too real. So much for being a tough guy.

Mia's scent lingers in my nostrils from when she was in my arms. The woman I love is on my skin and in the fiber of my clothes, but more importantly, she's chiseled into the chambers of my heart. Talk about slow torture.

Come on, Dante. What are you? A lovesick simpleton? Pull yourself together! You're a De Luca and you've got work to do. She'll come around. Mia loves you.

"Are you okay, Boss?"

"Mind your own business," I snap. "Just drive."

"Yes, Sir."

I'm not used to being vulnerable. The suit doesn't fit me terribly well. I refuse to show weakness in front of my men. That kind of Nancy pants shit gets you killed.

"Is the jet ready for take off?"

"Yes, Boss."

"Then let's get to it."

I left Paolo behind. He is the best man for the job, plus I know he'd give his life to keep Mia and Angelo safe. At least I know that no harm will come to my little family.

Family. It isn't official, but that's exactly what Mia and Angelo are to me. As soon as the woman I love tells me she's ready to join me in

Italy, I'm going to ask her to be my wife. So, instead of feeling sorry for myself I'm going to focus on securing a solid future for the three of us. This is my mission.

* * *

"Dante, my brother. It's good to see you."

Elio holds me in a bear hug. I've missed my little brother. He and I have always been very close. It felt odd being so far away from him for nearly half a year.

"It's good to be back, brother. You look good."

"I'm great, now that you're back. Come. Let's go home and have a drink. Mamma is at the house. She missed you."

"How is she?"

"Mamma's aged since you left. She's been so worried about you, out there all alone in the States."

"I feel awful about that. I plan on making it up to her."

My mother is old. She had us at a later stage in life. I think that this business has taken its toll on her too. First, she lost her husband, and then she nearly lost her oldest son. That must be tough on any woman, no matter how resilient she is.

"Does she know about Angelo?" I ask.

"No. It isn't my place to tell her. I thought I'd leave that to you."

"Thanks, Elio."

"She's going to be very pleased."

"Yeah. That's if I manage to convince Mia to move to Rome and join our family."

"She'll come around. I'm sure the news came as a shock to her."

"Yeah. She wasn't exactly thrilled about it."

"Let's get you drunk. You look like a man who could use a little distraction."

"You read my mind. I better not have had your stag night without me."

"Don't be ridiculous," he laughs and slaps me on the back.

"Excellent. I'll get cracking on the arrangements. Your last chance to squeeze some illegal titties, young man."

"Lisa's going to kill you."

"She'll have to catch me first."

"Fuck, it's good to have you home."

"La mia anima appartiene all'Italia! Let's drink."

* * *

"Hey, Mia."

"Hi, babe."

"How are you?"

"Okay. The house seems so empty now."

"Is Paolo taking good care of you?"

"Yeah. He's around but he doesn't say much. It's not the same here without you."

"How's my boy?"

"Angelo is the same as always. Crazy busy. He and Splash have moved their chaos to the indoor pool. It's a bit nippy out after dark."

"I miss you two so much."

"We miss you too, Dante."

I don't push. I'm not going to ask her to hurry up and make a decision. This relationship is important to me. I don't want to fuck it up by being a pushy asshole. But I don't know how long I can put off the inevitable question.

"How's your mom?" she asks.

"She's old. Chipper and full of sass, but old."

"She must be looking forward to the wedding."

"Very much. I wanted to talk to you about that. Will you and Angelo come? For the wedding."

"When is it?"

"The end of next month."

"That soon."

"Elio and Lisa have been together forever. It's about time they tied the knot."

"Are they planning on having kids?"

"Good question. I guess so. If Mamma has her way they'll have plenty."

"Have you told her about Angelo?"

"I did. I swear the news added at least ten years to her lifespan. She can't wait to meet her first grandson. It's a big deal here."

"That's sweet."

"Speaking of which. Have you told your parents about my…business?"

"No. Not yet. But, I will."

"I like them very much, Mia. They're good people. I hope they'll accept me for who I am."

"So do I. I'm sorry, babe, but I have to run. It's time to fetch Angelo from school."

"Okay. Call me tonight before he goes to sleep so I can say goodnight, will you?"

"Of course."

"I love you."

"I love you too."

The call leaves me wanting. I hate this. All I want is to be able to touch the woman I've fallen in love with and hold her closely but she is out of my reach—in more ways than one it would seem. I don't know why I don't just fly over to LA and fetch her. Why is this so complicated? Surely, we can work it out.

"What's with the long face, bro?"

"I miss Mia and my son."

"Come on, Dante. Don't let it get to you. She'll come around. Just give her some space."

"Space? It's been a month, Elio. I'm in Rome and she's in LA. How much more space does she need?"

"Women are a different breed. They think too much."

"Don't let Lisa hear you make such a Neanderthal-like statement. She'll dump your ass at the altar for sure."

"Nah. Not my little brood of vipers. Lisa is a true Sicilian woman. She gets it. I'm starting to think that that's your problem right there, Dante. You had to fall in love with a Californian rose, didn't you? You would have been much better off giving it to a local. They know how to handle the mafia culture."

"Don't you think I know that? You can't choose who you fall in love with, you idiot."

"I guess not. Mamma wants to see you."

"Okay. I'll go up after lunch."

I know exactly what my mother is going to say. It's going to be a long afternoon.

I find Mamma in her kitchen. She is baking cannoli and cassatella. The room is a feast for the senses.

"Ciao bella," I greet her and hug her gently.

"Ciao, Dante. Just just in time for a taste," she says and pushes a cannoli into my mouth.

"Ah! Heaven, Mamma" I smile once I've swallowed.

"Sit, my boy. I want to talk to you."

Oh, shit. She means business. This old Italian firecracker has something on her mind.

"Sure, Mamma."

I learned at a young age not to argue with my mother. Especially not when she's within reach of kitchen implements like knives and marble rolling pins. I sit down at the nook and accept an espresso from the De Luca matriarch.

"So, what are you doing, Dante?"

"What do you mean, Mamma?"

"Why haven't you fetched your woman and your son? What are you waiting for?"

An excellent question fraught with danger. Trust my mother to cut through the bull and get straight to the heart of the matter.

"Well, I'm trying to be respectful and give Mia the time she needs, Mamma."

"Ah, that's bullshit. Are you a man or a mouse? I didn't raise my boys to be mice. You need to call her and tell her and make her believe that this is the only place for her. I want my grandson to grow up with his father. Is that so terrible?"

"No, Mamma. I want that too."

"So, what are you doing?"

My mother, bless her frankness, is right. I've been pussy footing it, waiting for Mia to accept me for who I am, when, really, I should be showing her what she's missing. Rome, this life, the family, the love… Mia will love all of this. And my son will too. He's a prince here. This is his kingdom. He should be here to enjoy it.

"Thank you, Mamma."

"Don't thank me, son. Just go get your woman."

"Si, Mamma."

"Ti amo, Dante."

"Anch'io ti amo, Mamma."

"Now get out of my kitchen. I'm busy."

"Si, Mamma."

16

MIA

I wake up feeling like crap. This is my new normal. I'm stuck between a rock and a hard place. On the one hand, I miss Dante so much that my body literally aches. On the other hand, I know that if I decide to give into my feelings and move to Italy, I could very well be walking into the lion's mouth. And this particular lion has no shortage of razor sharp teeth.

What I *do* know, without an ounce of uncertainty, is that I can't do this for much longer. Dante calls me every day. The sound of his voice is nothing short of Chinese water torture. It's like being addicted to heroin—I can't wait for the next fix, and yet I know my addiction to this man and his love will most likely destroy me.

I'm not the only one who misses Dante. Angelo constantly asks me about his father and when he's coming back. The two have forged a strong bond in a very short time. Their connection is so powerful that it scares me. It's much more powerful than I ever anticipated it to be. I'm happy, of course, but I worry. Am I doing the wrong thing here? Keeping them apart is cruel. But the alternative is so frightening I cannot bear to think about it for too long before I have to suppress the urge to scream out at the top of my lungs in frustration.

LYDIA HALL

The problem, as I see it, is that Dante De Luca is not your average suitor. Not by any stretch of the imagination. The man is a Don in the mafia, for fuck's sake! What are the odds of me falling in love with someone so potentially lethal? How on God's green earth did I get myself into this mess? It was supposed to be a harmless one night stand. Not a lifelong connection to a crime boss! Had I not been so mortally wounded emotionally from my disastrous breakup, I would most likely have thought twice before diving into the unknown, vagina first!

But here I am in a perpetual state of anguish. Oh, love, you fickle bitch!

I have to tell my parents the truth. They've been asking questions I'm not comfortable answering. Normal, yet agonizing questions about why Dante left and why I didn't go with him to Rome. Ugh! Will this shit storm ever end?

I'm joining my folks for brunch this morning. I think it's about time I shared my agony with someone. Gina's been very supportive. I feel bad for shitting all over her after Dante told me the truth. I was so mad I couldn't see her side of it. I get that she was trying to do the right thing by allowing Dante to be the one to break the news to me, but in the heat of it all I was sorely tempted to throttle my best friend.

Angelo is having a playdate with his best friend, Max, today. I'm relieved. The discussion with Mom and Dad is bound to get a little heated and I cannot worry about what my son may or may not hear about his father.

I get out of bed and head for the shower. The warm water pelting my skin goes a long way to easing my physical maladies, but they're always there. My new companion—rage and regret, sugar coated with what ifs and blind hope.

After the attempt at washing away my troubles with scoldingly hot water, I head for Angelo's room. He's fast asleep. I watch him for a bit.

My baby is so beautiful. I imagine what he will look like when he's a man. He's a De Luca alright. Mothers lock up your daughters.

"Hey, monster," I whisper into his little ear. "Time to get up."

Angelo stirs and makes a muffled noise.

"You're going to play with Max today."

My words are like lighter fuel, causing my son's eyes to fly open.

"Yay!" he says and yaws.

"Come on. Let's get you dressed and ready."

"Good morning, buddy," he says as Splash licks him all over.

"Come on, boy," I call to the dog as I leave Angelo's room. "Breakfast time."

Splash follows the one who keeps him well fed, wagging his tail wildly at the prospect of a piece of bacon that may or may not end up on the kitchen floor.

"Good morning, Paolo."

"Good morning, Mia."

"Coffee?"

"I made a pot."

"Oh, thank you. That was sweet of you."

"No problem."

Paolo has become a fixture in our home. He doesn't speak much, but I can tell that there's a lot going on behind those dark brown eyes of his.

"I'm going over to see my folks today. Why don't you take the day off and go into town? I'll be fine."

"Will Angelo be going with you?"

LYDIA HALL

"No. He has a playdate with his friend, Max."

"I think I'll stay with him, then."

At first Paolo's constant presence irritated the shit out of me. It's just weird having a nursemaid following us around. But, I'm used to it now.

"Okay. But keep your distance please, Paolo. I don't want to freak Max's mother out."

"She won't even know I'm there."

"Thank you."

"Hey, Paolo."

"Good morning, Angelo," Paolo smiles warmly at the son of his Don.

"Mommy, can Splash come with me? Max says his mother won't mind. He also has a dog."

"No, my sweetheart. Splash has to stay here and guard the house," I smile.

"Ahhh!"

"Don't pout, sweetheart. Max's mom said she's taking you guys to the petting zoo today."

"Oh, cool! I'm going to feed carrots to the alpacas. Max says if you don't, they spit at you."

"Ugh!" I grimace.

"It's true. Suzie didn't give her alpaca a carrot and it snotted all over her hand."

"Okay. In that case, I'd better pack some wet wipes," I chuckle.

"Good luck," I whisper to Paolo as I pass him.

"Thanks," he grins.

* * *

"Hi, darling. Where's Angelo?"

"Hey, Mom. Nice to see you too," I smirk. "He's gone to the petting zoo with Max and his mom."

"Ah! I was hoping to see my little muffin. But you'll do," she grins. "Come in."

"Where's Dad?"

"He's in the den."

"Good. I want to talk to you both before we sit down to brunch."

"Is something the matter?"

"Kinda."

"Oh, no. Now you've got me worried."

"It's okay. It's not the end of the world."

No, but it's a close second.

"I'll get you father. Have a seat in the living room. I'll be right back."

I go ahead and take a seat in my favorite spot. I love to look at the photos on the mantelpiece. They chart my growth as a human, from playschool all the way through highschool and then my graduation.

Mom has photos of Angelo on there too. His baby pictures are front and center. He was so damn cute when he was a baby. His black hair was always poking out in different directions.

Mom returns a few moments later with Dad by her side.

"Hey, poppet. How's my girl?"

"Hi, Dad. I'm okay. How are you?"

"Fine. What's this I hear? Mom says you want to talk to us about something. What's wrong?"

"Sit down. I need to tell you something."

My parents take their place, side by side, on their favorite sofa. Seeing them like this I have a sudden flashback of when I snuck out one night and crashed into the fence with their car. It left a nasty dent in the fender. When I got home they were in this very position, waiting to rip me a new one. Oh, how simple those days were.

"Go ahead, baby. We're listening."

"It's about Dante—about what he does for a living."

"He mentioned that he's in finance. Right?" Dad asks.

"I guess that's one way of looking at it. But it's a little more complicated than that, I'm afraid."

"What is it, Mia?" Mom urges me.

I take a deep breath. There's no sense in delaying this. Best to just rip off the old bandaid and get it over with.

"Dante is in the mob."

There! I said it, and suddenly I feel weightless. Unfortunately, I've just handed the burden to two people I love very much. They stare at me in horror.

"What?" Mom whispers.

"The mob? As in the mafia?" Dad asks with a deadpan expression.

"Yes."

Dad leaps to his feet and starts pacing. Mom starts sniffling. Great. This is a bust.

"I don't understand," Dad says. "What do you mean, he's in the mob? Are you sure? How did you find out?"

"He told me."

"This can't be right," Mom says softly, shaking her head. "He's such a nice man."

"He's a goddamn criminal, Catherine!" Dad yells out.

"Calm down, Arnold. You're going to give yourself a heart attack. Besides, you're the mafia movie buff. This is karma, isn't it?"

"Please, guys. Calm down," I plead, well aware that this is all my fault.

"So, what now?" Dad asks.

"Can't he leave? He loves you and Angelo. Won't he change for your sake?" Mom adds.

"It's not that simple, I'm afraid. Dante is the head of the family. He can't just decide to change his profession. It's a mess."

"I'd say it, fucking is," Dad fumes.

"Arnold!" Mom snaps at her husband.

"Oh, come on, Catherine. Mia isn't a child. I'm sure she's heard plenty of colorful language."

"It's alright, Mom. I know just how Dad feels. It was a terrible shock to me too."

"I'm sorry, Mia," Dad says. "I'm being a selfish brute. I haven't asked how you feel about all of this yet. Are you okay? Did he hurt you?"

"No, of course not, Dad. Dante loves me and he's the gentlest man I've ever been with. He'd never hurt me or Angelo."

"That's something, at least," he sighs before he flops back onto the sofa.

"What exactly did he tell you, Mia?" Mom asks.

"He said that he's wanted to tell me for a long time, but he knew I may have an issue with it, so he put it off until he could show me who he was as a man."

"What are you going to do, my child? Do you love him enough to get into this sort of world?" Mom asks.

"I don't know what to do. I love him and he's Angelo's father and all, but I don't know if this is the kind of life I want for my son. What do you think? I value your opinion, guys. I'm at a loss here."

"What is your heart telling you, my darling?" Mom asks.

"Her heart! This is no time for your romantic machinations, Catherine. The man is a criminal. Get as far away from him as possible, Mia, and stay away. Nothing good can come of this relationship," Dad snaps.

"You forget that they share a child, Arnold."

"I haven't forgotten a thing. Angelo is better off growing up without a father than learning from one who's a crime boss."

"This is a nightmare," I say and drop my head into my hands in despair.

"If you need some time away to think this through, you could always go to my brother's house in Texas, sweetheart. It's a big house and he's never there. I'm sure he won't mind if you use it," Dad suggests.

"Yes, that's an excellent idea, Mia. Dad and I will help you with finances until you decide what you need to do."

"I can't ask you to do that, guys," I protest.

"You didn't ask, my darling. We're offering," Dad assures me. "Besides, if Dante knows where you are, he's bound to bug you until you give into him. What you need is distance."

"Okay. I think you're right."

"I'll call Uncle Ben and arrange everything," Dad says and comes over to hug me.

This is when I lose it and break down in tears. It's been a long time coming.

* * *

I have to talk to Gina. I can't leave her out in the cold. Besides, Dante is her cousin, and he'll almost certainly call her eventually after he hasn't heard from me for a while. It's bad enough that I'm icing him out. I can't do that to Gina too.

I call her after I leave my parent's house.

"Hi, M. What's up?"

"I need to talk to you. Can you come over?"

"What's wrong? You sound worried about something."

"Can you come over, please? I'll tell you when you get here."

"Uh, sure. I'll be there in half an hour."

"Thanks. See you soon."

I put Angelo to bed before Gina arrives. I don't want him to get wind of what I'm about to do. I can only pray that Gina doesn't spill the beans to Dante. But, I have to trust in our friendship.

"Hey, you. What's happening? You look like a fly spinning in a spider's web," Gina says as soon as she arrives.

I pour two glasses of wine and hand her one.

"Okay. I'm going to tell you something now but first you have to swear to me that you won't tell anyone. Especially Dante."

"O…k…a…y…" she says pensively.

"Also, don't talk too loudly. I don't want Paolo to hear us."

"Geez, Mia, What the hell is going on?"

"I'm leaving LA."

"What? Why?"

"I can't do this, Gina. I can't put Angelo in danger by moving to Italy with Dante. He's a Don for fuck's sake. The man has a target on his back. Had I known this at the start I never would have taken this relationship any further. I mean, what the hell was I thinking?"

"Mia, don't make any rash decisions. Think about this. You love Dante and I know he loves you. And, what about Angelo? He adores his daddy. What are you going to tell him?"

"I can't worry about that right now, Gina. All I can do is focus on the task at hand. One baby step at a time."

"Damn, girl. This is big."

"No shit. I'm a nervous wreck."

"Where are you going?"

"Texas. My uncle has a ranch there. He hardly ever uses it, so Angelo and I will have it all to ourselves."

"Texas! Talk about a change of scenery."

"Just a bit, yeah."

"What will you do for money?"

"I have savings. Also Mom and Dad are helping me until I find a job."

"M. I don't know about this. Are you sure this is a good idea?"

"No, but it's the only way I can get some peace and give my head a chance to clear."

"Clearing your head is the easy part. It's your heart that's the problem."

"Please don't tell him, Gina."

"Of course I won't, Mia. You're my best friend. I would never betray you like that. Just promise me you'll keep in touch so I know you're okay."

"I will."

"When are you leaving?"

"In three days."

"Wow, that soon?"

"Why wait? I want to get this done."

"Dante's going to go apeshit if he can't get hold of you. You must know that, right?"

"Yeah. I know."

"Well, darling Mia, I'm here for you. Please know that you can call on me at any time."

"I know. I love you, Gina."

"I love you more, M."

"What will I tell Dante?"

"I don't know. Just lie your ass off."

* * *

My escape has been arranged. The house in Texas is open to us for as long as I need it. The property is in a trust, so Dante won't know to look for me there. I feel awful for doing this, but I've given it so much thought. I love Dante, but I cannot allow his world to taint my son.

The only trick now is to escape Paolo's eagle eye. There's no way he'll let Angelo and me leave LA. But I have a plan. It's time to call in a few favors.

LYDIA HALL

"George, it's me. I need a favor."

"Sure, kid. How can I help you?"

"I need some kickass sleeping tabs."

"Do I want to know?"

I explain my situation to George over the phone. It's a long conversation during which I put my faith in the man who was there at the start of this mess. Afterward, I drive over to the pharmacy to collect the knockout drops.

I packed a bag for myself and Angelo during the night. All that's left to do is to pop a few drops into Paolo's morning coffee and I'll be home free. Oh, Lord, let this work. Please!

17

DANTE

"You need a few days' break, Dante. The other families are going to start thinking that you've got some sort of mysterious illness from the way you look.If your bottom lip grows any longer, you're bound to trip over it."

"I feel like crap, Elio. I miss my family and it seems that Mia is losing interest in the whole idea of coming to Rome."

"Why do you say that?"

"It isn't rocket science. Everytime we talk I feel as if she's gone a few more steps backwards. I don't know how much longer I can take this before I jump on the jet and drag her here by her hair."

"Yeah, I'd like to see that. I told you, brother, women have their own way of doing things. Not to mention taking their time while doing whatever those things are. You need to take a break. Let's go to the mountains for a few days."

"And be miserable there?"

"No, you idiot. We'll go to the ranch, saddle up the Caleberes, ride out for a few days, and camp under the stars. We haven't done that since we were kids. Come on. It will be good for you. And honestly, I could use a break myself from all this wedding planning crap. I tell you, Dante, if I have to taste one more wedding cake sample, or see one more flower arrangement, I'm going to throw up."

"So this is more a you problem than a me problem."

"Come on, man. Give a dog a bone!"

"Yeah, okay. It has to be better than moping around here, I suppose. Plus, the lake is good for fishing this time of year."

"There you go. Another silver lining. We'll catch our dinner. Bruno can run the operations while we're away."

"Thank you, Elio. You're a good brother."

Being out on horseback in the mountains can only cheer me up. There's nothing like it. That's the kind of tiredness that knocks you out at night. That and the good grappa made locally. That shit knocks you out cold. I feel a strong case of self medicating coming on.

The lake near the ranch is stunning. We slept there often as kids. Pappa would show us how to set up camp and then we'd build a fire and roast whatever we caught over an open flame. Such wonderful childhood memories they are.

Yeah, what the hell. Let's go have some clean fun. Or dirty, depending on the amount of mud Elio's horse kicks up as he sprints off ahead of me.

* * *

Elio and I are sitting outside on the porch of the ranch house, watching the sunset. It's old Italian architecture with raw stone and wood.

"I think we need to invest some money into bringing this place into the Twenty-First Century, brother," Elio says, sipping on grappa.

"Hell, no. This is history. It's just like I remember it. The modern world has no business intruding here. I can almost picture Pappa sitting there on the wall, swinging his legs back and forth, smoking his cigarette."

"Isn't it strange that neither one of us ever got into smoking?"

"I tried in high school. Vile stuff. Makes your skin all wrinkly and yellow too. A real babe repellent."

Elio laughs.

"Oh, please. With your looks, you could dress like a hobo and smoke a carton of fags a day and still bone the cutest girl in the room."

Elio is the opposite of me. Looks wise that is. I'm olive skinned with black hair and very dark brown eyes. My brother is sandy blonde with green eyes. He's a good looking guy, so I'm not sure what he's on about.

"So, you think I;m pretty, do you," I tease. "Wanna little kiss, blondie?"

"Fuck off," he laughs. "I'm just saying that it was tough growing up in the shadow of the unattainable older De Luca brother; the Don with the shlong."

"Oh, for fuck's sake. That's enough out of you, you dumbass. You have no reason to doubt yourself, Elio. You're equally as bright and competent as I am. If you were the firstborn, you'd be Don. That's all there is to it. In fact, sometimes I envy you."

"What? Why?"

"You have no idea how much pressure is on me to carry all the responsibility of leadership of this family on my shoulders. Wherever I go, someone has a hand out, wanting a favor, expecting me to solve everyone's problems. It may appear that I'm the king of my castle and loving all the attention, but trust me, it gets old."

"You've never complained."

"How could I? I want Mamma to be proud of me and I know my family needs me. I became the man of the house after Pappa died. That's no small thing."

"Dante, you put too much on yourself. I never expected you to be like Pappa, and I know neither does Mamma. I've always thought that you were the right man for the job. That's why I've never asked."

"I have nothing to complain about, brother. I'm a billionaire with the best of everything money can buy."

"Including this dilapidated, broke-ass ranch house," Elio grins.

"Exactly. So, why should I complain?"

"How very Zen of you. It's okay, Dante. You're allowed to throw out your toys occasionally. You can tell me whatever is on your mind. I'm here for you."

"Look at us. Bonding in the mountains with good grappa and the imminent threat of saddle sores."

"Glad I'm not alone."

"There's a reason we drive in plush SUVs, Elio. We've gotten soft."

"Pappa would turn in his grave," Elio laughs.

"He'd make us do manual labor, more like it."

"Tru dat. Let's go into town for a steak. I'm not in the mood to gut a fish. Besides, those sardines you caught would feed an ant."

"Oh, like yours was the catch of the day," Elio laughs.

"Face it. You and I are mafia men. We ain't no fishermen."

"Agreed. Right, off we go. I'm going to clean up quickly."

* * *

MERCILESS MONSTER

The ristorante at the nearest town is jam packed. Tourists love this part of the mountains. It's good for all sorts of outdoor adventures, especially around the national parks in the area.

Elio and I take a seat at the bar while we wait for a table. We haven't been to this area since we were teenagers so we aren't well known here. Honestly, the anonymity is a sorely needed distraction.

"Whiskey," Elio says to the barman over the noise of the diners and then turns back to me. "Looks like the whole of Europe is here tonight."

"I hope we get a table."

"Shall I move a few people?"

"I wouldn't recommend it. We're a tad outnumbered," I smile.

"Oh, please. These peasants! We'll kick their asses with one arm bound behind our back."

"I see all this fresh air has made you antsy, little brother."

"I see all that money has made you yellow."

I know what he's doing.

"Bating me isn't going to work, you trouble maker."

"Looks like I won't have to do too much bating," he grins and gestures to a table of diners.

"That sexy giovane donna over there can't take her eyes off you and her boyfriend doesn't seem terribly impressed."

"How do you know she isn't looking at you?"

"Could be. Either way we may get an opportunity tonight to flex a few muscles that have been laying dormant for too long."

"Don't start anything, Elio. It's tough eating a good steak with a split lip."

"Oh, come on. When did you become so boring?"

I laugh at my brother's challenge-filled look.

We order once we're seated.

"She's definitely got the hots for you, Dante."

"She is very pretty. But I'm taken."

"I don't think her boyfriend cares. He's starting to look like that bull we ran from in Pamplona. Remember that?"

"How can I forget? That thing's horns came way too close to my ass for comfort."

"I've never seen you run that fast," Elio cackles.

The boyfriend who's been checking Elio and I out since we walked in, gets up from his table and comes over with two of his mates.

Fuck. I'm not here to fight. I hope they listen to reason, because in the mood I've been in lately, I could easily push the cartilage of his nose through his stupid brain.

"You like what you see?" he slurs his accusation at us.

Elio and I ignore him. He's not pleased. Boneheads don't like that.

"Hey! I'm talking to you pretty boy," he says again, pokes me with his finger.

"I wouldn't do that if I were you," Elio threatens in a calm tone.

"Oh, yeah? And what are you planning on doing about it?"

I look down and shake my head. All I wanted to do was eat a steak and drink some whiskey. This asshole is pissing on my parade. Pent up rage is seething just beneath the surface of my otherwise cool and collected exterior.

I tell him politely to go fuck himself in Italian. He clearly doesn't speak the language because he doesn't react the way he would have, had he understood me.

"Why don't you go and sit down before I'm forced to teach you some manners?" I try again.

This time he gets my drift.

"Why don't you stop staring at my girlfriend, you dirty peasant?" he retorts.

I refuse to cause a scene in this nice restaurant. It was one of Pappa's favorite places to eat, and I won't sully the memory of us together by breaking this asshole's face here. So, quick as a flash, I jump to my feet, grab the dickhead by his hair, and drag him toward the exit. Elio does his bit to take care of the two friends who signed up for their friend's suicide mission.

The girlfriend starts yelling at us from their table, but it's too late for reasoning. I did my best, but the fool wouldn't listen. Now it's time for reckoning.

We're outside in record time. The man struggles, unsuccessfully, to free himself from my steely grip. I throw him down on the ground and kick him once in the ribs. I can feel the bones cracking under my boot.

You'd think that he would call it a day and apologize or something vaguely intelligent like that. But the booze is talking louder than his reason, so he hurls another insult at me.

I'm on top of him now, He's throwing wild punches at me. One grazes my chin and I taste blood. Like that bull in Pamplona, I see red and instantly my rage spills over. My anger at being ambushed by Kyle, my frustration over having left behind my woman and my son, the years of having to put others' happiness ahead of my own, all come flooding out.

I don't remember much until Elio pulls me off of the bloodied body on the ground.

"Okay, easy, brother," he shouts. "You don't want to kill him. I think he's learned his lesson."

I get up, out of breath and covered in his blood. My lip is stinging but I don't care. That was oddly cathartic.

"We'd better get out of here before the cops come. I don't think we need that kind of attention," Elio says and nudges me toward the car.

"I want my fucking steak," I say after we've been driving for a few minutes.

Elio starts giggling.

"What?"

"You already had your steak. That man's face is a mess."

"He asked for it. Besides, you egged me on to kick his ass."

"Guilty. But I suggested ruffling him up. You nearly killed the fool."

I smile.

"I bet he'll think twice before picking on a *peasant* again," I grin.

"Hoowy! That felt good. Let's find you a steak, brother. You've earned it."

* * *

"Good morning, Rocky. How are you feeling today?" Elio grins when I join him for breakfast.

"Like I had an intense therapy session."

"I bet your punch bag feels a little differently on this fine day. He's most likely forced to eat his breakfast through a straw."

"Fuck him. He's an idiot."

"How's your lip?"

"A little tender but nothing I can't handle."

"I had fun last night, Dante. Admit it. You feel better. Right?"

"Yeah."

"Nothing like a bit of horseplay to put some lead back in the pencil," Elio chuckles. "Lisa can thank her lucky stars she wasn't here last night. She'd be struggling to walk this morning."

"I think it's time we took you back to civilization, you reprobate."

"Ah, and miss out on more fun."

"You've had enough fun to hold you over for a while. I noticed two bodies hobbling away when we were walking back to the car."

"Oh, that."

"You weren't the only one getting your rocks off. At least mine walked away. Who knows if your hamburger meat lived to tell the story?"

"I think it's best we left today before the cops come looking."

"Like I said. You used to be more fun, brother."

18

MIA

Texas is not LA. For a start, it's huge. The house is big, the plains are vast, and practically everyone carries a gun. Perhaps if I'd grown up here I wouldn't have taken such issue with Dante's profession. I'd be accustomed to a good old shoot out at the O.K. Corral.

I decided that I'd be better off if I changed my number so that I don't have to explain myself to Dante. I hate to think about how heartbroken and no doubt furious the father of my child is with me right now. But, for now, I have to start over in Texas. One day, when Dante has given up on our love, and Angelo is old enough to make his own choices, I'll reassess. I just don't trust myself right now not to run off to join the man that I love.

I couldn't afford to fly to Texas, in case Dante checked the flights, so I drove. It was a long drive, but I broke it up into two stops, which made it more enjoyable. Angelo was excited when I told him that he, Splash and I were going on an adventure. I was exhausted by the time we arrived at our new abode, but Angelo and Splash were pumped.

MERCILESS MONSTER

Honestly, the ranch is bliss. There's so much space and the boys are having a blast. Uncle Ben's house is just spectacular. He made a good living and invested well, so this is his little gift to himself. I'm thankful that he's so generous. I'd be up shit creek without a paddle were it not for him.

"Angelo! Dinner time!" I call out into the wild blue yonder to my son and his canine sidekick.

It's very safe here. The property is large and it's nowhere near a thoroughfare, so no one would think to venture into it. Besides, if anyone tries, I'll whip out Uncle Ben's rifle and pretend I'm a Texan.

Angelo and Splash strom into the house like there's a raging buffalo after them.

"Oi! Shoes at the door, mister."

"Sorry," Angelo puffs and runs back to the door. "What's for dinner, Mommy? I'm starving."

"Cheeseburgers."

"Woohoo!"

How easy is it to please a kid? Meat and cheese in a bun and viola! I've given up on decorating the plate with cherry tomatoes and cucumbers. We're in Texas now.

"Wash your hands, sweetheart."

It looks like there is about a pound of dirt under my son's fingernails. I guess he's embracing the outdoors. I'm so relieved that he's enjoying himself. I live to make this child happy.

"How was school today?"

"It was great. There's a new boy. His name is Fred. Now I'm not the new kid anymore."

"Oh, okay. It's your birthday next week. I was thinking of baking some cupcakes for you and your classmates. What do you think?"

"Great idea, Mom."

"Mom? What happened to Mommy?"

"Hey, I'm almost six now. I can't call you that anymore. I'm old now."

My heart! I don't want Angelo to grow up. I wish I could bottle him while he's still cute and loves his mother more than anything else in the world!

"I see."

"Don't worry. I still love you," he mumbles nonchalantly through a mouth full of food.

"Well, that's good news," I smile, ruffling his hair.

I have an early appointment tomorrow morning for a job interview at a doctor's surgery. I know my way around medication, so it will be an easy adjustment. I didn;t want to make it too easy for Dante to find me so I'm steering clear of pharmacies for now.

I don't like this life of hiding and overthinking my every move. It's getting to me. The other day I could have sworn I saw someone following me. It turns out he was one of the dad's from school who happened to shop at the same store as me. I felt like a drama queen all day.

"Can you drop me off early tomorrow, Mom? I'm playing a new game with Fred."

"Okay. What's the game?"

"It's complicated. You won't understand."

Well, excuse me.

"Sure, honey. We'll leave early. Are you done?"

"Yup. Can I go watch some TV?"

"Put your plate in the sink and then have a bath. When you're clean you and Splash can watch some TV. Okay?"

"Okay."

* * *

"Hi, Mom. How are you?"

"Hi, Sweetheart. I thought I'd call you for a quick catch up."

"That's nice. I'm all good. How are you?"

"Missing you. Is Angelo still up?"

"No, I put him to bed about half an hour ago. He's exhausted. Or is that me?"

"I imagine you must be, darling. It's been a crazy few weeks. How are you adjusting to Texas?"

"Pretty good, considering. I got a job today."

"Oh, wonderful! Well done, Mia. Where?"

"A doctor's office. He's very nice."

"Is the pay decent?"

"It's not going to make me fabulously wealthy, but it's a good job. I'm happy."

"How are you really?"

"Sad, mostly. I miss Dante so much, Mom. I didn't think it would hurt this much."

"I'm sorry you're having such a tough time of it, my child. But you're doing the right thing for Angelo."

"Am I?"

"Yes, you are."

"I hope so, because that's the only thing keeping me here—and halfway sane."

"It will get easier. Hang in there."

"I'll try. How are you and Dad?"

"We were thinking of coming over to visit soon."

"No. Please don't do that, Mom. Paolo will be watching you guys."

"Are you sure? He must be back in Italy by now."

"I doubt it. Dante will no doubt order him to stay until he finds me."

My mom sighs.

"I'm sorry, Mom. We miss you too. But I have to be careful. Dante isn't in the boy scouts."

"Understatement."

"I'm bushed, Mom. Think I'll hit the hay early tonight."

"Sleep well, darling. Keep in touch."

"I will. Thanks for the call. Love you."

"Love you too. Goodnight."

I'm not the best company or conversationalist at the moment. I'm tired and depressed. Not a good combination. And to make it worse, I don't have Mom or Gina here to talk me off the proverbial ledge. It's lonely.

Cut the pity party, Mia. It could be a lot worse.

It could be worse. Not by much, but hey.

I fall asleep the minute my head touches down on the pillow. It's a deep sleep until about 2 a.m. when I wake up from a dream. Dante and I were walking together on the beach, holding hands and kissing every few steps. My heart aches when I realize it wasn't real.

I stumble out of bed at 6 a.m. My head feels fuzzy from spending half the night staring up at the ceiling. I drag my weary bones to the kitchen and put on a pot of coffee. It's my morning ritual. Coffee and toast with butter—my lifeline. It's too early to wake Angelo, so I switch on the TV and settle in for a bit until the caffeine kicks in.

No news sells like bad news. Suddenly, out of nowhere, a thought pierces my brain. What if I switch to the news channel one day and see Dante's face on the screen with a headline that reads, *Mafia Kingpin sought by Interpol.*

Come on now, Mia. Let's not get ahead of ourselves. This isn't a Mario Puzo novel.

That's it. I have to get a life. I can't sit around like this, holding my breath for the rest of my life. This is bullshit. I'm a fighter. I have to decide to either make a success of my new start or just go to Rome. Anything in between is pointless.

With a newfound resolution I switch off the TV and move upstairs to get myself dressed and Angelo ready for school.

Today is going to be a good day. The first of many if I can stop pining for Dante.

* * *

"Hey there! It's so good to hear your voice, Gina. I'm missing you like crazy."

"Hey, M. Missing you more. How's life in the lone star state?"

"Biiiig!" I chuckle. "How's LA? I miss the ocean so much, you won't believe it."

"Texas has an ocean, you know."

"I know, but it's so far away. I could practically walk to the beach back in LA."

"You're not missing much. It's the off season here now, so not much happening. How's my favorite godchild?"

"Getting old. He told me he can't call me Mommy anymore cause he's too old for that now. So, now I've been downgraded to Mom," I chuckle.

"Oh, no! You must be heartbroken," Gina laughs.

"Shattered. I tell you, Gina, they grow so fast. I don't suppose you and Jeff are planning any babies soon?"

"Nah, I don't know if I want to have kids. Besides, I have Angelo."

"Fair enough."

"Listen, I wanted to talk to you about something."

"Yeah?"

"Dante called me."

The mere mention of his name sends a current through me. I nearly drop the phone.

"What?"

"Yeah."

"What did he say?"

"He's pretty pissed."

"I see."

"He wanted me to tell him why you left LA and where he can get a hold of you."

"Shit. You didn't tell him, did you?"

"Of course not. I told him to be patient and wait until you're ready to talk."

"Thank you, Gina. I'm sorry to put you in the middle of this."

"Don't worry about it. I'm a big girl. I can handle my cousin. How are you feeling about the whole mess?"

"Well, I nearly dropped the phone when you mentioned his name, so I guess I'm still hung up on him. Big time."

"Oh, M. I'm sorry you're hurting."

"I got myself into this mess. It's not your fault."

"He misses you."

"Okay, no more helping."

"Sorry. How's the new job?"

"Fine."

"That good, huh?"

"No, it's okay. I'm just feeling a little sorry for myself right now. In fact, I'm getting pretty good at it," I sigh. "If it were an Olympic sport, I'd walk it."

"You're a hell of a fighter, M. You're braver than I could ever be. What you're doing is admirable."

"Tell my fractured heart. Do you know if Paolo is still around?"

"I don't know."

"I feel awful for drugging him. He's a nice guy."

"He's a mafia henchman. Don't feel too sorry for him. He'll get over it."

"I hope so. I wouldn't want to make an enemy of him."

"Paolo would never hurt you. Dante would kill him. Damn. Gotta run. There's a call on the other line. I love you, my friend. Chat soon."

LYDIA HALL

"Love you back."

Damn! And my day was going so well. Now, I'm right back where I started. Feeling like shit and missing Dante.

I fly into the kitchen and whip out the cupcake trays. I may as well do something with this nervous energy bouncing around my insides. I wasn't going to bake until tomorrow evening, but the cupcakes will hold. The recipients are six-year-olds for goodness sake, not connoisseurs. Angelo's classmates will probably lick off the frosting and toss the cupcakes anyway. That's what usually happens at these juvenile shindigs.

It's 10 p.m. and the smell of vanilla is wafting through the house. I'm on my thirst glass of Chardonnay—not the good stuff Dante and I brought back from the vineyard, but it's palatable. The memories of that week come flooding back, leaving me feeling rather short changed.

Oh, well. At least my son will have killer cupcakes with sprinkles galore for his birthday party in class. Bless him, the little darling.

"This is for you, my love," I say softly as I finish decorating the last one. "This is all for you. Everything. I hope you will understand one day how much this hurts. I hope you won't hate me for keeping you from you Daddy."

I take the last sip of wine, switch off the kitchen light, and go to bed. Another day in Texas, done and dusted. I feel good. Not great, just good. I'm making this work. So, I'll have my time to be happy. It will come. Not sure when, but there's always hope.

Splash is on my bed when I enter my room. He curls up at my feet, as if he senses that I need companionship tonight. I scratch him behind his ear before I close my eyes and drift off to sleep.

19

DANTE

"You're kidding me!" I scream into the air. "How the fuck do you manage to lose a woman and a child, Paolo?"

"I'm sorry Boss but she drugged me. I had no reason to think she would run. I'm sorry, Boss."

"Not as sorry as you're going to be when I get my hands on you. How can you be hoodwinked like this? Fuck! I'm surrounded by idiots!"

"I'll start looking immediately, Boss."

"You do that. And, Paolo, if you don't have answers for me by the end of the day, then do yourself a favor and hide."

The tight feeling I've had in my gut for a week makes sense at this moment. I knew something was wrong. I could hear it in Mia's voice. She was distant, distracted, cool even. Elio kept banging on about how women need time and space and all that bullshit, but I knew in my heart that Mia was distancing herself from me emotionally.

All I can do now is wait. I can't fly off to America again. Not now. I'll do serious damage if I disappear again. I'll lose face with all my investors. No. This time I have to sit tight and hope that the woman of my dreams comes to her senses.

**

"She's ghosting me," I say and throw down my phone.

"Are you sure, Dante? She could be having trouble with her cell. It happens."

"No. There are untold ways of getting in touch with me if she wanted to. I'm telling you, Mia has given up on us. Why else would she leave LA and not tell me where she is?'"

I haven't heard from Mia since Paolo called me over a week ago. Everytime I call, I get a voicemail service. My texts aren't going through, neither are my WhatsApps, and she hasn't been seen on any of the other social media platforms. Mia is definitely icing me out.

The worst of it is I don't know why. I haven't said anything too pushy or offensive in the least, so I can only deduce from her silence that she's having second thoughts about us.

"Dante, you have to focus. I'm really sorry to be a dick about this, but we have a very busy week ahead of us with regards to business."

"How can I focus on work if I'm out of my mind with worry? What if something's happened to them? What if someone took them?"

"Her family would have called you by now if that was the case."

"I'm going to call Gina and find out if she knows anything. Give me a minute. I'll join you downstairs as soon as I've spoken to our cousin."

"Fine, but hurry up. We can't be late for this meeting. Corelli is gunning for our family as it is. We can't afford to give him ammunition to use against us."

"Yes, yes, Elio. I said I'll be right there!"

My brother leaves the room in a huff. I can't worry about that now. I dial Gina's number. It's late in LA, so I hope she's still awake. This can't wait a moment longer.

'Hello…" she answers in a sleepy voice.

"Gina, it's Dante."

"Dante? It's the middle of the night. What is it?"

"Where's Mia?"

"Good to hear from you too, cousin."

"Gina, I don't have the time for your sass right now. Where is my son?"

"I don't know, Dante."

"You're lying!"

"don't you yell at me. I'm not one of your lackeys."

"I'm sorry. Please forgive me."

"I don't know where Mia is, Dante. I only know that she said she was thinking of leaving town for a while to get her head straight."

"She's your best friend. Do you expect me to believe that she didn't tell you where she was going? Do you take me for a fool?"

"No, I don't. I also know that Mia is no fool either. Do you really think she's going to confide in me after I kept my mouth shut about what you do for a living, cousin? I betrayed her once. She isn't likely to turn the other cheek so I can do it to her again."

"Fuck it all. I'm worried about her, Gina. Mia has no idea what kind of danger she could be in if my enemies find out who and where is."

"Whose fault is that, Dante?"

"That's a low blow, cousin. You know I love her. I won't let anything happen to her. That's why I wanted Mia and Angelo to come with me to Rome. I never should have left her behind."

"Mia will be fine, Dante. She's tougher than you think."

"So are the people who hate me."

* * *

If I was pissy before, I'm now a raving lunatic waiting for a place to explode. The meeting today with the Don's from the other families in the area is bound to get a little explosive.

Don Corelli hates me. He's been systematically working his way through the group, spouting shit about me in their ears for months now. But I'm ready for him today. I'm not taking anymore shit from that treacherous bastard. Come to think about it, I would be at all surprised if it was Corelli who was behind Kyle's attack on me.

The mob business isn't always as transparent and predictable as it would seem. Thugs hide behind respectability and donations to charities, when all they truly are, are low lives who will betray their mothers to advance.

Corelli is such a rat. There isn't an ounce of honor in that bastard.

"What did Gina say?" Elio asks as I get into the car.

"Mia left LA for a while. She says she doesn;t know where Mia is. Only that she needed time away."

"Do you believe her?"

"Does it matter? What am I going to do? Torture our cousin until she spills the beans?"

"Yeah, Mamma may be a little pissed if you tried that."

"Gina's mom is Mamma's favorite cousin. She'd skin me alive."

"Blood women and their sisterhood bullshit. Can you imagine what men could accomplish if we had that kind of bond between ourselves?"

"What are you going to do?"

"What can I do? America isn't Italy. It's a big place. Lots of states to hide in. I would know where to start."

"The best thing you can do now is be patient and try not to lose your mind, brother. If Mia loves you, like you said she does, she'll come around."

"I don't know if I can wait that long. In the meantime I'm losing precious time with my son. I already lost the first five years of the child's life."

"He's not going anywhere, Dante. Be patient. I need you to focus on what we're about to walk into. I hear Corelli is making alliances. We have to be careful of that snake."

"Oh, please God let him challenge me today. I'm so ready for him. I'm itching to pop a cap in that man's skull."

"Looks like I created a monster."

"What are you talking about?"

"Have you already forgotten Rocky Gate in the mountains, slugger?"

"Oh, that. Corelli wishes he could walk away with a broken jaw and a fractured eye socket. He's be so fucking lucky."

"There he is. The Don with the ten pound hammer fist. I feel the same as you do, bro. I think it's high time Corelli reaps the rewards for his meddling."

The casino conference room is heavily guarded. It stands to reason as some of the most important players in Italy's mafia underworld are present within her cash cow walls. Elio and I take our places around the large table.

Corelli sits across from us. It's lucky for him that the table is so wide, otherwise I'd reach across and snap his neck. We glare at each other while we wait for the others to arrive. My mentor once told me never to show emotion as it makes a man weak, but today I'm tossing caution to the wind. I loathe this worm.

"I hear you have a problem with me, Corelli," I say in a calm voice.

"We all do, De Luca. Some of us just don;t bother hiding it."

"I see. What's the problem?"

"You are. Your boys are encroaching on the other families' territory."

"That's bullshit, and you know it. That's the kind of baseless rumor that could advance your position, Corelli. Whoever finds themselves in alignment with such fuckery will reap the rewards of their lies. I'll see to that. Personally."

"You don't scare me, De Luca. You're soft."

I'm clenching my hands under the table. I refuse to give Corelli the satisfaction of showing him my fury. Not yet. That will come later.

* * *

I check my watch. It's 10 p.m.

"Corelli should be staring down the barrel of a gun right about now," I smile, taking a sip of my brandy.

"Uh-huh. I hope he enjoyed his last blowjob. That little whore of his will probably send us flowers tomorrow," Elio adds.

"I'm sure his wife won't be too sorry to see him gone either. On top of all his charming qualities, he likes to smack her around. I loathe a man who hits a woman. Pick on someone your own strength. Coward."

"The community is going to blow up after this."

"I don't give a damn. Let them. Corelli is an arrogant, narcissistic megalomaniac who deserves what he's about to get."

"Cheers to that, brother."

My cell rings.

"Hello."

"It's done, Boss."

"Excellent."

"And?" Elio asks.

"Corelli is officially swimming with the fishes, bro."

"Couldn't have happened to a nicer guy."

20

MIA

"Come on, slowpoke! Get in the car. We're going to be late."

"Coming, Mom!" Angelo yells from upstairs.

"Oh, no, buddy. Not today," I say as Splash, tries to jump into the car via the open back door.

It takes all my strength to hold onto his collar as he wiggles and thrashes to get in. The dog has grown to be quite the little ninja when it comes to slipping by me. He and Angelo are inseparable.

I march Splash back to the house and put him into the kitchen long enough so that Angelo can hop into the car.

"We're going to have to take your shadow to a trainer, my boy. Soon he'll be too strong for me to handle."

"Cool. Can they teach him to sit, and roll over, and play dead, and all that cool stuff?"

"I think you should teach him that."

"Okay. I'll start today, after school."

"We've got plenty of treats to motivate him," I smile.

"I'll use a spoonful of peanut butter. Splash always tries to steal my peanut butter and jelly sandwiches."

"He's a real scrounger, that's for sure. Ready to go?"

"Yup."

"Do you have your lunch?"

"Uh-huh."

"Okay, let's go."

"I'm working a little later than usual today, sweetheart, so you'll hang at aftercare for an hour."

"Okay. I like it there. We get to play cool games with Mrs. Martin."

"That's great, honey. I'm glad. Buckle up now."

Weekday mornings are akin to being caught up in a whirlwind. I'm looking forward to the weekend so Angelo and Splash can sleep in a bit. Being a single mom is tiring and I sneak in every ounce of peace and quiet I can get. Tomorrow is Saturday. Thank God!

I head off to work as soon as I've dropped Angelo at school. He's at that age now where he talks incessantly. My ears are still ringing when I get to work. Hang in there, Mia! It's almost Miller time.

"Hey, Mia."

"Hi, Julie."

"Hey, hey! It's Friday!" she says in her southern drawl.

"I was just thinking the exact same thing."

"It's been a doozy of a week, girl. How about joining us for a drink later?"

"I'd love to, but I can't."

"Oh, yeah. Angelo. I forgot. I could give ya the number of an excellent babysitter, if ya like. Her name's Hannah. She watches my niece. Great girl. Brilliant with kids."

The idea is so tempting. I haven't had a night out in…hell, I can't even remember. But I'm not sure I'll feel comfortable yet with leaving my darling with a stranger, no matter how reliable she is. I'm just not there yet.

"Thanks, Julie. That's very thoughtful of you but I'll give this one a miss."

"I understand. I'll forward ya her number anyway. Just in case you change your mind or ever need a break. Okay?"

"Thanks, you're a sweetheart."

"Hey, we moms gotta stick together."

"Tru dat."

* * *

"Julie, I'm going to take my lunch hour now. Is that okay with you?"

"Sure, hon."

"Okay, see you later."

"Enjoy."

I'm craving a nicoise salad. I found a place close to work that has a brilliant selection of salads. You take the girl out of LA but you can't take LA out of the girl. The store is close enough so I walk rather than drive. It's a nice day out.

I check my messages while I walk. Mom sent me a few links to recipes on a budget—that's so Mom—and Gina sent me a few dirty jokes— how very Gina. My wallet slips out of my hands while I'm texting

Gina. I stoop to pick it up and notice a man watching me. Has he been there the whole time?

Come on, Mia. Don't be paranoid.

I'm probably being a little sensitive. No one knows I'm here. I've been extremely careful in all my movements. I even registered Angelo under my mother's maiden name. I haven't taken any chances.

The man smiles when he sees me looking at him and then he passes me and moves off down the street.

You see. All that panic for nothing.

I pay for my salad in the store, and take it with me to the park where I open the container and dig into its delicious contents. This is definitely an outdoor salad. The whiff from the boiled eggs and anchovies would spread through the office like a plague. I could never do that to poor Julie.

The park is lovely. Dog owners have their furry kids chasing balls and frisbees and couples are out on picnic blankets, enjoying a quick snack before returning to their nine-to-five. What a lovely way to spend an hour.

I check my watch. Time to start my slow walk back to the office. I throw away the empty container, swish some water around in my mouth to get rid of the remnants of the tuna, and head to the office. I happen to glance over my shoulder at a dog leaping into the air to catch a frisbee when my eye catches a familiar face. It's the same man from earlier!

No, this can't be a coincidence. I don't believe in coincidence anyway, and this is just too close to the mark. He must sense my trepidation, because the smile he gave me earlier isn;t quite so bright this time around. I pick up the pace. A few meters into my walk, I look back. He's still there.

Now my heart is racing. The stranger is definitely following me. I'm not imagining it. I even crossed to the other side of the street and I couldn't shake him. I can do one of two things here. I can run, or I can stop in my tracks and ask him what he wants. I choose to do the latter. Not sure where I get the sudden surge of bravado, but, hey.

"Excuse me. Why are you following me?"

He's much taller than I am, so I have to crane my neck to look him square in the eye, but I puff myself up and keep my course.

"Hello, Mia," he says with a somewhat menacing grin.

I can feel the blood leaving my face and pooling in my lower body.

"How do you know my name?" I bark, scared shitless, but determined not to show it.

"We share an acquaintance."

I'm pretty sure I would know about it if that were the case. Perhaps he knows Uncle Ben. Is that even possible?

"Who would that be?"

"Dante De Luca."

I want to run. I want to run and never stop. How the actual fuck did Dante find me?

"Tell Dante to leave me alone," I snap and turn to walk away.

A forceful hand on my shoulder stops me in my tracks.

"Get your hands off me," I growl at him.

"You misunderstand," he says with his hands in the air in surrender.

"What do you mean?"

"Dante didn't send me."

Wait, What? I'm confused.

"Then who did?"

"Someone who really wants to see the De Lucas pay for their sins."

I pray for the earth to open up and swallow my whole, but no such luck. This is exactly what I feared would happen. I have no hand in this war. Why am I being punished? This is crazy.

"Look. I don't know who sent you or what his beef is with the De Luca family, but I have nothing to do with them, so I'm going to go and you're going to leave me alone. Okay?"

"No."

Okay, that was spoken with far too much conviction for my liking. What do I do now? I turn to walk away, but the next few words out of the man's mouth stop me dead.

"Angelo is such a sweet boy. What is he now? Six?"

No! Please, no! Not my boy.

"Stay away from my son!"

"You mean Dante's son."

How the fuck does he know this?

"Good news travels fast," he grins.

"What do you want?"

"The De Lucas are big on family. We want you to invite Dante here. We'll take it from there."

I stare at him in disbelief. I cannot betray Dante like that. I won't!

"I can tell you need some time to think about this. I'll give you the weekend to think it over. I'll contact you again on Monday."

And, with that, he unceremoniously turns and walks away, leaving me standing with my bottom jaw scraping the curb. I sit down because I'm sure my legs aren't going to hold me up much longer.

I jump when I feel someone touching my shoulder.

"Oh, I'm terribly sorry, Ms. Are you alright? Did that man upset you?"

A young woman is standing over me. She must be in her early twenties. She looks concerned.

"Oh, that's alright. I'm fine. Thank you for checking."

"Are you sure?"

"Yeah. Thanks."

She smiles and walks on. I'm so not fine.

I pull out my cell phone and call the office.

"Hi, Julie. It's me. I'm so sorry, but I have to take the afternoon off. I feel terrible. Must be something I just ate. I'm so sorry. Will you cope without me?"

"Oh, honey, ya sound awful. That's fine. Feel better. See ya Monday."

"Thanks, Julie."

"You bet, sugar."

I get up as soon as I'm confident enough that I won't fall down again and knock out my teeth. I have to get to Angelo. The man scared the living shit out of me. I have to make sure my son is safe.

It takes me a few minutes of speed walking to get to my car. I'm all sweaty by the time I start the engine and race off to Angelo's school. He's in class when I get there. The school secretary looks at me oddly. I must look like a mess.

"Hello, Mia. It's lovely to see you," she smiles.

"Hi, Jacqui. I wonder if I could take Angelo a little early today?"

"Of course. Please, take a seat, I'll get him for you."

"Thank you."

I sit down on one of the chairs outside the office while she fetches my boy. I have no idea what I'm going to tell him but I'll cross that bridge later. All I know is that I want him with me now.

"Mom?"

"Hi, baby."

"What are you doing here?"

"I'll tell you in the car. Thank you, Jacqui."

"No problem."

"I thought I was going to stay at aftercare today."

"I got off work early, so I thought we'd go on an adventure," I smile.

"Like what?"

"Well, how does a pizza and ice cream followed by a movie sound?"

"Wow! Awesome."

Thank God he's only six. It's so easy to bribe them at this age.

"Great. Let's go. Buckle up."

I wasn't paying too much attention before but I won't make that mistake again. I keep a close eye on the traffic around me, making sure that I don't see anyone following us. Damn it! They probably know where I live too. I feel like an idiot for having been so naive.

I spend the rest of the afternoon looking about like a criminal. The sinking feeling in my stomach that started at lunch is now a permanent fixture. It seems that all the eyes around me are on me. Paranoid much?

I'm utterly shattered by the time Angelo and I get home. All I want to do is crawl into bed and stay under the covers until all this blows over. But it isn't going to blow over, is it? Oh, no. Dante De Luca has made some powerful enemies and I'm going to pay for it. Either by losing my child or losing my lover. Fuck!

"Bedtime, tiger. Did you have a good afternoon?"

"Yeah, thanks, Mom. That was so much fun."

"You're welcome, sweetheart."

"Mom."

"Yes, my love?"

"When are we going home? I miss Max."

"Oh, sweetie. I don't know. Don't you like your friends here?"

"Yeah. They're okay, I guess."

My heart aches. My poor baby. I wish Dante had never come into our lives. He's brought nothing but chaos with him. Damn the mafia! Damn my love for Dante!

"Goodnight, sweet boy. I love you very much."

"I love you too, Mommy."

I smile as he closes his eyes. Angelo must be pretty tired as he let that one slip. I don't mind. I love being Mommy.

Now that he's asleep, I'd better call my parents and tell them what's happened. This is going to be a tough call.

21

MIA

"Hello, Mia. How are you, darling?"

"Hi, Dad. Not good."

"Why? What's happened?"

"I'm in trouble, Dad. I don't know how, but they found me, but they did."

"Dante?"

"No. Worse. Someone who is clearly looking to settle a score with the De Luca family. I'm scared."

"Tell me exactly what happened, my love."

I fill Dad in on the details of what happened on the street with the stranger. I can hear in his voice that my father has switched over to paternal protective mode.

"You have to go to the police, Mia."

"I can't do that. They're watching me. I can't do anything to upset them or they'll hurt Angelo. I'm stuck, Dad!" I blurt out.

"Call Dante and tell him what's happening. He's Angelo's father. He must come to his son's rescue."

"If he comes here, they'll kill him."

"Oh, Lord, Mia. I'm booking a flight tonight. I'm coming to keep an eye on you both."

"No. I don't want you hurt, Dad."

"Nonsense. You can't be out there on your own. You need protection."

"No offense Dad, but what can you do? These men are dangerous."

"I don't care. I'm coming."

"Please, don't bring Mom. She's too emotional."

"I won't."

"What will you tell her?"

"I'll think of something."

"Okay. Thank you, Dad."

"I love you, sweetheart. Hang in there. I'm coming."

★ ★ ★

"Good morning, my little lovebug. Did you sleep well?"

Angelo has his little sleepy face on. He's so adorable I just want to squish his cheeks until they pop. Kids are extra cute when they wake up from a deep sleep. They look so discombobulated, as if they have no idea where they are or where they've been for the past few hours.

"Hi, Mom," he says in a crackling voice.

The weekend is over and Monday has circled around once more. I enjoyed having Angelo close to me. It's the only time I can breathe

MERCILESS MONSTER

deeply. Even after six years of motherhood, I still suffer from separation anxiety. Now it's worse than ever.

I checked the windows all weekend to make sure that no one was lurking about. Dad arrived on Saturday afternoon and took a taxi to the ranch. Angelo and I were over the moon to see him, even if it was for different reasons.

I placed a loaded shotgun next to my bed at night. Of course, I waited until Angelo was asleep before I took it out. I don't want to scare my child. It's bad enough that one of us is scared shitless.

Dad's downstairs, doing what he does when he's nervous—cooking. It's the oddest thing, but that's his coping mechanism. This morning he's scrambling eggs, frying bacon, and making toast. Not that I'm complaining. It smells like home down there.

"Grandpa is cooking eggs and bacon. Are you hungry?"

"Yum. Yes."

"Okay, then. Let's get you dressed."

Dad and I decided that Angelo would be better off going about his day as if nothing was different. So, he's going to go to school and we'll be there to fetch him straight after. I'll go to work and Dad will hold down the fort on the homefront.

I'm a ball of nerves by the time Angelo and I get in the car.

"See you later, Grandpa," Angelo says excitedly. "Bye, Splash. Be good for Grandpa!"

"See you soon, my boy," Dad says and waves.

"Be careful out there, Mia," Dad whispers to me once Angelo is inside the vehicle.

"I will."

I watch my father waving at us in my rearview mirror.

"It's so nice of Grandpa to come visit us, Mom."

"Yes, isn't it?"

"Why didn't Grandma come?"

"She has a few things to do but she'll probably come a little later."

"Oh. Okay. We're going to the zoo today. The whole class."

"That sounds like fun. Stay close to your teacher, sweetheart. Don't wander off."

"Never."

I walk Angelo into the building once we get to school.

"Have a fun day, hon."

"You too, Mom."

I get a quick kiss on the cheek before he spots a group of friends and then I become a distant memory. I'm glad he has no idea of the shitstorm raging around us at the moment.

I find it almost impossible to focus at work.

"Man, that bug got ya good, huh?" Julie coos. "Ya look a little green, darlin'."

"I'll be okay."

"Well, you let me know if ya need to head on home, ya hear?"

"Thanks, Julie. I will."

I watch the door and listen out for my phone. The man said he'd be contacting me today. My stomach is a mess. I wasn't able to keep down the eggs and now my gut is screaming and growing like a wildcat in a bag.

"Here, drink this," Julie says and puts down a mug of coffee on my desk. "It's strong, but it will get the job done."

"Thanks."

Julie wasn't kidding. The coffee is so strong I'm amazed that the teaspoon didn't lose its stainless steel coating. But it does the job alright. The caffeine pulls me straight in no time.

"There. Now don't ya feel better, honey?" Julie smiles after I down the last sip.

"Ready for a marathon," I smile back.

I tense up when my phone rings. It's 11 a.m.

"Hello," I answer hesitantly.

"Mia, it's Angelo's teacher. I'm afraid we have a situation."

My heart sinks into my feet and I immediately break out into a cold sweat.

"What do you mean? What's wrong? Is Angelo okay?"

"I think you should come to the school immediately."

"What is it?!" I yell.

"Angelo is missing."

I drop the phone on the floor. It bounces and lands a few meters away. Julie comes running when she hears my screams.

"What is it?" she implores me.

"I have to go," is all I can manage.

I don't stop to answer her questions. All I can think of while I'm running to the car is Angelo out there somewhere, in the hands of Dante's enemies.

I call my father on the way to school and tell him what's happened. He's in as much of a state as I am by the time we meet in the school parking lot.

"Don't worry, Mia. We'll find him," he says and throws his arms around me.

The principal is waiting for us in the lobby. She's pale. Clearly, this isn;t something anyone in her position is used to.

"I'm so sorry," the treacher babbles. "He was right there and then he was just gone," she says through tears.

"Have you called the police?" my father insists.

"Yes, we have. They are on their way."

Fuck! I was hoping to keep the cops out of this mess, but now it's too late.

My cell phone rings. It's not a number I recognize so I answer.

"Hello."

"Hello, Mia. Listen to me very carefully. Tell the teacher to call the police and tell them that Angelo's aunt has him and that it's all okay."

"What?"

"If you want to see your son again, then do it."

The call ends.

My hands are shaking so violently, I can barely hold onto the phone.

"Uhm, it's okay," I stutter. "My sister just called. She says she has Angelo. I'm so sorry. It's a long story. I'm so sorry about this," I tell the principal.

Dad stares at me as if I've gone mad. Probably because he of all people knows I don't have a sister, and also he no doubt knows who that was who just called. He nudges me.

"Are you sure you want to call off the police?" he whispers to me while the principal consoles the teacher.

I nod.

"This is highly unorthodox, Mia," the principal says with a stern face.

"I know. I'm so very sorry. My sister does that sometimes. I do apologize again for the fuss."

It takes a lot of apologizing and consoling before Dad and I are able to leave the school without further chastising.

"You want to catch me up?" Dad says as soon as we're out of earshot of the school staff.

I share with him what the caller said.

"What are we supposed to do now? Those bastards have Angelo!" he barks out of frustration.

"I know, Dad. I'm sure he'll call again with instructions."

"We better pray that he does."

I'm in too much shock to cry. All I can do is stare out blankly into space, white knuckling my phone.

"Let's go back to the house and wait for the call there. No point in hanging around the school," Dad says.

"Okay."

"Are you alright to drive, my love?"

"What? Yeah. I'm fine."

"They won't hurt him, Mia. They aren't fools. They need you and you need Angelo. This is a warning, is all."

I nod.

Oh, God. Please don't let them hurt my boy, Please.

Dad follows me home. It's all I can do not to drive into a ditch. I'm beside myself with stress and grief. I did not see this coming.

I'm still trembling all over by the time I pull into the driveway. I notice something at the front door. The closer I get to the house the bigger and clearer the object becomes. Oh, God! It's Angelo!

I slam on the brakes and switch off the engine. I leap out of the car before I have a chance to engage the handbrake. The car rolls slowly until it comes to a stop against a hedge. I don't care because I'm running at full speed to get to my son.

"Angelo!" I yell before I get to him.

My child isn't moving.

"Oh, no, Oh, no," I keep saying over and over, cradling him and rocking back and forth.

"Is he okay?" Dad calls as he comes running.

"I'm not sure."

Now I'm balling.

"He's breathing," I say.

I move Angelo around so I can check his body. There are no signs of physical trauma. He simply appears to be fast asleep.

Dad takes him from me and carries him into the house. I follow after.

"Put him over there on the couch, Dad. I'll get some water."

Dad and I hover over Angelo for about half an hour before my son opens his eyes.

"Baby!" I say, hugging him tightly.

"Mom? Grandpa? When did we get home?"

"Are you alright, my love?" I ask.

"Sure."

"What happened champ?" Dad asks.

"A nice man at the zoo gave me ice cream. When did I get home?"

"Oh, uhm, not too long ago," I say, trying to stay calm. I don't want to freak Angelo out.

"You must have been really tired from all the fun, champ," Dad smiles. "You fell asleep."

My cell phone rings again.

"Hello."

"Cute kid. Very talkative."

"Okay," I acquiesce. "I'll do what you ask."

"That's better. I'll call you tomorrow with the details. Have a good night, Mia."

I want to tell the man to go fuck himself, but think better of it. He may not be open to such a suggestion. Instead, I end the call and turn my focus back to my son.

"Are you hungry, sweetheart?"

"No. I'm sleepy. I think I'll go to bed."

Wow. This is one for the books. Usually it takes a lot of negotiating and plenty of convincing to get Angelo to agree to go to bed. Whatever those bastards gave him must have been strong. I hope the substance doesn;t cause any permanent damage. But I cannot worry about that now. I have my son back and that's all that matters.

The next hurdle looms large on the horizon. I'm going to have to call Dante and tell him everything. But how can I betray the man I love? The father of my child.

I go downstairs as soon as Angelo is asleep.

"Is he okay?" Dad asks.

"Seems to be. Thank God."

"Here," he says and places a tumbler in front of me. "Whiskey. A double. I think you and I have earned it."

I throw back the amber liquid in one go. Dad pours me another.

"Are you going to call Dante?"

"I have no choice now."

"What are you going to tell him?"

"Everything."

"I'm proud of you, Mia."

"Thank you, Dad. It's kind of you to say, but I'm not so sure I'm liking myself much at this point."

"This is not your fault."

I wish I could agree with my Dad. I should have gone to Rome with Dante. None of this would have happened if I had just done as he asked. I'm so tired. So tired.

22

DANTE

My phone is ringing. At least I think that's the sound I'm hearing. I open my eyes and look across to the clock on the nightstand. It's just after 3 a.m. What the hell? This better be important.

I reach across and pick up the blasted thing. It's not a number I recognize.

"Hello."

There's silence on the other end. This had better not be a crank call. I'm in no mood for…

"Dante."

My heart skips a beat. I'm instantly awake.

"Mia? Is that you?"

"Yes, it's me, Dante."

Mia's voice tells me there's something wrong. I've been planning my response since I found out she left without saying a word to me. I've been so furious with her that I was determined to rip her to pieces as soon as I had the chance. But now, hearing her sweet voice, all I can do is thank God that she's talking to me.

"Are you okay?"

"Not really."

"Where are you?"

"We need to talk. I'm in trouble."

"Okay. Tell me where you are. I'll come to you."

"Wait. I have to tell you something first."

"Okay. I'm listening."

"First off, I'd like to apologize. You must be so angry with me."

"I'm not, Mia. I…"

"Wait. let me finish."

"Sorry. Carry on."

"I had to do it, Dante. I was afraid that your lifestyle would harm our son. And now I realize it was all for nothing. I should have listened to you and joined you in Rome. But it's too late."

"What are you talking about? Why is it too late?"

"They know, Dante. They know."

"Mia, you're not making any sense. What are you saying? Who knows what?"

"You enemies, Dante! They know who I am and where Angelo and I are. They threatened our son's life! They just took him. They took him…"

Mia is crying. I can barely understand what she's saying. My stomach is in a mess. I feel sick. All I heard was that my family is in danger.

"What?"

"They took Angelo from school and then I found him unconscious at my front door a few hours later. I'm so scared, Dante."

"Mia, where are you? I'm leaving right now. Tell me where you are."

"They want you to come here. They want to set a trap so that they can kill you. This is a lose lose situation. Either you die or our son does."

Mia is positively sobbing now. My heart aches for her. I wish I could wrap my arms around her and make her feel safe.

"Mia. Listen to me. Don't worry about a thing. I'm going to get you out of this. I promise. You have to trust me. Please tell me where you are so I can fix this."

"Okay."

"Where are you?"

"In Texas. I'll send you a pin location."

"I'll leave as soon as I can."

"Okay."

"I love you, Mia. I'am sorry this has happened to you. I truly am. I swear I'll make this right."

I'm up and ready within the hour. There's no time to waste. I make a few calls before I leave the house. The first one I wake up is Elio.

"Brother, I need you."

"It's 3 a.m. What is it?" he groans.

"Yes, I know it's early. Mia is in trouble."

"What? How do you know?"

"She just called me. It seems that whoever was working with Kyle tracked her down somehow. They took my kid, Elio! My fucking son!"

"Fuck, Bro. Is he okay?"

"Yeah. Mia says it was a warning, but I'm not going to allow them to take a second bite at the apple. I'm flying to Texas right now."

"Okay. What do you need from me, brother? How can I help?"

"I need you to be on standby, Elio. I don't know what's going to happen when I get to texas. I may be walking into a trap. So, I need you to be my eyes and ears here in Rome. Okay?"

"Of course. Anything."

"And, for God's sake, don't tell mother what I'm doing. I don't want her to stress about me again."

"Sure, I won't say a word."

"Thanks, Elio."

"Please be careful, Dante."

"I will. I'll call you when I land."

The next call is to Bruno, who helps me to arrange for a few of our best men to accompany me on the rescue mission. I'm going to need some serious muscle. Paolo is one of them. I know he's desperate to make up for his fuck up in LA.

It's 5 a.m. when the jet takes off with all of us on board. I give the men a quick talk to bring them up to speed.

"I'm sure that by now you all know that Angelo is my son."

I don't hear any gasps and no one flinches.

"My son and his mother are in danger and I intend to get them back to Rome without incident. I need you all to give me your best. Any questions?"

"We're with you, Boss," Paolo says, followed by a roar of affirmation from the rest of the party.

"Good. Your loyalty will be handsomely rewarded."

Hang in there, Mia, my love. I'm coming.

* * *

Bruno arranges transport for the men and me, so that we don't have to announce our arrival in Texas with too much fanfare. I don't know how entrenched the enemy is over here, so I prefer to keep my arrival a secret.

I've had ten hours to contemplate what I'm going to say to Mia, but now, sitting here in the car, speeding my way to her, I'm a little less confident than I was when I left Rome.

I still don't know if she called me because she wants to be with me or if it's a knee jerk reaction to the danger she's in. I hope to God it's the former. I cannot imagine losing her again, especially now that she's within my grasp once more. And Angelo! My son. My fatherly heart aches for my son. The fear he must have felt when he was taken from his mother. I don't know who did this yet, but whoever it was had better pray to their maker that I never find them.

I call Mia from the house Bruno arranged for me. It would be foolish to go straight to Mia's as she is most certainly being watched.

"I'm here. How are you feeling?"

"Nervous."

"Don't worry. I think we need to arrange a place where we can meet. Better make it public. Somewhere the people who are following you won't suspect anything."

"Yeah, we can do that. I'll send you a location."

"Okay. I'll see you soon."

"Right, boys. Time to dress like tourists," I say once I end the call. "We can't go around looking like a Don and his muscle."

I hardly recognize myself by the time we leave the house. I hope Mia does. I look like a female German tourist in full regalia. The men don't look like they've ever seen the Italian mainland either.

It's 6 p.m. when we get to the aquarium. There must be a visiting school program in progress because there are kids everywhere. Good news for us, as it will be easier to get lost in a crowd.

I make my way to the rainforest exhibit, where Mia told me she'd meet me. I see her standing at one of the glass partitions, watching a school of Red-bellied piranhas. She is even more gorgeous than I remember. She sees me approaching and nods slightly.

We agreed to meet in the women's bathroom. I feel like a pervert, but hey, it's the safest option right now. Mia follows me in and waits until I go into a stall. I close the toilet door but I leave it unlocked. She follows me into the stall.

"This has to be the weirdest thing I've ever done," I grin, wrestling with the stockings bunched up in my crack.

Mia chuckles before she grabs me and holds onto me.

"Oh, Dante. I've missed you so much."

She lets go before I can answer and punches me hard on my arm.

"Ow. What was that for?"

"I'm fucking mad at you! They took our son, Dante. Our son!"

"Shhh. I know. I'm so sorry. I swear I'm going to make them pay."

"Damn right you will," she says before she kisses me passionately.

If I thought the stockings were tight before, they're positively tortuous now. I have to get out of this getup so I can show Mia how much I truly missed her. We're in the handicapped stall. I pity the handicapped person who needs to use the facilities in the next fifteen minutes because I'm not letting Mia out of here before I make her toes curl.

"You smell so good," I whisper into her ear, as she's kissing neck.

"I want you, right now," she moans.

"No problem."

I pull off my blasted stockings and underwear, and then claw at her jeans. Mia helps and soon we are naked from the waist down. I cup her beautiful ass cheeks as I lift her up. She wraps her legs around my waist. We're kissing passionately.

I secure Mia against the basin before I slip into her. She is so warm and wet I could just cum right now, but I want this to last so I focus. We're rutting like wild animals, desperate for the feel of one another.

She cums quickly—hard. I'm not far behind. I can hear the voices of young girls as they enter the bathroom. I smirk and place my finger over Mia's mouth. Together we grin quietly so as not to give ourselves away.

"I love you," she whispers breathlessly.

"I love you too," I smile, then I kiss her slowly and delicately.

"Thank you for coming."

"If you'll pardon the pun," I chuckle.

"Come on. We'd better get out of here and back to the ranch."

"Not so fast. It's going to take a mammoth effort to get me back into these stockings."

"You make a very handsome woman, Mr. De Luca."

"Bunched up stockings in my crack notwithstanding."

I'm back in my female attire. Time to get out of here.

"We'll casually stroll back to your car and then I'll follow you home in mine. Okay?" I say as before we leave the bathroom stall.

"Okay."

"Keep the chatter going for the benefit of whoever may be watching you."

"I can do that. Remember, women talk with their hands. Can't have you looking all butch," she chuckles.

"You weren't complaining about my butchness a few minutes ago."

"It was fun a few minutes ago."

We link arms and walk out of the bathroom, chatting and smiling. To all intents and purposes we're just two gals who bumped into each other in the bathroom. We keep up the pretense until we get to the carpark, where we keep it jovial before getting into our cars.

The men are in the back of the large American brand vehicle. They kept out of sight the whole time I was inside so no one would suspect a thing. It's about a twenty minute drive until we get to the ranch turn off. I stay close to Mia's vehicle.

It's a beautiful ranch, albeit out in the sticks. I had no idea Mia and Angeko were so secluded. I shudder to think what would have happened if they were ambushed. Anyway, I'm here now and no one is going to harm my family.

Tomorrow we'll put our plan into action. I'm not going to allow anyone to get away with this crime against me and my family. Someone is going to pay with their life. Probably more than one person. I'll kill a whole army if I have to. Fuck it, what do I have to lose?

I park the car and get out. The men stay put. They'll follow later under the cover of darkness. I follow Mia and together we walk into the house.

"Where's Angelo?" I ask.

"He's upstairs with my Dad."

I'm not too excited about seeing Mia's father. I can only imah=gine what he must think of me right now. But I have to confront him sometime.

"I think you should get out of that dress before our son sees you."

"Good thinking. Give me a minute."

I change while Mia goes upstairs. I can't wait to see my son. I wipe the makeup off my face and wash away the last bits of German female tourist from my being. Thank God for stage makeup. I must remember to thank Bruno for the clever suggestion. A raise may even be in order.

I can hear little footsteps on the stairs and Mia's voice.

"I have a surprise for you, my boy."

"Ohhh, how exciting."

My son. Finally.

23

MIA

"Daddy!"

Angelo launches himself at Dante and with that I finally crack the vault that has held me back from trusting the man I love and giving myself to him fully. How could I have thought that keeping our son away from his father was even remotely a good idea?

"My boy," Dante says as he nestles his son. "Let me see how much you've grown," he crows proudly as he holds Angelo at arm's length.

"I'm six now, Daddy! I'm big."

"I can see that. My goodness, how you've grown. Let me see your muscles."

Angelo pulls up his pj sleeves and strikes a strongman pose.

"Phooweet!" Dante whistles. "Those are some serious guns, my boy."

"I can swing from the monkey bars without even getting tired, Daddy. Lexi says I'm the strongest boy in the class."

"Oh? Who's Lexi?" Dante smiles.

"Just a girl."

Dante winks at me. I know what he's thinking. Daddy's boy.

"Are you staying?" Angelo asks excitedly.

"Yes, son. I'm staying."

"Cool! Will you take me to school tomorrow? Mom, can Daddy take me to school tomorrow?"

"I was thinking you could take the day off so we can do some things around the house," Dante answers.

"Oh. Okay."

Splash stretches out against Dante's back while he's kneeling in front of Angelo.

"Hey, you trouble maker," Dante smiles and ruffles Splash's fur.

He stops when he sees Dad standing on the landing at the top of the staircase.

"Angelo, will you do me a favor, son?"

"Sure, Daddy."

"Would you take this bag upstairs for me? There's a surprise in it for you. Open it and I'll be up in a few minutes to join you. Okay?"

"Oh, wow. Okay. Come Splash!"

Dad waits until Angelo is upstairs before he comes down.

"Arnold," Dante says in greeting and holds out his hand.

"Hello, Dante."

Dad doesn't shake Dante's hand but rather walks past him and takes a seat in the living room.

"I'd like to talk to you, Dante," Dad says.

"Yes, Sir."

Dante follows my father to the living room and sits down across from him. My heart is racing. This could go either way.

"Dante, I'm spitting mad."

"I imagine you would be, Arnold."

"Aside from the fact that I'm disappointed in you, to say the least, I'm mad as hell! If I were a younger man, I'd beat the crap out of you."

I've never seen my father so angry. I'm quite taken aback.

"How could you put my daughter and my grandson in this kind of danger?" he continues.

"It was never my intention. I apologize. I love Mia and Angelo dearly."

"I don't doubt your love for them, Dante. But, what are you going to do to dig them out of this hole? How can you ever keep them safe now that your enemies know about them?"

"I have a plan, Arnold."

"I would bloody well hope so!"

"Dad." I say, hoping to calm my father down.

He looks at me as if he forgot that I was in the room. His expression softens a bit.

"Fighting amongst ourselves isn't helping. We need to focus on a solution."

"You're right, Mia. I'm sorry."

"I love you, Dad. I know you are worried about us, but we're going to get out of this. I promise."

"Alright," he says. "I'm going upstairs."

"I suppose that could have gone worse," Dante says once Dad is out of earshot.

"Your nose is still in place," I add.

"I'm so sorry, Mia."

"I know you are. I think we should get some rest. It's been a very long week."

"You go up. I'll be up in a while. I want to talk to my men first."

"Men? What men?"

"The ones hiding in the car."

"Dante! Have those poor guys been in there all this time?"

"Uh-huh."

"Shame on you. They must be so uncomfortable."

"They're fighters, Mia. This is nothing."

"I will never understand your world, Dante."

"You just leave that to me."

"Fine. But don't be too long. I want to finish what we started earlier on."

"You don't have to tell me twice," he grins before I go upstairs to bed.

* * *

I'm so tired I'll just close my eyes for a few minutes. I'm fast asleep when I feel Dante's body sliding into bed. He's naked. I'm instantly aroused. All it takes is one touch of his skin to send me into a tailspin of passion.

"Hey, babe," he purrs.

"Hmm."

"Wanna fool around?"

"Always."

Dante slides on top of me. His body is so warm. It feels good to have him touching me again. I missed our closeness most of all. He feels like home. Everything about him sets my mind at ease. It's as if we were made as a solid piece of tapestry, torn asunder by circumstance, reunited to fit perfectly together once more.

"I missed this," he coos.

"What's that?"

"Being close to you. You have no idea how much."

"I think I may have some idea."

"You're all I've thought about for months, Mia."

"Stop talking and make love to me," I whisper.

Dante chuckles as he moves under the covers. Sliding his tongue steadily down the length of my body as he goes. I'm in Heaven. I'm trembling with excitement at his touch. He cups my breasts as he stops at my core, caressing and teasing me with his tongue until I want to scream, More!

I spread my legs wider so that he can move his body in between them. I rake my hands through his soft wavy hair while he brings me to the brink of ecstasy and back down again. I moan when he stops, but I know he's getting ready to slide into me, making us one once more.

I gasp as he glides his shaft into me. My lover is kissing me now. It's an urgent kiss; a hunger that will stop at nothing to be filled. I grab onto his strong, firm buttocks and rock back and forth with him, faster, harder.

His tongue is in my ear, his breath racing as we chase the ultimate high.

"I love you," Dante calls out as he climaxes.

My lover's body shudders violently as he surrenders himself to the joy of knowing that he is completely fulfilled and truly loved. I yield to the same force a few moments later.

We lay together in perfect peace. Neither one of us needs to say anything. Our bodies did all the talking for us. I'm happy for the first time since Dante told me his truth. I know instinctively that everything will work out just fine. My man promised me it would and I believe him.

"Sleep well, my beautiful Mia."

"Sleep well, Dante. Welcome home."

* * *

I have to give my dad credit for his willingness to forgive. He's in the kitchen, putting together a breakfast fit for a king's court.

Angelo has been up since the crack of dawn. He's playing with the Lego set his Daddy bought him. I haven't seen him sit still for this long in forever.

I'm downstairs, making coffee when Dante enters the open plan kitchen.

"Good morning, all," he smiles and kisses me on the cheek. "Something smells good."

"Good morning, Dante," Dad greets. "Take a seat. I made bacon and eggs."

"Thank you, Arnold. That's very kind of you."

"I made enough for your men too."

"They'll be thrilled, thanks."

"Did you sleep well, my boy?" Dante asks Angelo.

"Great. I'm building a tank."

"That's wonderful," Dante smiles.

"Come have your breakfast, sweetheart," I call to Angelo.

"Aah."

"Come, son. You can carry on playing afterward," Dante encourages him.

"Okay."

"Wow. Magic touch," I smile.

"It's a man's thing," Dante smiles and winks as our son hops onto the chair next to his father.

"So, what's the plan for today?" Dad asks.

"We'll stay put and make a few calls," Dante answers, careful not to say anything that might upset Angelo.

"Okay."

"Dad, would you mind going into town and getting a few things from the store?"

"Sure, my love."

"Thank you. I'll give you a list."

We don't need that much, but I want to get Dad out of the house for a bit. He's been very understanding but I don't want him and Dante in each other's hair for too long. It's still early days.

"Can I go to town with Grandpa?" Angelo asks, crunching down on a piece of crispy bacon.

"No," Dante and I say all at once.

Angelo puts down his piece of bacon and stares at us in confusion while Splash lifts his head up and looks at us.

"I mean, I'd like to have you here, my love. You and Daddy are going to build some Lego," I add, hoping to diffuse the sudden storm with a modicum of calm.

"Yes, I'd love to build something with you, son," Dante adds.

"Okay," Angelo smiles and carries on eating.

The three adults at the table share a knowing look. The last thing we need is for our son and grandchild to get snatched again. I don't think my nerves could take anymore nasty surprises.

"Okay, I think I've had my fill," Dad smiles and takes his plate to the kitchen sink. "Do you want to play ball with me before I go to town, champ?" he asks Angelo.

"Sure, Grandpa. I'll get my mitt."

He jumps off the seat.

"Hey! What do you say?" I stop him.

"Oh, thank you for the food, Grandpa. May I be excused, Mom?"

"That's better. Yres, my love."

Angelo hops off the chair and rushes up the stairs to fetch his baseball mitt.

"I see he still runs everywhere," Angelo chuckles.

"That boy is allergic to walking," Dad grins. "Excuse me."

"Thank you for breakfast, Arnold. It was delicious."

"You're welcome."

Baby steps.

"Did you sleep well, my gorgeous woman?" Dante coos once Dad is outside with Angelo.

"How could I not after what you did to me?" I smirk. "You?"

"Like the dead."

"So. What are you doing today? I assume you have a plan."

"Indeed, I do."

"I'm expecting a call soon from the bastard that took Angelo. In fact, I'm surprised he didn't call me yesterday," I say, sipping my coffee.

"I need you to make careful notes on everything he says, Mia. It's important that I know everything he says."

"I could put you on speaker phone when he calls."

"No. He'll know that something's up if you do that. My plan is contingent upon the element of surprise. He mustn't know that I'm here already."

"Okay. I'll take notes. What do we do in the meantime?"

"I think you should go to work."

"Really? Are you sure?"

"Yes. He'll be watching you."

I don't want to go. The idea of leaving the house makes me nervous.

"Angelo will be fine," Dante assures me. "I'll be here with him. Trust me. No one will get to him under my watch. No one. They already know that your father is here. They'll assume Angelo is here with him."

"Okay," I agree, more than a little reluctantly. "If you're sure."

"I'm sure. Now get your delicious self upstairs and get ready for work. Need someone to wash your back?"

"No, I can manage," I sniff.

"Oh, are you punishing me now," he laughs.

"If the Italian shoe fits."

"Haha."

I arrive at the office an hour later.

"Hey, baby doll. Well, don't you look as good as a new penny. Feeling better?"

"Hey, Julie. Much better. Thank you."

"Good, cause the doc has a full program today."

Wonderful. I don't know how I'm expected to focus on anything but my cell phone today. It's going to be a tough slog.

"I'll take the first few patients' vitals so long. Would you man the desk, sugar?"

"Sure thing, Julie."

The minutes become hours while I try to get on with my job as well as listen out for that all important phone call. Lunchtime arrives not a moment too soon. I do my usual and make my way to the diner for lunch, although I have no idea how I'm going to stomach food with my stomach in this knot.

Keep calm, Mia. Act normal.

Normal. Ha! What a joke. I haven't experienced normal since after Sam and before Dante.

I'm on my way out of the diner, carrying a takeaway nicoise salad, when I come face to face with the man who scared the crap out of me a few days ago. My first instinct is to claw out his eyes as payback for taking my boy. But I know that's a really stupid idea, so I glare at him instead.

"Hello, Mia."

"What do you want?"

"What? No small talk?" he grins.

I don't respond for fear of cursing him into oblivion.

"Here are the details," he says and hands me an envelope. "Date, time, location. Get De Luca to come to you."

"He will know it's a trap," I offer to cement the deal.

"Only if you blab. And I don't have to remind you what will happen to Angelo if you do that. Do I?"

"No."

"Good. Enjoy your salad," he smiles then walks away.

24

DANTE

"Here," Mia says and hands me an envelope.

"What's this?"

"My instructions for delivering you like a shameless stool pigeon."

"Where did you get it?"

"It was hand delivered to me by the man who took our son."

"Son of a bitch! Did he threaten you? Are you okay?"

"No, I'm fine. Just seething. I wish I could have gouged out his condescending eyes. "

"You're not alone. Don't worry, though. He's going to wish you had once I get a hold of him. In fact, I may even put them in a jar for you."

"Ugh! Gross. Wait, yeah. Make him suffer, Dante."

"And here I thought you were all sugar and spice and all things nice."

"I am. Until you fuck with my kid."

"Sexy."

"Yeah, yeah. Go on. Go work on getting this scumbag."

"I'm going to call Elio. Why don't you and Angelo relax together for a while. Watch some TV or something. Try and get your mind off this whole business. You look like you could use a little Angelo therapy."

"Trying to get rid of me?"

"Never."

"Okay," Mia smiles and leaves the room her uncle fashioned into an office.

I dial Elio's number and wait while it rings.

"Dante. Is everything okay?"

"Hey, Elio. Yeah. Everything is under control in Texas."

"Good. What do you want me to do for you? How can I help?"

"The scumbag bastard gave Mia instructions today on when and where I'm to be offered up. Like a lamb to the slaughter. I don't know who this is, but I'm going to wipe out his whole fucking family."

"I almost feel sorry for the fool. Any ideas yet on who it is?"

"No. But whoever it is, seems to know an awful lot about me. How else would they know about Mia and Angelo?"

"That is very concerning."

"They have been watching me since LA. I assume they waited until I was gone to formulate their plan of attack. I should never have left Mia and Angelo alone."

"How were you to know, Dante? Besides, what were you going to do? Club Mia over the head and drag her to Rome? She needed time. Neither of you is to blame."

"I guess you're right. I'm just so frustrated."

"I understand. But we have a plan. Right?"

"Damn right. I need you to send the jet with a few men in it to the Houston airstrip."

"Alright."

"I want this clown to think that I'm onboard. Then, when he attacks, we'll ambush him. He'll never see it coming. I have a feeling he's going to try and get to me as soon as he thinks it's me getting off the plane. That's when he's at his most vulnerable."

"Are you sure you have enough men and firepower to accomplish this?"

"Absolutely. Bruno's been rather industrious on this side, using his connections to secure arms and ammunition. I swear that man can make it rain in a drought."

"Yeah. Makes me glad he's on our team."

"Absolutely. How are Mia and Angelo?"

"They're both fine. Mia's a little edgy, but she's a brave woman. She has been much better since I arrived. Or so she says anyway."

"Good. I can't imagine what she must have been through when she thought her child was going to die."

"I can't imagine. This situation has done damage to all of us. I tell you, Elio. Sometimes I wonder if it's all worth it."

"You can't think like that, Dante. This is our life and we have to live it the best way we can. It's our family legacy."

"I'm sorry that you had to postpone your wedding, Elio. I hate that you have to delay it on my account."

"Don't worry about the wedding, brother. You would do the same for me, brother."

"I would."

"Please tell Lisa I'll make it up to her."

"Of course. She sends her love."

"Thanks. Okay. I'll send you the details of the times and the men I need you to send via text. Let me know as soon as you're ready to take off."

"Will do, brother. Be careful. If they're watching the house as you suspect, they'll be looking out for anything off."

"Well, listen to you, all reconnaissance schooled and all," I laugh.

"All those years watching and learning from you had to pay off eventually," Elio chuckles.

"Gotta go. Chat later."

"Ciao, Dante."

I text the time and other details to Elio as soon as I end the call. He sends me a thumbs up. I feel better after having spoken to my brother.

The trap is set for two days from now. It's going to be hard to wait until then to exact my revenge, but there's no fast track to vengeance. It's a waiting game and I've flexed my patience muscle over the years into a substantial one.

I'm tired but amped at the same time, so I join Mia and Angelo in the den to watch a movie. Mother and son are sharing a bowl of popcorn, so I grab a bottle of wine and pour out some for the adults. Angelo is sipping on a juicebox.

A sudden feeling of warmth and belonging tugs at my heartstrings. I'm used to the highs of making a million, or the thrill of taking out the opposition. This 'normalcy' is foreign to me, yet it feels as intense, if not more so, than anything my business life has to offer.

"A penny for your thought," Mia whispers. "You look like you were far away for a moment."

"I was just thinking how good this feels."

"There's nothing like it, is there?" she smiles, knowingly.

"No, I can't say I've felt this before."

"It's called love," she says and winks.

"Oh, really," I smile. "And, exactly when did you become so wise?" I tease.

"Haven't I always been? How's Elio?"

"Ready to come to my rescue."

"Sure, as if you need rescuing from anyone."

"I needed it from you once. Remember?"

"How can I forget?"

"I have a feeling you rescued me in more ways than one."

"Oh?"

"Uh-huh. You rescued me from both physical and emotional death, my American beauty."

"Careful. You don't want your rivals to find out that you have a heart, do you?"

"You're right. I'd better stop all this mushy business then."

"Don't you dare," she chuckles and kisses me.

"Ugh!" Angelo says and pulls a face.

"What? Mia laughs.

"Kissing!" he says with more noises to highlight his repulsion.

"One day, all you'll be able to think about is kissing a girl, son," I grin.

"Oh, no. Not me," he smiles. "Girls are just too weird."

Both Mia and I laugh at our son's naivete.

"It's true," Mia reinforces.

"I'll kiss a girl when I have to. When I'm old."

"Hey! Are you calling me old?" I laugh.

"Yeah. You're my dad. That makes you old."

"Wow, that's a sledgehammer to the groin," I whisper into Mia's ear.

"From the mouths of babes, old man," she grins.

"Oh, yeah? Meet me upstairs. I'll show you old."

* * *

"Good morning, my handsome *and* more than young enough man."

"Hey, sex kitten."

Meah is snuggled up against my back. I reach behind and around to touch her soft butt cheek. Her skin feels like satin. Amazing. I'm instantly aroused—no blaming this one on morning wood.

"Tomorrow is D-day," she says, and I can tell from her tone that she's afraid.

"Yeah."

"I'm scared, Dante."

"I know, my love. Don't be. I won't let anything happen to you. Or to our son."

Mia's cell phone rings, interrupting our cuddle.

"I better get that," she squeals as I pinch her bottom.

"Fine, but don't be long," I say, getting up to take my morning tinkle.

"Hello," I hear her saying while I'm in the toilet.

I look back to see her face growing pale. I know who is on the line. Mia holds up her finger to her lips, signaling me not to make a sound. I walk quietly back to the bed and sit down next to Mia so I can put my ear to the phone and listen.

"I need to see you today," the man says.

I don't like his tone and I want to grab the phone from Mia and demand he reveal himself to me. But that would be the worst thing for all of us. If I'm going to catch this bastard and his associates and kill them, I have to exercise more patience now than I ever have before in my life.

"Why?" Mia asks. "You gave me the information I need. What do you want from me now?"

"Careful, Mia. I don't like your attitude."

Mia bites down hard on her lip and I'm afraid she'll spill blood if she doesn't ease up.

"When?" she relents.

"Noon. At the diner. I'll meet you inside."

"Fine."

The man ends the call and Mia throws down the cell phone on the bed. It bounces before it drops to the ground.

"Are you okay?" I ask.

"No! I'm mad, Dante! And scared."

I don't know what to tell Mia. I know that words of apology are meaningless and empty right now, so instead, I hold her in the hopes that my arms around her will bring her a modicum of comfort.

"I'm so sorry, Mia. Please forgive me. I never meant for this to happen to you."

I mean this sincerely. I've always been on the other side of the hammer. Never have I considered the emotions that go hand in hand with the kind of violence the men in my world afflict on their women and children. I don't give any man's family a moment's thought as I slit his throat from ear to ear. To me, it's business. If you get in my way, I will take care of you.

It feels different now. It's an uncomfortable feeling that creeps glacially into your gut and rests there. I don't care for it.

"The thought never even occurred to you, did it, Dante? But then again, does it ever when it comes to men and their ego? You men placate your consciences with the illusion that you're taking care of your family, creating wealth so you can give them a better life. But is it, Dante? Is it a better life?"

Mia gets up, goes to the bathroom, and slams the door shut, leaving me feeling lower than snake shit at the bottom of the ocean. Is she right? Is it better to have love rather than money and power?

She can't possibly think that! Love amidst poverty and squalor is a romantic notion suffered only by those who have not lived it. Money buys security. It keeps families fed and protected. Granted, my wealth may seem excessive to most, but it isn't even about that for me. It's about being on top; being the best and what I do. That's what drives me.

I get off the bed and move toward the bathroom. I turn the handle. The door is locked.

"Please, Dante. I just need a few minutes," Mia says from the other side.

What can I do? I get dressed and go downstairs where Arnold is busily preparing breakfast. He's a sweet guy. I don't hold his harsh words toward me against him. I'd be dead had the roles been reversed and I were him. What father wouldn't want to keep his daughter safe from a mobster.

"Hi, Arnold."

"Morning. Coffee? You look like a man who could use one."

"Yeah. Thanks."

"Everything alright upstairs?"

"Could be better."

"You have to be patient when it comes to the women folk, Dante. Times may have changed, but a woman's heart remains the same."

"Yes, well I don't know if I'll ever forgive myself for breaking Mia's. Unintentionally as it may have been."

"You have an opportunity to fix it. I sincerely hope you appreciate that. Not many women would have given you a second chance."

"I know. Mia is special. I love her deeply."

"Then make this go away, Dante. And just a little friendly advice. I'd think long and hard on changing careers if I were you. Is this really how you want your son to grow up?"

I don't have an answer for Arnold. Face it, there are none that would make sense. None that would justify the means. Meeting Mia has changed me. I think that's quite evident in the niggling thoughts I've had of late about where I am in my life.

I've got some introspective thinking ahead of me. But that will have to take a backseat to the task that lies before me. I have to find and kill the men who are threatening the wellbeing of my family. And soon.

25

MIA

"Where are you going, Mom?"

"I have to go by the office for a bit, my love," I lie.

"But, it's Sunday."

"Yeah, I know. The doctor needs me to help him with something quickly. I won't be long, sweetheart. Grandpa and Daddy are here."

"Your job sucks, Mom."

Angelo stomps off, dejected. He's been looking forward to a game of catch all week. He wants us all to play, like a big family, he said. Now I feel rotten.

I also am not particularly looking forward to meeting with the enemy right now, but I don't have a choice. Seeing Angelo's disappointment makes me mad all over again. This day is getting worse. Who knew that was even possible?

Guilt and regret is a malicious creature. It takes a hold of you with its sharp teeth and holds on for dear life while you writhe in pain. I feel bothered by my reaction toward Dante this morning, but what's done is done.

"It's okay, champ. You Dad and I are going to run you ragged," Dad says with as much excitement in his voice as he can muster.

I look across to him and give him a wry smile. The poor man is trying his best. If anyone should win the award for best father and grandfather of the year, it's my dad.

"He'll come around, Mia. Don't let it get you down. It's important to focus. Are you sure you don't want me to come along and watch from a distance?"

"That's sweet, Dad, but no. If they suspect I'm being followed, the whole plan is shot to hell. Besides, how would it look if we leave Angelo alone on the ranch? They'll know for sure that something's up."

"I guess. Promise me you'll be careful. Don't be alone with him. Stay in the crowd."

"Yes, Arnold," I play-mock before I hug my sweet father.

Dante is in the office. He's trying to keep out of my way, I imagine. Smart boy. I can't leave without saying goodbye to him. He's sitting at the desk, staring into space when I open the door.

"Hi," I say.

"Hi."

"I'm leaving now."

Dante looks so vulnerable, which is ridiculous considering who he is and all the crazy things he's done in his life.

"I'm sorry," he says, and I know with every fiber of my being that he means it.

"I know. I'm sorry too."

"What are you sorry for? You've done nothing to apologize for."

"Yes, I have. I picked on you when it wasn't your fault."

"This *is* my fault, Mia. I should have left the moment I was well enough to travel and never looked back."

"You don't mean that, Dante."

"Yes, I do. I've brought nothing but fear and danger into your life. I should have known from the start that I was never the kind of man who deserves a family. It's selfish of me to think that I could ever love someone like you without hurting her."

"Now you listen to me, Dante De Luca. I'm glad you're in my life. I don't regret it for a single moment. Look at what we have. We have a son and more love than most people will ever have. That can never be a mistake."

"I'm afraid of what they'll do to you, Mia."

"Don't you worry about that. I'll be fine. They need me. Remember?"

"Please be careful, Mia. I love you so much. I can't imagine living without you. Fuck, I couldn't live with myself if anything happened to you."

"Don't talk like that. We have a child and he needs you. Promise me that whatever happens, you'll be there for him, Dante."

Dante gets up and walks over to me. He throws his arms around me and holds me so tightly I can hardly breathe.

"I promise."

We stay like that for the longest time. Two lovers, bruised by the world, desperate for comfort.

"I have to go or I'll be late."

"Call me when it's over."

"I will."

* * *

My legs are wobbly as I enter the deli I visit every day of the week and buy my standard nicoise salad. The waitress who serves me smiles brightly when she sees me.

"Working on a Sunday?" she asks with a smile.

"Yeah. Doctors never rest, I guess."

"Your usual, to go?"

"Uhm, no. I'll have a double cappuccino, thanks. I'll have it here."

"Sure. A sprinkle of cinnamon?"

"Thanks."

She walks away. I check my watch. I'm a few minutes early. My stomach is in a mess. I think a quick trip to the bathroom is wise. The deli is pumping. It's the perfect meeting place for brunch, especially on a beautiful day like today.

There are a few ladies in the bathroom. I wait for a stall and go inside as soon as one opens up. I'm cold even though it's warm out. Must be the stress. There's a beautiful blonde at the basin when I come out. She smiles at me.

"Isn't it great out?" she comments.

"Yeah."

It's one of those awkward moments when you find yourself alone in a bathroom with a stranger who's trying to initiate small talk. The last thing I feel like doing right now is shooting the breeze, so I keep my head down while I wash my hands, hoping she'll get the hint.

"That's a gorgeous top," she gushes. "There's a loose strand though. I hate it when that happens. Let me just get that for you," she says with too much chipper for my liking.

"No, that's okay. I'll…"

A sudden sharp pain to the back of my neck sends me reeling. What the hell? I look at her in horror.

"What are you doing? What was…"

I can't seem to focus. Everything around me is spinning. An intense wave of nausea overtakes me and I stumble. There's no time to stop myself. I don't know if I could even if I tried to. The last thing I remember is the woman's voice.

"Okay, she's out. Quick, get her feet…"

* * *

I can hear myself moaning. My head is fuzzy and my tongue is thick and heavy. And dry! It feels like I've been sucking on cotton balls. The metallic taste isn't helping any.

I open my eyes but I'm finding it difficult to focus. Everything is blurry—objects have a halo around them. Where am I? What happened? My last memory is sketchy. I was in the bathroom, talking to the blonde. I felt a sharp sting, like a needle…

A needle! The woman stabbed me with a needle. That's what happened. That explains my sudden tanking. I try to sit up. The world is still spinning far too quickly. This is possibly the worst hangover I've ever had.

I sit up—considerably slower this time and touch the spot where the needle entered my skin. There's a nasty welt. Who was the woman? Where is she now? Who was she talking to?

Fuck! They tricked me! They've taken me. But, why? What good am I to them? I've already agreed to go along with their plan to lure Dante to the US. What do they want from me this time?

I have to get out of here. My purse must have stayed behind in the bathroom. It's a good thing I had the presence of mind to hide my cell phone in the car. If they find it and somehow manage to unlock the screen, they know that Dante is in fact here already. That would be a fuck up of note.

Where am I? I gaze around the room. It looks like a room in a house. It's very basic. I get up very slowly as my legs are still unsteady. The earth is spinning. It must have been some strong shit they gave me. I look at my wrist. My watch is gone. I have no way of knowing what the time is or how long I've been here.

There are no windows and one door, so I figure I must be in a basement. Great. How long before my host shows up? What will he want from me?

Angelo! Oh, hell. I hope they haven't been to the house. Then again, I know Dante will protect our son with his life. He also has his men there so I put that chilling thought right out of my mind.

Come on, Mia. Keep it together. You can figure this out. There must be a way of escaping. Stay calm.

The door is locked. Obviously. All I can do now is wait and pray. I'm sure I'll get my answers soon enough. There's a jug of water on the nightstand. I'm so thirsty I could drink it all in one go. Is that a good idea? Oh, hell. I'm here, what good would it do to drug me some more? Right?

The water goes down like a fat kid on a swing. Thankfully, I feel fine after ingesting it. There's nothing much for me to do at this stage but contemplate my fate with as much optimism as I can muster.

The sound of footsteps approaching and muffled voices snaps me out of my funk.

Oh, Lord, Please don't let them hurt me!

The sound of a key in the lock tells me I'm about to come face to face with my abductor. I'm sweating bullets. Not sure if it's the drugs or my nerves failing me. The door handle turns. This is it. I refuse to look the part of a victim so I make myself taller than I am.

"Hello, Mia."

It's him!

"What the hell are you playing at?" I growl, radiating hatred.

"How are you feeling?"

"Just great, thanks. What woman doesn't dream of being drugged and kidnapped by a psychopath?"

"I see the drugs haven't beveled your sharp tongue any," he grins.

"What is your name?"

"I don't see what difference that makes to your current situation."

I don't comment.

"Franco."

"Well, Franco. What the hell am I doing here? I did as you so politely asked. What more do you want from me?"

"You're insurance."

"Insurance?"

"Yes. Leverage."

"For what?"

"Just in case your boyfriend thinks of doing anything foolish. You're my insurance policy."

"This is ridiculous! Let me go! I have a child to care for."

"Your father can look after Angelo just fine. I know he's still here."

"So. You've been watching me?"

"Of course."

Thank God he hasn't discovered Dante and his men at the ranch. That's one thing in my favor, at least.

"Stay away from them."

"You're in no position to order me around, Mia. Haven't you figured it out yet? I own your pretty little ass, bitch. You will do as I say and that's all there is to it."

"He's going to kill you, you know."

"Who? De Luca? Please! He's an idiot. He's going to watch you and your son die before I carve his heart from his chest with a blunt knife."

The look in this maniac's eyes tells me that he isn't fucking around. A chill comes over me as his cruel, cold eyes arrest mine. I can't look away. It's like watching a car approaching a baby's stroller—I want to avert my gaze, but I'm powerless to do so.

I refuse to show fear. I'm defiant. It's the only weapon I have.

"So, what's the plan, Franco? Are you going to dangle me as bait?"

"If I have to. You'd better hope that Dante loves you as much as you think."

"Will you let me and my son go when this is over?"

I ask the question, even though, instinctively, I already know the answer.

Franco smiles.

"I'll see you a bit later. Someone will bring you something to eat."

He turns his back to me and heads for the door.

"No! Wait! Franco!"

He ignores me and keeps moving. I have a sudden urge to throw something at him or at the very least scratch the skin off the back of his neck!

Stay calm, Mia. The man's a mountain without a soul. He WILL kill you and you're no good to anyone if you're dead.

I let out a feral scream as soon as the door locks behind Franco.

If ever I needed Dante, it's now. I collapse to the ground where I sit with my head in my hands for the longest time. Angelo. My baby won't know where I am. I don't even know how long it's been since I left the house? Will Dante know that I'm gone yet? Is he looking for me?

"Please, Dante," I whisper. "I need you now more than ever. Find me."

26

DANTE

Bruno and the men I brought with me from Rome came to the ranch under the cover of darkness on the second night after we'd landed in Texas. He and the others have been dressing and working as ranch hands ever since, replacing the regular staff after Mia's uncle agreed to help us.

The permanent staff have all been paid extra and are enjoying a well earned holiday in the meantime, courtesy of the De Luca family empire. This was done in case whoever may or may not have been watching the place wouldn't think anything had changed.

The two of us are sitting in the office, enjoying our morning coffee while talking about the call Mia received earlier.

"This is crazy, Boss. I should go with her," Bruno says.

"I know, Bruno, but I can't take any chances."

"Come on, Dante. No one will see me."

"You don't know that, Bruno."

"Let me send someone else then."

"Okay. But don't tell Mia. I don't want her to panic. If she knows someone is watching over her, she may give him away."

"Agreed. I'll send Lucian."

"Thanks, Bruno."

* * *

Watching Mia leave was one of the hardest things I've ever done. She had no idea that Lucian was following her from a distance. I feel a bit better knowing that she's not out there all alone, but one man isn't an army.

I check my watch. Mia should have called by now. I wonder what's keeping her. I call Lucian's phone, but he doesn't answer. He may be unable to speak to me now, so I take a deep breath and try to hold it together.

"For Heaven's sake, Dante. Will you stop pacing? I'm nervous enough as it is. I don't want to have to replace my brother's expensive Persian rug on top of everything else that's going on."

"I'm sorry, Arnold. I don't know what's keeping Mia. Something is off. This doesn't feel right. I should never have let her go."

"What other choice did we have? Do you think *I* wanted to let her go out there by herself? But if they see either of us, she's as good as dead."

Mia's father is right. I had no choice. But it's been two hours. What could be taking so long? I daren't call Mia's cell either, in case she's not alone.

"When's Mom coming home, Daddy?" Angelo asks as he and Splash mosey into the living room where his grandfather and I are struggling to maintain our sanity.

"I'm sure she'll be along soon, son."

"How about we play that game of catch now?" Arnold suggests.

"Good idea," I add. "Angelo, go fetch your mitt, son."

"Okay," he says excitedly, dashing off to his room.

"If I don't hear from Mia in half an hour, I'm going down to the deli," Arnold insists.

"I should go."

"You don't know where it is."

"I do have a GPS."

"No. If they see you, it's all over."

"Are you sure, Arnold?"

"Of course. Wouldn't you do the same for your child?"

"Of course. But I can't let you go alone. You'll take one of my men with you."

"Fine."

"I'm ready!" Angelo calls from the back door.

"Coming," Arnold calls back.

The back of the property is fenced off, so no one can see into that part of the yard. That's where we play catch for a while until I just can't take it anymore. Something is wrong. My gut tells me so.

Arnold keeps looking at his watch too. There's no more time to dick around. Mia should have called by now. It's time to spring into action.

"I'm not waiting one more minute. I'm going," Arnold says as soon as Angelo goes inside to get a drink.

"Yeah, you're right. Something's wrong. Mia should have contacted me by now."

I call my men into the office. My cell phone rings unexpectedly. It's Lucian.

"What's happening? Where are you? Where is Mia? Is she okay?"

"I'm sorry, boss. She's gone."

My blood pressure shoots up instantaneously.

"What the fuck do you mean?!" I shout at the top of my voice.

"She went into the bathroom and then she just vanished. I've been driving around looking for her."

"You're a dead man, you fucking idiot! A dead man! Don't come back here. I never want to see your face again! If I as much as smell you, I'm going to kill your whole family. Do you fucking understand me?"

I throw the phone against the wall. The glass shatters into a thousand pieces.

Bruno is the first to speak.

"Leave the room," he says to the men, who don't need to be told twice.

"What happened, Boss?" he asks as soon as we're alone."

"That fucking halfwit you sent with to watch over Mia has managed to lose her. Fuck!"

Arnold comes running into the office.

"What's happening? Why are you shouting?"

He's ashen when I tell him what's going on.

"I knew I should have gone with her. I knew it!" he says as he sinks down onto the chair.

"Okay, I'll go and meet with Lician, Bruno says. It doesn't matter if they see us now. It's too late now for hide and seek."

"I'm coming," I say.

"No, please, Dante. Wait here for me. I'll call you as soon as I know anything. I swear."

"I want you to put a bullet in Lucian's head!" I bark.

"Mia wouldn't want that, Boss. I'll find her. Lucian and I will find her."

I'm seething with rage.

"You won't kill one of your own, Dante," Arnold say, as if he's giving me an order.

I'm not used to taking orders from anyone. Especially not civilians like Arnold. People like him don't understand what it's like in my world. I have to uphold my mob boss image. If I go soft on anyone word gets around and I may as well walk around with a target on my back—strap a fucking bull's eye to my designer shirt and fire the starter's pistol.

But I love Mia, and I respect Arnold, so I bite my tongue.

"Arnold, you don't understand how this works," is all I say.

"I understand plenty. I don't care what you did in your past, Dante. But if you want to be with my daughter and grandson, you had better damn well know that I won;t stand for this kind of violence."

He has a look in his eyes that tells me he means business.

"I hope you understand what I'm telling you," he says.

"Would you feel different about the man who has taken her? What if I told you I was planning on wiping him from the face of the earth?"

"At the risk of sounding like a hypocrite, I'd say that he is a different matter altogether."

"I'm glad we agree on that," I say firmly.

"Some people are just bad, Dante, and the world is a better place without them. But those people are few and far between."

"In your world, perhaps."

"I choose to live in my world, Dante. I told you that you'll have to decide if this is the world you want to live in. One thing I can tell you for certain, is that my daughter and grandson have no place in that world."

What is he telling me? Will he stand in our way if I asked Mia to marry when this is over?

A sudden idea interrupts my thinking. It's like someone just switched on a lightbulb.

"Arnold, do you know what Mia's pin code is for her cell phone?"

"What? Why?"

"I'll track her cell."

"Can you do that?"

"Yes. I can't believe I didn't think of it sooner. There's a feature on a cell phone called find my phone. We joked about it once when she said...never mind, not important. Anyway, if I can get into her phone then I can track it and find her location."

"Hang on. Mia has a list in her drawer of her pin codes. She's almost as bad as I am when it comes to remembering that sort of thing."

Arnold and I leave the office and go to Mia's bedroom. I open the nightstands drawer and start looking. Arnold goes through the desk drawer.

"Here," he says, "found it."

He hands me the paper.

"Great. Here it is. I need to use the PC in the office."

"Of course."

I dial Bruno's number. It rings a few times before he answers.

"Boss?"

"Bruno, I'm going to track Mia's cell phone and see if I can nail down a location. Where are you?"

"I just left the deli. I spoke to a waitress there who said she saw Mia going into the bathroom. She says she' didn;t see her after that. I checked and there's a backdoor to the place. I found Mia's scarf in the parking lot behind the deli. Whoever took her, brought her out the back."

"Fuckers! Okay. Come back to the ranch."

"What about Lucian?"

I look at Arnold. He can't hear my conversation, but I know what he'll say if anything happens to Lucian.

"Bring the fucking idiot with. I'll deal with him later. He's lucky I need all the manpower I can lay my hands on. Tell the asshole he's just hit the jackpot. He'd better be of use to me or else."

"Yes, Boss."

"Okay, the PC is on."

"Thank you, Arnold."

I take a seat at the desk and open the website where I type in the details of Mia's phone.

"Let's pray Mia hasn't changed her pin code since writing down this one," I say.

"Please, God."

"There! Found it!"

"Oh, thank God. Where is she? Can you see it?"

"Yeah. There she is," I say, pointing to a location on the map on the screen. Now we know where to look."

"We'd better hurry, Dante. Who knows what kind of people these are and what they're subjecting my daughter to. We have to leave as soon as possible."

"Oh, no. You're not coming with us, Arnold. I'm sorry, but I need you here with Angelo. You're his grandfather and he is comfortable with you. He needs you more now than I do. I've got this. Trust me."

"But…"

"Please, Arnold. Do it for Mia. She must be out of her mind with worry for our son. You know how much she loves him. Please."

"Fine. I'll stay here. But you better keep me up to date, Dante."

"I swear it."

Bruno and Lucian are back. I can hear them talking downstairs. Only Bruno comes up to the office.

"Where is Mia?" he asks.

"There," I say, pointing to the spot on the map.

"Okay. It isn't too far away. I'll get the men armed and ready."

"Tell Lucian and two others to stay behind and guard Arnold and Angelo."

"Yes, Boss."

"I'll take Angelo into the bunker. We'll lock ourselves in there until you come black with Mia. It's an old war bunker. No one can get in there. We'll be safe."

"Thank you, Arnold."

"Be careful, Dante. Bring my daughter back to me and his son. I'm putting my trust in you, son. Don't let me down."

"I won't. We'll be back soon. When this is over, we'll all go back to LA. How much have you told Catherine?"

"I haven't told her about Mia's kidnapping yet. I don't think I have the heart to do that to my wife. Mia is her only child. It will break her heart."

"Don't tell her now. We'll tell her once we have Mia back."

"Agreed."

"Just a few more hours and it will be over. I promise you that, Arnold."

I have to talk to my son before I leave. God forbid anything should happen to me and I didn't see his perfect little face one more time.

"Angelo!"

"Yes, Daddy."

"Where are you, son?"

"I'm in the den."

He's watching a movie with Splash.

"Son, come sit with me."

"What's wrong, Daddy?"

"Nothing, my love. I just wanted to give you a hug before I went to town."

"Why are you going out?"

"Bruno and the boys and I need to go get something quickly. Grandpa will stay here with you until Mommy and I return."

"Oh, okay."

"See you later. Daddy. Will you bring me something nice?"

"Sure, son. What would you like?"

"Uhm, ice cream."

LYDIA HALL

"Then ice cream you shall have, my love," I smile and press my nose into his hair while I hug him tightly.

"I love you, Angelo."

"I love you too, Daddy."

"Be a good boy for Grandpa."

"Sure."

27

MIA

I'm tired and still a bit woozy from the drugs. I have no idea what the time is but I know that I've been here for at least a few hours. A young man brought me a sandwich and a bottle of water. I can't eat now. I couldn't even if I were hungry, which I'm not. My gut is clenched tighter than gnat's chuff with fear and worry.

Then there's the anger that keeps seeping through every so often, and I'm tempted to take a run at the door and gnaw through the wood.

I haven't seen Franco since I arrived. He must be around somewhere, working his evil. Will Dante ever find me here, wherever here happens to be? I hope so. I don't know how much more of this I can take. If I was tired before, I'm positively circling the emotional drain right about now.

I wonder what Angelo is thinking. He must be so confused. I was supposed to be back home a long time ago. Is my child fretting for his mother? Thank God my father and Dante are with him. I'm thankful to Dante for that much. I draw strength now from knowing that the three men in my life are together.

LYDIA HALL

I lie down on the pillow for a bit. I have a splitting headache that's been developing all afternoon and most of the evening. It has now reached full blown migraine status and I'm doubled up in pain. Thank God it's dark in here. I tear off a piece of the sheet and dip it into the jug of water. Then I lay it across my eyes. It's soothing and brings some relief.

I allow myself a short respite as I drift in and out of sleep. I have to be rested when the time comes for me to escape. How I am to do this is unclear to me right now, but I trust that an opportunity will present itself soon.

I wake up with a start. Was that? Yes! I hear it again! Shouting and gunfire. What the hell is happening?

I have to hide. If there's a turf war going on outside that door, I have to hide. I squeeze myself under the very low bed frame and close my eyes tightly. I can barely manage under there. It's tight. The voices outside are loud. Men are screaming and rushing about. I can hear objects crashing to the floor and suddenly, without warning, the door to the room bursts open.

I'm too afraid to look. Is it Franco? My answer comes soon enough.

"Where are you, you bitch?"

"Yup. It's my gracious host, alright and he sounds pissed."

"Mia! Where are you?"

I have no intention of coming out from the safety of my hiding place. Franco is going to have to flip the bed if he wants to get to me.

The next noise I hear is of another set of footsteps rushing into the room. Someone else is in the room. I hear Franco hurling insults at someone in Italian before he lets out a groan as someone clearly punches him.

"You!" Franco gasps.

The men are on the floor now, in a skirmish to the death by the sounds of it.

I'm too afraid to look. The level of noise coming from outside of the room is almost deafening. Screaming, shouting, gunfire, fighting. I cup my ears with my hands and close my eyes. All I see in my mind's eye is my son. It's as if I'm watching his life story on a reel on a large screen. I see him for the first time when he's born. He's so small in my arms. I see him crawl for the first time and then I watch as he takes his first wobbly steps.

I watch as he throws a ball for the first time and rides his bike without training wheels. He crashes onto the grass and I run to him to make sure he's not hurt. I watch as he writes his name for the first time and how he learns to swim without his water wings.

Mom and Dad are there too. They're talking to Angelo and laughing as he gets into Dad's grease bucket and rubs it into his hair. I see my son's face when he tells me that my job sucks. That's the last thing I remember. No! It can't be the last memory. It can't. There are so many more we need to make. Many more happy memories, more milestones. High school, his first kiss, college, finding the love of his life, getting married and having his own children. This can't be the end. It can't be.

"Who put you up to this, you scum?" I hear a man's voice asking.

I know that voice! Is it Dante, or am I hearing things?

"Did Corelli's gang put you up to this?"

"Fuck you, De Luca!"

The noise escalates. Franco is making a gutteral choking noise, like someone who can't breathe. Suddenly, the fighting in the room has stopped. I notice the sound of someone looking for something. Pillows are scattered, the blankets and sheets are pulled away. Then an arm reaches under the bed and touches my foot. I scream.

LYDIA HALL

"Mia!"

I keep screaming.

"Mia! It's me. It's Dante."

What? Is this another trick of the mind? Like the reel of Angelo's life I just watched? Is it real? Is Dante really here?

"Dante?" I say softly, hesitantly.

"Yes, my love. It's me."

"Can you get out? Are you stuck?"

My lover reaches under the bed again and pulls at me very gently until I;m all the way out from my hiding place.

It's true. It's Dante. The man I love. He's here! He's really here.

"Dante," I cry and throw myself into his arms. "How did you find me? Where am I?"

"We'll talk about it later. Let's get you out of here."

"Okay."

"Are you hurt, my love?"

"No, I'm fine."

This is when I see Franco's perfectly still, lifeless body on the ground. He looks like a wax doll. His eyes are open in a panic filled stare and there's a knife protruding from his chest. His throat has been cut too.

"Don't look, Mia," Dante says, steering me away, but I want to look upon the lifeless face of the man who nearly destroyed my world.

"I'm glad he's dead," I say, as I spit on him.

"You don't mean that, Mia. This isn't who you are."

"Oh, yes I do. I would have killed him myself had I had the opportunity."

The adrenaline is coursing through me. I suspect I may feel different in the light of day but right now, right here, I would have killed Franco myself if I had the chance.

"Come, my love, we have to go."

Dante dials my father's number from his cell phone and hands it to me while he drives.

"Dante? Is Mia okay? Did you find her? Is she safe?" my Dad fires off his questions in rapid successions.

"It's me, Dad. I'm fine."

"Oh, Mia! Thank God! I was so worried about you, my love," he says in a shaky voice.

"Is Angelo okay, Dad?"

"Yes, he's fine. He's asleep. Where are you?"

"We're on our way back to the ranch."

"I'm so relieved, Mia. Are you hurt, my darling?"

"No, Dad. I'm fine. Really."

"You have no idea how scared I was."

That makes two of us. I'll see you soon, Dad. I love you."

"I love you too."

* * *

I roll over in bed to find Dante staring at me.

"Hey," he says softly. "How are you feeling?"

"Hi. Much better after I got some sleep. How are you?"

"A little stiff from wrestling Franco. But I'll recover."

"We're going to have to have a conversation at some stage, Dante."

"Yeah, I know."

"But first, I'd like to get some coffee and Dad's eggs into my system," I smile.

"You must be hungry."

"Starving."

"Good morning, Mom. Hey, Dad. Wow, you worked really late last night," Angelo says as he rushes into the room and jumps onto the bed.

"Hello, my sweet boy. Yes, I did. I'm sorry. I'll never do that again."

"Good morning, son," Dante smiles as our baby crawls in between us and snuggles in.

"Grandpa and I had a campout in the bunker. It's so cool down there, Mom. There's a big steel door and everything."

"Wow. That sounds like quite an adventure."

"Yeah, it was until Splash farted," he says and holds his nose.

"Oh, ugh!" I laugh, happy that Angelo has no idea how close he came to losing his parents.

"Is that Grandpa's special huevos rancheros I can smell?"

"Yes, I think so."

"Have you had breakfast yet?" Dante asks.

"Yes, I had some cheerios. Grandpa said it was a special occasion so he let me have some."

"Special occasion?"

"Uh-huh. He didn't say what, but I'm sure he'll tell me later."

"I think I know," I smile.

"Really? What?"

"How would you like to go back to LA?" Dante asks.

"Really? Home? I'd love that," Angelo beams. "Max will be so happy to see me! And I miss Grandma too."

"So do I," I say. "And Aunty Gina."

"I miss our swimming pool."

"Of course you do, " Dante laughs.

"Will you take me and Splash to the beach, Daddy?"

"I'd love to."

"Woohoo! I'm going to tell Grandpa the good news," Angelo says and leaps off the bed. "Come Splash. Here boy!"

"Someone's excited," Dante smiles happily.

"Yeah, I think he misses his friends more than he's let on. I must say I know how he feels. Texas is one state I don't mind seeing in the rearview mirror."

"Yeehaw."

I can't help laughing at the Italian stallion's impression of a cowboy.

I feel lighter today than I've felt in months. It's crazy how one can get so used to feeling awful. I don't think I realized how unhappy I've been the last while. Having Dante in my life has been both a blessing and a curse. Whatever happens next, I have to talk to him about our future together, and how I see that play out.

But that's a conversation for another day. Today I want to eat breakfast with my family, pack up my things, and head for home. Everything else can wait.

I move to get up but Dante stops me by placing his hand on my back.

"Wait," he says gently.

"What is it?"

"I want you all to myself for a little while longer," he says. "I cannot put into words how afraid I was when I didn;t hear from you yesterday. I think I'm still reeling."

I was exhausted last night when we got home. Neither Dante nor I spoke much. I think we were in too much shock at the time. Now, by the light of a new day, the pent up fear is pushing toward the surface, like a pressure cooker about to blow off steam.

"I must tell you, Mia. I've never felt this way about anyone. I never knew that love could be this way. Yesterday, when I thought I'd lost you, I could hardly breathe. I was ready to kill blindly for you."

Dante's eyes are so vulnerable. I can see into his soul. He's never shown me this side of him before. Who knew that a man who ruled his empire with such an iron fist would allow himself such a luxury as complete vulnerability.

"I feel it too, Dante. All I could think about was how I was about to lose everything precious to me. The only ray of hope I clung to was knowing that you and Angelo were together. That's why I fought to keep myself alive."

Dante reached up and pulls me gently toward him. I'm on my back now, staring up into his deep, soulful pools. My lover strokes my face before he reaches down gently and kisses me on the lips. It's a tender kiss. A rare moment between two people who have fought so hard to hide behind the curtain of self preservation.

"Ti amo, Mia," he whispers tenderly into my ear as his hands move down my abdomen toward the sweet spot.

"Ti amo, Dante," I whisper back.

My beautiful man gets up and locks the bedroom door. I don't take my eyes off him for a moment while he walks back to me and slips off his boxers. My lover is ready for me—his powerful erection standing proud. He is so beautiful. His olive skin takes my breath away. I understand the scars he carries on his body now that I know where he's been and what he's seen. It makes me appreciate him all the more.

His hand caress me gently. These are the same hands that killed a man to protect me. He's hovering over me now, ready to make our bodies as one. I position my body in a way that tells him in no uncertain terms that I'm willing and longing for him to take me. I belong to this man—body and soul. No matter where we go from here, what we decide about our future, I know I will always belong to Dante. Whether I'm with him in person or not.

28

DANTE

"Oh, It's good to be back," Mia smiles as we wake up in our home in LA."

"It is, isn't it?"

"Gina and Jeff are coming over for dinner tonight. She's dying to hear all about my *adventure,* as she put it."

"Only Gina could come up with that," I say, shaking my head.

"Your cousin is made from tough stuff. Must be a family trait."

"Indeed. Forged in the mountains of Sicily, the De Lucas," I grin.

"Hmm, and chiseled from granite," Mia coos and slaps me on the backside as I get up.

"All yours, baby."

"Yummy."

"Listen, I don't want you slaving in the kitchen today. Okay? You've done enough of that for a while. Please call the caterer and order whatever you're in the mood for tonight. No expense spared."

"Aren't you sweet?"

"All I want you to do today is relax, potter around in your studio, and enjoy our son. That's an order."

"Hey, Don. Easy on the orders," Mia grins.

"Honey, you haven't seen me rule with an iron fist yet," I chuckle.

"Do you have any special requests?"

"You mean for food?"

"Yes, you horny man, requests for food. I can read your bedroom eyes just fine. Your gut, not so much."

"Something Italian would be nice. I miss Mamma's cooking."

"You got it."

"She is looking forward to seeing us at Elio's wedding. Mamma can't wait to meet her grandson."

There's that look again. Every time I bring up Rome, she gets the deer caught in the headlights look and I can't help feeling that it has something to do with the *conversation* we've both been putting off.

I know what the woman I love wants me to do. She doesn't have to say the words, yet I feel she must in order for me to move forward. It isn't going to be easy. I don't know how I'm going to leave behind everything I've ever known to start over again.

But if that's what it takes to keep my family happy and safe, I'll give it the earnest contemplation it's due.

"Angelo is excited about meeting his other grandma," she settles for.

"There certainly are plenty of kids to play with. All the4 cousins and their families are attending this wedding. If you thought that Gina's wedding was big, it pales into insignificance compared to what Elio's one will be."

"Okay. I guess I'd better brush up on my Italian skills."

"My love, you could speak Swahili for all I care. You are the Don's woman, the mother of the heir apparent. You will be the envy of all."

What am I doing? Am I trying to push Mia to say what's on her mind? When did I become this coward? America has made me soft.

"I think it's time we had that conversation, Mia."

"Yeah, I think so too."

* * *

We're in the car, on our way to the airport where my jet is waiting to take us to Italy. Dinner with Gina and Jeff was pleasant. My cousin has decided to give me a break, but the looks of it. No more hairy eyeballs or snide comments from her.

Angelo is as excited as I've ever seen him. This is my son's first airplane ride and he's beside himself with excitement. He wasn't impressed when we told him that Splash couldn't come along for the trip.

I'm looking forward to seeing my family again. Mamma has been cooking for days, even though she has a more than full complement of staff to help. She insists that no one but the mother of the groom should ever prepare the feast of the best day of his life. Elio daren't argue with a Sicilian Mamma. Men have been found at the bottom of the ocean for less.

There's so much happening at the moment but all I can think about is the conversation that Mia and I had about our future. I'm thinking about it now as Mia and Angelo chatter away to each other about all the plans our son has for the two weeks that we'll be in Rome.

"You know what I'm going to say, don't you, Dante?"

"Yes, I have a pretty good idea."

"You know we can't carry on like this, don't you?"

"What do you want me to do, Mia?"

"I want you to leave the mafia, Dante. Everything bad that's ever happened between us has been a direct result of the people with whom you've surrounded yourself. Our son was kidnapped, my love. Our son! And God knows what would have happened to me if Franco hadn't driven my car to where they were holding me hostage."

"I hear what you're saying, my love. I do. But, a Don doesn't just grab the keys to his jet and fly off into the sunset. Who will run the organization if I'm not there? What you're asking me to do isn't as simple as you think."

"You wouldn't be the first one to do it, Dante, and I'm guessing you won't be the last. Men make sacrifices for their families every day. The question I have for you is, are you willing to do this for Angelo and me?"

"You Amricans see things in black and white. I'm Italian. There are a host of colors in between for us."

"Well, Dante. Then, you're going to have to make your family an offer they can't refuse."

"Did you just quote from The Godfather?" I grin, thankful for the temporary break from this tough discussion.

"I did. I know them all, including 'Leave the gun. Take the cannoli.' I'm begging you, Dante. Take the cannoli, Do it for me. Do it for Angelo."

"Okay. I'll talk to Elio when we're in Rome."

"Thank you, Dante."

"Don't thank me yet. This is by no means a done deal. But, I'm willing to try."

Yeah, if only that were as easy as it sounds.

"Hey, Daddy. Is that your plane?"

"Yes, my son. Do you like it?"

"Wow! It's big."

Mia chuckles at the wide eyed wonder of our little man.

"Do you think he's excited?" I whisper.

"What was your first clue? He's been talking about this trip since we first broke the news to him. He's been driving me nuts."

"Yeah, I'm sorry I've been missing in action the last few days. Been catching up on everything I missed in Rome. The time difference does make it a little tough."

"It's fine. All I'm saying is he's your baby once we get in the air. I'm going to take a well deserved nap."

"No problem."

*　*　*

"Mamma, this is Angelo, your grandson. Angelo, this is my mother, your nonna."

"Oh, Dante. He's beautiful. Ciao, Angelo. Come here, let Nonna see you."

"Hello, Nonna," Angelo beams and walks over to my mother so she can touch his little face.

"You are a strong boy, no?" she coos. "He looks just like you when you were a boy," Mamma says with pride.

"I'm six, Nonna. How old are you?"

"Angelo, that's not polite," Mia says.

"No, it's okay. The boy has an enquiring mind," Mamma counters, already madly in love with my son.

"I am seventy-two years old, my little nipote."

"Wow! That's old!"

Mamma laughs from her gut.

"Sì. One day you will be that old too, my darling."

"Really?"

"Sì."

"Where is Grandpa?"

"Your Nonno died when your father was young,"

"Do you miss him, Nonna?"

"Very much."

"It's okay. I love you, Nonna."

My mothers eye fill with tears.

"What a beautiful child you've raised, Mia," she says.

"Thank you."

I've never been as proud of a woman as I am of Mia right now. Getting the stamp of approval from Mamma is no small thing. What my mother is saying is that I've chosen well. I agree. I just wonder what she'll think once I tell her that I'm going to talk to my brother about handing the leadership over to him. But that's a topic for another time.

* * *

"Hi, Lisa. It's so nice to meet you in person."

"Ciao, Mia. Nice to meet you too."

"Elio, can we talk?"

"Sure, brother. Come, let's leave the ladies to get to know each other better. To tell you the truth, I've had my fill of wedding talk."

"Ah, get out of here, you ingrate," Lisa chuckles.

"Goodbye, my love," Elio grins as he and I leave the two women to it.

"Lisa thinks I'm just kidding, but holy crap! The shit a man has to go through just to put a ring on a woman's finger!"

"You're lucky Lisa said yes, you brat," I laugh.

"You think I'm joking. Wait until it's your turn, my brother. Then we'll talk again."

"Let's go to the office."

"Office? Sounds serious."

"It is. I don't want to be disturbed."

This is going to be hard enough without interruptions.

"What's up, Dante?"

"I want to talk to you about the future."

"Okay. I'm listening."

"Brandy?"

"Sure."

I pour two snifters and hand one to Elio.

"This doesn't have anything to do with a certain American woman, does it?"

"Smartass. Yes, it does."

"What's on your mind, brother?"

"Mia wants me to step down as Don."

Elio nearly chokes on his brandy.

"What?"

"Uh-huh."

"Have you lost your mind, Dante?"

"Can you really blame her, Elio? After what she's been through I'm amazed that she's still with me."

"I get it, Dante. It was a rocky start for anyone who isn't Sicilian. But leaving the organization? That's crazy talk."

"Is it? I've had a good run. I have more than enough money to live comfortably for more than one lifetime. Is it really so terrible for me to want to retire while I'm still young and full of life and enjoy the fruits of my labor?"

Elio stares at me as if he has no clue what I;m saying.

"I have a son, brother. A son who almost lost his mother. A son who was kidnapped. I want to take them away from all of this, Elio. Does that make me a bad son and brother?"

"Of course not."

"You and Lisa aren't that keen on having kids. You don't understand what it's like to wake up every morning and fear for your son's safety."

"Who will take over from you?"

"Are you kidding? You, you dunce. You're a smart man, you work hard, and there's no reason a man like you should live in the shadow of an older brother just because you were born second. You'll have Bruno to help you. Come on, Elio. You've learned from me for years, but you are equally as capable as I am to run this family."

"Are you sure you want to do this, brother?"

"No, but I want to do it anyway. If you agree, of course."

"When will you step down?"

"As soon as you and Lisa are back from your honeymoon."

"That soon?"

"Why wait?"

"I guess."

"I want to ask Mia to marry me. I know she will say yes if I'm no longer the Don. It's what I want too, little brother. Hey, maybe I'll take a crack at property development or something like that."

"As if the racketeers won't get to you there," Elio grins.

"Yeah, but I know a wise guy who will protect me," I wink.

"Okay, Dante, You win. I'll talk to Lisa."

"Thank you, Elio."

"You're telling Mamma."

"You tell her and I'll throw in the jet to sweeten the deal."

"Oh, no. Nice try," Elio chuckles.

"Sure. Give me the impossible task, why don't you."

***

"I swear he was half asleep all through dinner. The last time I saw him this tired we'd just moved into the house in LA and he'd spent the whole day in the pool."

"Our son loves family."

"His cousins adore him too."

"Your family is lovely, Dante. So warm and inviting."

"Thank you. I spoke to Elio today."

"And?"

"He thinks I'm crazy, but he's agreed."

"Oh, Dante. That's wonderful news. Thank you. I know it must have been difficult for you. I'm going to make you so happy. I promise."

"Are you kidding? Happier than this? I doubt it."

* * *

"Ciao, Mamma."

"Ciao, Dante."

"Can I talk to you, please, Mamma?"

"Sure, my son. What is it?"

It's time to tell my mother of my plans to hand over the torch to Elio. My biggest fear is that she's disappointed with me. Ever since my father died, I've taken on the mantle of family leader. I've done my best to grow and protect our business interests and to foster good relations with the other families in the area.

I've been successful, too. For the most part. But now it's time to live my life for my young family; my own wife and son.

"Sit, my son. What is on your mind?"

"Mama, I love you. I want to say thank you for everything you've done to make me the man that I am."

"Is something wrong, Dante? Are you ill?"

Mother looks worried.

"No. I'm not ill."

"Spit it out, son. You're giving me more gray hairs."

"I'm stepping down as Don and handing it over to Elio."

That should rip the bandaid right off.

Mamma doesn't say anything. Her face gives nothing away about what she's thinking. What a card player she could have been.

"Mamma. Say something, please."

"Is this what you want or is it what Mia wants?"

"It's what we both want. I want to dedicate myself to my family, Mamma. When we lost Pappa I promised myself I would try and be the best father I could be if I ever had a son. Angelo means the world to me, Mamma, and I almost lost him."

"Son, there are many dangers in this world. Stepping down doesn't automatically guarantee the safety of your family."

"I know that. I'm not naive enough to think that everything will be wine and roses ever after, but stepping down does give me more time to be the kind of father Pappa was. Before he went too deeply down the mafia rabbit hole."

"Have you spoken to Elio?"

"Yes. He is happy to take over from me."

"Have you told anyone else?"

"No, Mamma. I wanted to talk to you first."

"If this is truly what you want, Dante, then you must do it. I am an old woman. I lived my life the way I saw fit and I won't stand between you and your life choices. You have my blessing."

"Grazie, Mamma."

"Prego, il mio forte figlio."

29

MIA

Dante told me last night that he had spoken to his mother about stepping down. It's sweet how he loves and respects her so much that he won't make a move like this without discussing it with her first.

He said she gave him her blessing, which was a great relief. I don't want to be *that American woman* everyone will resent after the fact. I feel as if a weight has been lifted from my shoulders. The thought of Dante and I starting a new life, untainted by the violence that touches his world on a daily basis, fills me with tremendous hope.

Today is Elio and Lisa's wedding day and the little coastal town is teaming with De Lucas and Antonellis. Angelo was quite overwhelmed by all the new faces at first, but he soon got into the swing of it. My son isn't at all used to such a large gathering. We don't even get this kind of crowd at one of his little league games.

My family is miniscule in comparison. Being an only child makes the circle rather small. The time to leave for the church is ticking away and I'm getting Angelo ready for the big event.

"Ah, Mom. Why do I have to wear this suit? I feel silly."

"You look very handsome, my boy. Today is a big day for your uncle Elio. You are a man now, remember? You have to look the part, Master De Luca," I tease.

"You're funny, Mom," he grimaces, pulling at his collar.

"Is Daddy also wearing a suit?"

"Of course. He's the best man."

"What does that mean?"

"Well, he is the most important witness to the wedding today. He's the one who ties the ribbon to the church door so the guests know where to come to celebrate the ceremony. He also presents the rings to the bride and groom."

"Really?"

"Uh-huh. And then once Elio and Lisa are married, Daddy will do the first speech to wish the couple a long and happy marriage."

"That's a very important job, isn't it, Mom?"

"It sure is, my love."

"Daddy is important here, isn't he?"

Interesting observation. Smart boy.

"Why do you ask that?"

"I see how everyone waits outside Daddy's office so they can talk to him. He must be really clever, hey."

"Yes, Angelo. Your Daddy is very clever."

"I want to be strong and clever like Daddy when I grow up."

Angelo's words both thrill and frighten me. It's beautiful when a son wants to follow in his father's footsteps, but my son doesn't know what he's saying. This is the last thing I'd ever want for him.

"I'm sure you're going to be even stronger and smarter than your Dad, my angel. Now let me take a look at you. Oh, my goodness. You are a handsome young man."

"Can I go now, Mom?"

"Only if you promise not to get dirt all over this suit, Angelo. I want you to look nice today."

"Ugh! Fine. I'll be careful," he moans.

"Promise?"

"I promise," he sighs.

"Okay, off you go then."

Angelo takes off like a rocket. He's probably miffed that he's missed out on playtime with the other children.

"Knock, knock."

Dante walks into the room.

"I just saw a very handsome little De Luca shoot out of here like a man fired from a canon," he chuckles.

"Yup. It took me forever to get him dressed. That boy is like a slinky."

"You did a good job, mommy. He looks adorable."

"I know," I smile, proud as punch.

"I'm going to join the other men. Will you be alright to come on your own?"

"Of course."

Dante comes closer so he can kiss me.

"You look very sexy," I note as he wraps his arms around me.

"Oh, this old thing," he grins.

"Nothing like a man in a suit," I tease some more.

"Woman, if you don't let go of me, this very expensive suit will be a crumpled mess on the floor in a few minutes," he coos, his eyes heavy with desire.

"So, no quickie for the best man's plus one then?" I purr.

"Woman, you are more lethal than a Sicilian with a grudge," he says and places my hand over his erection to prove his point.

"I'll be quick," I whisper in a husky tone brimming over with lust.

"I'll be quicker," he says, lifts me off my feet, and props me up between his body and the wall.

"Careful," I pant. "It took great effort to fix my hair. Don't mess it up."

"I wouldn't dream of it," he says as he unzips his pants, and frees his engorged penis.

I take a hold of him and stroke while he pulls aside my panties.

"Ah, so wet and warm," he breathes into my ear.

"All for you, my queen."

It's a quickie, alright. Not that I mind—eleven out of ten for intensity.

"All that, and my hair still looks fabulous," I pant while I check the mirror and Dante zips up his pants.

"I'd better get out of here before Elio calls a search party."

"Is he nervous?" I laugh.

"Like a slab of chocolate in a room where PMS reigns."

"Haha."

"See you in the church, gorgeous," Dante says and gives me a quick peck on the cheek.

"See you later."

My lover gives me one last lusty grin, and then he's gone.

* * *

"Lisa looked so beautiful. What a dress."

"She did."

"I swear I could see the beads of sweat from where I was sitting in the first pew."

"You should have seen how his fingers trembled when he took the ring. I was sure he would drop it," Dante laughs.

Dante, Angelo, and I are in the car, on our way to the reception.

"So, what did you think of the ceremony, son?"

"It was so long," he sighs.

"Forty-five minutes isn't that long, sweetheart," I interject.

"It felt like forever," Angelo says again.

"Don't worry, my boy. All that's left for you to do now is play and eat," Dante chuckles. "You look very handsome today. I saw a few of the girls checking you out."

"No they weren't!" he insists, with a great amount of disgust at such a vile thought.

Dante and I laugh heartily at our son's expression. He even throws in a few eyerolls to drive home his point.

"You look so beautiful, Mia," Dante coos. "Don't you think your mom looks stunning, Angelo?"

"Yes, Mom looks very pretty."

"Thank you, my boys."

The car comes to a stop.

LYDIA HALL

"Okay, Angelo. Hold my hand until we're inside the venue, please."

"Ah, Mom! I'm not a baby."

"Listen to your mother, Angelo," Dante says in a stern voice.

"Okay, Daddy."

Dante and I are very careful with Angelo after the kidnapping incident. Thankfully, he doesn't seem to remember anything other than the excellent strawberry flavored ice cream he ate that knocked him out. I'm so relieved about that and so is his father, who is still struggling to forgive himself for the chaos he introduced into our lives.

The reception hall is stunning, with an outside lawn area that leads onto a private beach. White marquees, white tables, bright flowers, food, a live band—postcard perfection.

"Your family sure knows how to throw a party."

"That we do. How about a glass of champagne to wet your whistle?"

"You read my mind."

"Okay, sweetheart. You can go play now," I tell Angelo after I take off his jacket and I'm happy that he's safe.

"Thanks, Mom," he says and rushed off.

The happy couple is surrounded by well wishers, all shoving envelopes into a bad Lisa's holding. It's an old Italian custom that is alive and well in these parts of Italy. The wedding guests bless the newlyweds with cash. Some give lavishly, some generously, and some as they can afford to; but everybody gives. It's considered an insult not to give.

"Ciao, bella."

"Oh, hello, Mrs. De Luca."

"Basta! Call me Mamma."

"Sorry, I will. The food smells delicious, Mamma. You did an amazing job."

"Grazie, Mia. Come. Let's talk for a moment."

Oh, crap. I hope this isn't going to be awkward. I don't know this woman well enough to be able to tell if she's on my side or not. I guess I'm about to find out.

"Sit," she says and points to a sofa away from the noise.

I don't know what's keeping Dante.

"Mia, I want to talk to you about my son."

"Okay."

"He loves you very much."

"I love him very much too."

"I hope you love him enough, my dear. He's about to give up his whole world for you."

"And for his son."

I'm a little irritated by her comment. It's not as if I'm asking Dante to leave his family behind and never see or speak to them again! I'm asking him to stop stealing and killing, for fuck's sake.

"I am not angry, Mia. I just want to know that you love my son enough to support him in this new way of life."

"Mama, I adore Dante. I will do whatever he asks, but I cannot, no, will not, subject Angelo to any further danger. We almost lost our child."

"I see that you have a fire inside of you. That's good. Dante needs a woman with fire. He is a strong man."

"I have plenty of fire. But more important than fire, I have love. We have love. More than enough for us and our son."

"Bene. Come let us eat. You are too skinny."

She gets up and holds out her hand to me. I imagine that's the pep talk over and done with.

"Ah, there you are. My two favorite girls," Dante smiles and hands me a glass of champagne. "Champagne, Mamma?"

"Grazie, darling."

"It's almost time for the speeches. Join me," Dante says and takes my hand.

He kisses his mother on the cheek before we walk away.

"Was I interrupting something?" he asks.

"No. All good."

"Great."

Dante and I take our seats at the main table, next to Elio and Lisa. Angelo sits with his friends at the children's table. It's time for the speeches. Dante speaks first. A hush falls over the onlookers.

"Welcome everyone. It's good to see so many friends here today. May I be the first to congratulate the happy couple. Lisa, you are a brave woman."

A collective chuckle rises from the crowd.

"I struggled a bit to find stories about my baby brother that I could share with this group," Dante says with a grin. "I was always the quiet, oldest child, you see. Not so when it came to little Elio, who was really a hurricane waiting for a place to happen.

Then came the dating years, at which point Elio discovered the various ways in which the fairer sex could enlighten a man's world. Well, it's fair to say we didn't see much of Elio after that. Not for about a decade.

Then, he met Lisa. After that, we couldn't get him out of the house with a crowbar. The two of them were basically bunked down in Elio's room for weeks on end, doing God knows what, eating all Mamma's food, and drinking my expensive alcohol.

But, we grew to love Lisa like she was one of us, and I'm so happy to be here today to wish the two of them the very best life together. And, Lisa, one more word of encouragement as you take on the great responsibility of keeping my brother out of trouble. Remember, the woman cries before the wedding, the man afterwards.

Saluti!"

"Saluti!" the crowd echoes as one.

Dante bends down and kisses Elio on both cheeks. The two are laughing and lovingly slapping each other's backs. It's been a good day.

* * *

Dante carries Angelo into his bedroom and lays him down gently on the bed. Our son is fast asleep.

"Let me take off his clothes first," I whisper.

"Leave it, my love. It's so dirty we'll have to throw it away anyway," he smiles. "A few more hours in these soiled clothes won't hurt."

"Okay," I whisper, kiss my son's sticky forehead, and close the bedroom door quietly.

"I'm shattered," I say, slipping off my pumps and rubbing my toes.

"How about a nightcap before bed?"

"I'd love one, thanks."

We walk hand in hand to the living room.

"It was a great day."

"Yes, it was. Elio and Lisa looked so happy. So did your mom."

"She is. Both her boys have found the love of their lives. How can she be anything but joyous?"

"Love of your life, am I?" I coo.

"You are, my sweet."

"Does that mean you'll rub my toes for me?"

"Sure, but I can't guarantee that it will end there."

"You bad boy," I giggle.

"Where did you disappear to for so long after the speeches?"

"I had a meeting with the four families."

"Who?"

"The Dons of the other families."

"Oh."

"I told them that I am stepping down and that Elio is the new Don. I wanted to make sure everyone knows before we leave Italy."

"I still can't believe it's real."

"Oh, it is now."

"Thank you, Dante. I can't tell you what this means to me."

"Honestly, I thought at the beginning that this was all you. But now that it's done, I'm happier than I thought I'd be. I have a whole new future planned for us. It's exciting, actually."

"I'm glad you feel that way. What are you thinking of doing now?"

"The first thing I want to do is this."

Dante reaches into his pocket and pulls out a little box.

"I've been wanting to do this for a long time, but the timing never seemed quite right."

My heart is thundering in my chest as I open the box.

"Oh, Dante. It's beautiful!"

"I'm glad you like it."

He gets down on one knee and takes my hands in his.

"Before I met you, Mia, I never thought I'd want to be a husband. Now I cannot imagine a world in which I'm not. Will you do me the honor of becoming my wife, Mia, the love of my life, the mother of my son, and the owner of the sexiest ass I've ever had the pleasure of biting into."

"Yes, you beautiful, crazy, man. I'll marry you."

He slips the ring onto my finger. It's a perfect fit. We're the perfect fit.

30

DANTE

"Where shall we live, my darling fiancé?" I ask Mia.

We're back in LA. I thought a clean break from Italy would be best. At least for a while until the organization starts to forget about me. Granted, it may take a good few decades, but I'm a patient man. Besides, LA isn't so bad. I may even open an Italian trattoria.

Today, we're out shopping for a permanent home, or a forever home, as Angelo likes to call it. He's given his parents very specific criteria for this home too. He would like a pool, lots of space for Splash to dig holes, oh, and a beach if that's possible. How cute is my kid?

Of course I'll give him any and everything he wants. He's my son!

I wish my father was alive to meet his grandson. Angelo is everything I ever could have dreamed of. I'm so proud of Mia for raising our child so well. Tonight we're having dinner with her folks. We'll share our good news with them then. I wanted to ask Mia's father for his permission, even though Mia has already said yes. Arnold was good to me when I needed an understanding and forgiving heart.

We thought it best not to tell Angelo about our wedding yet, either. He'll blab for sure, because that's what six-year-olds do.

"I really like this one," Mia says as we're walking through a newly built, ten bedroom home with a pool and private access to the beach. "But I'm not sure we need all these rooms."

"We do if the De Luca clan decides to descend on us for the holidays. You've seen the mob, no pun intended. They're huge."

"And what are we supposed to do with eight of them during the rest of the year?"

"Well, you could convert one into a pottery studio. The other seven we'll use alternatively for rampant sex, experimental type stuff. A new one for every night of the week. Starting with this one," I purr and pull her in for a kiss.

"Ooh, I like your thinking."

"Ma'am, we'll take it!" he says and pats me on the tush.

* * *

"You're not nervous are you?" Mia says as we pull up outside her parents' home.

"No."

"Then why are there tiny beads of sweat on your brow?" she giggles.

"Ugh! Busted," I admit.

"Oh, my word, you are so adorable."

"Of course I'm nervous. I don't want to have to elope if your father chases me out into the street."

"Oh, rubbish. He'd never."

"I hope not. I gave up my job for you, you know," I smirk.

"Oh, ha...ha... Very funny."

Mia walks into the house, carrying a bottle of whiskey I bought for Arnold and chocolates we bought for Catherine, who I'm told is a complete chocoholic.

"There you are," Mom says and hugs little Angelo.

"Hey, Grandma. Look what I got."

"Wow, That's a lovely catcher's mitt, darling. What happened to your other one?"

"I think Splash buried it in the garden."

"What a naughty dog," she fusses.

"Hi, Mia. Hello, Dante. Welcome. Arnold is out in the back starting a bushfire," she says and rolls her eyes. "I swear that man is a recycled pyromaniac."

"Thanks, Catherine. I'll make sure he doesn't set the house alight."

"Thank you, darling."

"Hey, Dante," Arnold greets me happily as I join him outside at the fire pit. "How are you? How was Rome?"

"Hi, Arnold. It was good, thanks. My brother's wedding was lovely. So good to see the family together. How are you?"

"Much better, thanks. Mia told me the news. I'm proud of you, Dante."

"Thank you, Arnold. That means a lot to me. There's something I want to discuss with you."

"Okay. Grab us a beer over there in the cooler before we'll chat."

"Sure."

I take two beers from the cooler and hand him one.

"Thanks. Okay, I'm listening."

"Firstly, I wanted to thank you for the classy way in which you handled the whole situation out at the ranch. You could have lost it with me, but you didn't. I really appreciate that."

"I can't say it was my pleasure, but you're welcome."

"Secondly, I wanted to ask you something."

Arnold starts to smile.

"Uh-huh."

"I want to ask you for Mia's hand in marriage, Arnold. I love her very much and I want her and I and our beautiful Angelo to be a family. Officially."

I'm sweating bullets. Imagine that. A tough ex Don afraid of Mia's father's answer. It would be hysterical if it wasn't so damned important to me.

"What did Mia say? Will she take your raggedy ass for a husband?"

"Yeah, she will. Crazy, isn't it?"

"Insane."

"Come on, Arnold. You're killing me here."

He laughs out loud, then slaps me on the shoulder.

"Yes, Dante. You have my blessing."

"Thank you, Arnold."

"I think you'd better start calling me Dad. Don't you?"

"It would be my honor, Dad."

* * *

"Angelo. Angelo! Where is that boy?"

"He's getting dressed, Mamma."

"Are you sure? I saw him bolt past the window a few minutes ago."

"Don't worry, Mia's mom said she'd deal with it. How are you feeling?"

"I'm happy."

"You look beautiful, Mamma."

"Oh, you old charmer. Just like your father," Mamma smiles. "He would be so proud of his boys."

"I wish he were here too, Mamma. But I have you and that's all that matters."

"You're such a good boy," she says and cups my face in her hands.

"Thank you, Mamma."

"I like your choice of women, Dante. Mia's got spunk."

"I was wondering what you were talking about at Elio's wedding reception. Testing her, were you?" I grin.

"Of course."

"I'm glad she passed the Mamma De Luca test."

"What is this nonsense about you living here in America?"

"It's best for now that I stay out of Italy. It won;t be forever, I promise."

"I;m not getting any younger, Dante."

"Oh, yes you are," I laugh. "You have more gusto now than ever before."

"That's because both my boys are happy. I'm happy. But I'm an old woman now, my boy. I want to spend time with my grandbabies. How can I do that if I live in Italy and they live in America? Hey?"

"You're welcome to spend as much time with us as you like. We have plenty of room for you."

"No! My life is in Italy. My friends are there. I can't move now. I'm too settled in my ways."

"Okay. But, the offer stands. You are always welcome."

"I'll think about it. Now go get dressed. You can't be late for your own wedding."

* * *

Elio is standing next to me at the altar. I'm less nervous now than I was when I asked Mia's father for her hand in marriage—but not by much.

"Scared she's going to leave you standing at the altar, are you," Elio asks in a low voice, smirking like a naughty kid.

"Shut up! Sorry, Father."

The priest gives me a knowing wink. I'm sure he's heard worse from the pulpit.

Elio chuckles. Now that he's married he's getting his dig in with more fun than I'd like to grant the little shit. The wedding march starts.

"Here we go," Elio says and straightens up. "Showtime, big bro. Too late to run now."

The procession of bridesmaids start their walk down the aisle, followed by Arnold, and on his arm, my stunning bride. Mia takes my breath away. She took her time choosing a wedding dress and I have to give it to her, it's the most beautiful garment I've ever seen on a bride.

I watch as she walks slowly toward me, her veil covering her precious face. How did I ever get this lucky? Of all the women in the world, how was it that she was the one to steal my heart right out from under my nose? Angelo is standing next to Elio. He looks like a movie star in his tux, his mop of black hair perfectly quaffed.

She's so close now, I can see her piercing blue eyes radiating through the thin fabric of the veil. Mia is radiant.

Arnold lifts the veil and kisses his daughter on her cheek. He looks so proud. And so he should be. His child is an angel.

I hardly hear a word that the priest is saying. He may as well be reciting the Gettysburg Address for all I know, or swearing me into a secret society of giant slayers. All I see is Mia. All I hear is the sound of my heart thundering in my chest as I gaze into the eyes of the woman I adore.

"Do you, Dante Anthony De Luca, take this woman, Mia Martin, to be your wife, to live together in holy matrimony, to love her, to honor her, to comfort her, and to keep her in sickness and in health, forsaking all others, for as long as you both shall live?"

This part I hear. Only because Mia's grip on my hand intensifies.

"I do."

"And, do you, Mia Martin, take this man to be your husband, to live together in holy matrimony, to love him, to honor him, to comfort him, and to keep him in sickness and in health, forsaking all others, for as long as you both shall live?"

Mia smiles.

"I do."

"Then, by the power vested in me by the state of California, I now pronounce you husband and wife. You may kiss the bride."

Hey, you don't have to tell me twice.

"Come here, Mrs. De Luca."

* * *

"Good morning, gorgeous."

"Good morning to you too, handsome."

"You were sleeping so peacefully, I didn't want to wake you," I say, kissing Mia;s bare shoulder.

"Hhmm, that's nice. Where's Angelo?"

"He's gone with the winemaker. They're driving through the vineyard on a tractor. I haven't seen our son this excited since yesterday when he was allowed to press a small vat of grapes."

"His toes looked an awful mess last night. He had grapes under his toenails."

Mia decided to bring Angelo along on the first week of our honeymoon. Mia chose to come to the vineyard where we'd enjoyed time before. I am happy that the sleaze I punched in the nose when we visited before is no longer working here. Not that I'd mind a second go at him. You can take the Don out of the mob…

"He's had such a lovely few days. I feel a little guilty about sending him back to LA to be with my folks while you and I carry on honeymooning."

"Don't be. We have the rest of our lives to dote on him. I want to be able to do unspeakable things to my stunning bride without worrying about a stealthy child busting in on us," I purr.

"Good point. Yesterday was far too close for comfort," she giggles.

"You think he bought the nap explanation?"

"I hope so."

"He's on a tractor now, you know," I whisper suggestively.

"We're bound to hear that sucker approaching," Mia grins.

"I'll lock the door, just in case. I must say, I do like retirement."

"Ditto."

* * *

Eighteen Months Later

"Dad! Come see! They're here!" Angelo yells from the den.

"Oh, my goodness," I say when I bend down and look at Splash's new puppies.

Angelo talked us into getting Splash a *wife*. With all the wedding business last year, first Elio's and then our, I think my son thought it only fair that his bestie, Splash, start a family of his own too.

"Aren't they cute, Dad? Look how small this one is," he coos and points to the runt of the litter. "I'm going to call this one Nugget."

"That's the perfect name, sweetheart," Mia gushes.

"You're a good girl, Lucy," Mia says and strokes the tired new mommy.

Splash is strutting around like a proud father, his tail wagging wildly.

"Careful, Splash," Angelo commands in a stern voice. "Babies are delicate. don't stand on one."

Our son knows all about babies and how delicate they are. He handles his baby sister, Leila, with such skill and care that it makes my heart melt whenever I watch them together. It would seem that Angelo wasn't the only child who joined us on our honeymoon.

Leila is my pride and joy. There's something about a daughter that captures her daddy's heart like no one can. Leila is a carbon copy of her beautiful mother. She has the same blue eyes. I can see that I'm going to be as powerless against my daughter's charms as I am to her mother's.

It's only been a year, but my life has changed so dramatically, I can hardly believe it. I made the right decision in walking away from the life I knew in Rome. I wouldn't change what I have now for the world.

My property development company is up, and running very successfully. I've even talked Elio into considering joining me in America. I'm happy to report that he's thinking about it. It would be wonderful if the whole family were together again. I do miss my brother very much.

"Puppies are such a gift, aren't they, son?" I smile.

"They sure are."

"I have something for you too, my love," Mia whispers to me.

"Oh? What's that?"

She puts something into my jacket pocket.

"Intriguing," I smile.

I feel for the item and pull it out.

"What? Are you serious?"

"Uh-huh."

"Splash isn't the only one that's been busy," she grins.

"The legend of Erice strikes again!" I laugh.

"Guess what you're getting for Christmas, Angelo," I beam.

"What?"

"Another baby!"

EXCERPT: RUTHLESS BEAST

The death of my brother brought me face to face with a commanding mafia leader.

Lucas had all my attention from the moment our eyes met.

He saw the sadness in mine and embraced me.

I felt protected.

But Lucas is way older… *and* dangerous.

Still, he's not the one I have to be afraid of.

My brother's death was, in fact, murder.

And my own life is in the hands of the rival gang.

Lucas has always felt like a protector.

But his mystery sends shivers down my spine.

He's anything but innocent.

And he would go to any lengths to ensure my safety.

Even if that means taking me in without my will.

But there's one thing that even Lucas has no control over.

A secret – a baby that's growing inside my belly who would call him daddy.

Chapter 1: Emily

"Oh, wow! That's amazing, Ems. You are such a fabulous artist."

"Ooh, fabulous, hey? Thanks, Dannie. You're my biggest fan," I coo in appreciation of my best friend, Daniella's encouragement.

"It's true. Next to yours, my drawings look like something a two year old would deposit on a canvas with pureed broccoli."

"Funny."

"How's the assignment coming along?"

"I'm almost done. This is the last in the collection I have to submit by Friday. I'm nervous."

"You're crazy. You're always nervous when the truth is that your art professor would be so lucky to have more students like you in his class. You're going to ace it. No sweat."

My one-woman fan club smiles brightly at me. Dannie and I couldn't be more different if we tried. We are polar opposites in every way, but we are cut from the same cloth when it comes to friendship and loyalty.

Daniella is a math nerd. With her eyeglasses and pullovers, she'd be perfectly at home on the set of The Big Bang Theory. I zone out when she starts waxing lyrical about equations and stats. She may as well be speaking a foreign language, for all the sense it makes to me. The light dances in her eyes, and I swear her voice goes up a few octaves as she chatters on about all things mathematical. I nod my head and pretend to be interested, but truthfully, I'd be happier watching paint dry.

I painted a canvas for Dannie for her twentieth birthday. It was my artistic interpretation of an equation she'd been particularly fascinated with at the time. I have to say it was pretty damn impressive. Even I was amazed at how good the end result was. The canvas hangs over her desk now. Dannie insists that it serves as her inspiration when she's feeling a tad unmotivated.

"Are you working this afternoon?" she asks, a red gummy worm dangling from her lips.

"No. Pierre is working an extra shift. He's going to visit his parents next weekend, so he asked if I'd swap shifts with him."

"Uhhh, Pierre. That man is too beautiful for his own good," Dannie gushes.

"That he is. Pity he bats for the other side."

"Hey, give me one night with him, armed with a bottle of wine, and I'll change his mind."

"You're far too horny for a math major, Daniella Freeman."

"It might interest you to know that apparently old Einstein got around quite a bit in his day," Dannie grins. "Genius is horny work, my dear woman," she says, staring mockingly down at me over the rim of her glasses.

"Is that so?"

"Yup. Speaking of horny work, How's your love life? What happened to that tall drink of water you met at the gallery? Paolo, was it?"

"Ah, yes. I'm afraid the delicious Paolo went back home to Italy."

"Oh, darn it. Never mind. It's a good thing you have a best friend who has your back."

"You're referring to that enormous vibrator you bought me for my birthday, aren't you?" I sigh, rolling my eyes.

"Don't knock it til you've tried it, hon. Not all of us have access to lovers of art with deep pockets who enjoy lazy afternoons filled with champagne cocktails and oodles of rampant sex."

"Do you even know what I do at the gallery?" I laugh.

My phone rings, cutting our conversation short. It's David.

"Hi, Big Bro."

"Hey, Ems."

"What's up?"

"I was just wondering if you were free for dinner."

"Hey, gorgeous man!" Dannie yells out loud. "The answer is yes. Yes, I'll marry you!"

"David says hi," I say as she cackles and leaves the room.

LYDIA HALL

"That girl is one fraction short of a whole number," David laughs.

"And the horse it rode in on," I add. "Anyway, I'd love to join you for dinner. Where are we going?"

"You decide. I'll swing by at 6 p.m. and pick you up. Okay?"

"Great. See you then."

David's and my parents died suddenly when I was twelve and he was twenty. For the last twelve years, my older brother has been dad, mom, brother, best friend, bodyguard, guardian, and all the other things my parents aren't able to be for me. I'm so proud of him.

David is handsome and very clever. He's done well for himself when it comes to finances. And the most impressive part is that he did it all while raising his little sister like a boss.

It's 5:55 p.m. when I hear his car engine's telltale roar outside my apartment.

"I'll see you later, Dannie!" I call out in the direction of her bedroom.

"Have fun!" she calls back. "Give my future husband a sloppy kiss on the cheek for me!"

"Will do!"

Dannie has a serious crush on David. They have a very playful relationship where he pretends it's annoying, and she embarrasses him at every opportunity. It's cute.

"Hiya," I say, jumping into the passenger side of the Mustang.

"Hey, Sis. You look lovely."

"Thanks, Davy. Let's make some girls jealous," I giggle.

"You're not going to pretend you're my hot girlfriend again, are you?"

"Of course I am. It's the least I can do to pay you back for all those times you scared the crap out of my dates."

"Hey, thanks to my vigilance, you were never disrespected, were you?"

"Yeah, yeah. I also never had a serious boyfriend until college, thanks to you. Moving on, what's new with you?"

"Nothing much. I work too hard to get into any trouble. How's school?"

"You mean university. I'm twenty-four just in case you missed it," I smirk. "School is school. I'm looking forward to getting my last assignment in. It's almost time to dust off the old tux, Bro. Your baby sister is graduating soon."

"I can't believe the time has gone by so fast. I'm super proud of you, Ems."

"Thank you, David. I couldn't have done it without you. I love you so much, you old stinker," I smile and slap him playfully on the knee.

"Woah! Don't get me all misty now. You'll ruin my reputation as a tough guy."

"Tough guy! Oh, please. You're a softy, Mr. Thornton. And don't let them tell you anything different."

"Where would you like to go?"

"I'm in the mood for Mexican."

"Then Mexican you shall have, young lady."

"Do you ever wonder what our lives would be like if Mom and Dad were still alive?" I say after a few moments of silence.

"All the time."

"Do you think you and I would be this close?"

"I'd like to think so."

"I miss them, Davy."

"I miss them too, Ems. They'd be very proud of you, you know."

LYDIA HALL

"What about you? You've done incredibly well for yourself. You're so young, and look at the life you've made for us."

David is far away. I can see that he has something on his mind.

"What is it?" I ask, resting my hand on his knee.

"Nothing," he says after a while. "Just thinking about work stuff."

"Are you sure?"

"Yes, of course."

"You'd tell me if something was wrong, wouldn't you, Davy?"

"Probably not," he grins.

"Come on. I'm an adult now. You don't have to protect me from everything anymore. I'm tougher than I look."

"Don't I know it! Trust me. It's nothing serious. I'm just preoccupied. Come on. No more talk of work or studies. It's tequila and loaded nachos time."

"You don't gotta tell me twice, Amigo."

"It's a good thing you're not a language major," David chuckles.

"Oh, come now. I talk English so very deliciously."

David is making light of things, but I sense there's something he's not telling me. I hope that in the course of the evening I'll be able to pull out of him whatever it is that's bothering him.

I don't know much about David's work. He doesn't speak much about his clients, but I understand that. Client confidentiality is key when you're an accountant, and my brother is nothing if not honorable.

The restaurant is packed, but the owner always makes a space for David and me. It used to be our family's favorite place to eat, so after the owners learned of our parents' accident, David and I were pretty much guaranteed a permanent table no matter what.

"Hello, you two. So nice to see you."

"Hi, Pedro. It's always good to see you," David smiles.

"It smells heavenly in here as always," I chime in.

"The usual for my special friends?" Pedro asks.

"Oh, yeah. And keep 'em coming," I grin.

It isn't long before I'm in Mexican food heaven.

"I could so die deliriously happy right now," I grin after licking the habanero sauce off my fingers and washing it all down with a healthy glug of margarita.

"No one wears habanero better than you, little sis," David laughs.

"Ain't that the truth? Are you going to eat that?" I ask, pointing to a perfectly untouched chili popper.

"Go ahead," he says. I eagerly scoop up the treat before he changes his mind.

It isn't like my brother to leave food on his plate. What's more, he's been absent minded all evening. I try one last time to get it out of him.

"Davy, what's wrong? You're not yourself. You know you can talk to me, right?"

"I'm fine, Ems. Really. It's been a busy week. I'm tired."

I raise one eyebrow while sipping on a margarita.

"Don't give me the hairy eyeball, Inspector. I'm serious. I'm just tired."

"Okay. I'll let you off the hook this time. What's keeping you so busy?"

"A new client. They're a big deal. I'm snowed under."

"Well, you can relax. I'm sure they know, as do we all, that you're the best. You don't have to work yourself to death to prove anything, David."

"You're sweet."

"Okay, now I know there's something wrong," I cackle. "You never call me sweet."

"Haha. Are we having dessert?"

"I am. No dessert for you, Davy-boy. You didn't finish your meal. Mom will turn in her grave if I allow you to break that golden rule."

"You're in a good mood. I take it you're excited about graduating next month."

"I can't wait. I'm done with studying. It's time to make some money."

"My poor starving artist sister," David winks. "Are you going to work at the gallery full-time after that?"

"Yes. They've offered me good money. Also, Adam told me I'm free to paint while I'm there, and I can display my work."

"Of course he did. Having you there is a winning scenario for him. Your art is stunning, Ems."

"Ahhh... Thanks, Davy. Why don't you have dinner with Dannie and me next Saturday? I know she's dying to perv over you," I tease.

"As much as I'd love to fulfill Dannie's fantasies, I'm afraid I'm busy next Saturday."

"A girl?"

"No, I'm afraid it's much less exciting. My new client invited me to his place for a function."

"You know who to call if you need a date," I tease some more.

"Thank you, Cupid, but I've got this."

"I'm just saying. I have a team of friends who are all more than willing to keep you entertained."

"So, what you're saying is that you don't believe that I can scare up a decent date? When did my little sister lose faith in her stud of a brother?"

David pulls a face of mock devastation. He's so handsome. I love my brother so much.

"No doubts here, Bro. You're da man."

The waitress comes over and asks if we'd like to see the dessert menu. I watch her eyes as they explore David's body. I'm used to it. I'm very proud of him.

"Two shots of Tequila, please," I say, snapping the cupcake out of her lascivious thoughts. "Don Julio."

She smiles bashfully at me, as if she forgot for a moment that I was there.

"That's telling her," David says, laughing once she's out of earshot.

* * *

It's 11:48 and I'm in bed with a lovely little buzz, courtesy of faithful old Don. Dannie raps on the door twice before she pokes her head inside the room.

"How's my future husband?" she grins.

"Still as handsome as ever."

"Did he ask you for my hand in marriage?"

"Not yet. Any day now."

Dannie giggles and plops herself down at the foot of the bed.

"Did you have a good time?"

"I did, thanks."

"What is it? Your mouth is saying one thing, but your eyes are telling a different story."

"You know me far too well."

"Spill it, Mildred."

"I'm worried about David. I get the feeling he's keeping something from me."

"Did you ask him?"

"I did. He waffled on about a new client and being very busy, but I know it's more than that."

"Woman's intuition is a curse."

"It is when you can't put your finger on the problem."

"You know what men are like, Ems. I'm sure David will tell you if it's serious. They don't like to talk about feelings and shit."

"I guess not."

"Well, I'm paste. Sleep tight, Ems."

"Good night, Dannie."

I decide to send David a text before I turn off my nightlight.

Hey, Davy.

Thanks for a lovely evening. I miss you. Let's do this more often. Sleep tight.

Love ya.

Read the complete story here!

SUBSCRIBE TO MY EXCLUSIVE NEWSLETTER

I hope you enjoyed reading this book.

If you want to stay updated on my upcoming releases, price promotions, and any ARC opportunities, then I would love to have you on my mailing list.

Subscribe yourself to my exclusive mailing list using the below link!

Subscribe to Lydia Hall's Exclusive Newsletter

Made in United States
North Haven, CT
21 February 2024